ROBYN

Also by Glen R Stott

Dead Angels

Heart of the Bison
Neandertals Book One

Spirit Fire
Neandertals Book Two

Search for the Heart of the Bison
Neandertals Book Three

Timpanogos

ROBYN

GLEN R STOTT

Copyright © Glen R Stott.

All rights reserved. No part of this book may be reproduced in any form or by any electronic or mechanical means, including information storage and retrieval systems, without permission in writing from the publisher, except by reviewers, who may quote brief passages in a review.

ISBN: 978-1-64713-525-6 (Paperback Edition)
ISBN: 978-1-64713-526-3 (Hardcover Edition)
ISBN: 978-1-64713-524-9 (E-book Edition)

Some characters and events in this book are fictitious. Any similarity to real persons, living or dead, is coincidental and not intended by the author.

Book Ordering Information

Phone Number: 347-901-4929 or 347-901-4920
Email: info@globalsummithouse.com
Global Summit House
www.globalsummithouse.com

Printed in the United States of America

To
Chi*Ki

In loving memory of
Jane and Shirley

CONTENTS

Acknowledgements ix
Introduction xi
Prologue July, 2012 xiii

Chapter 1:   1984 – Thursday Games; Karriane 1
Chapter 2:   1958 – The Wedding; Dianne 17
Chapter 3:   1984 – The Accusations; Darlene 40
Chapter 4:   1980 – The Divorce; Dianne 69
Chapter 5:   1985 – The Goodbye; Darlene 85
Chapter 6:   1977 – The Runaway; Karianne 102
Chapter 7:   1998 – The Hat; Robyn 120
Chapter 8:   1950s – The Letters; Janice 138
Chapter 9:   2012 – The Three Sisters; Robyn 149
Chapter 10:   July/August 2012 – The Trip to Paris; Robyn 184
Interlude   Joshua Godwin 214
Chapter 11:   August 2012 – The Box 218

Epilog—July 27, 2015 263

ACKNOWLEDGEMENTS

A lot of people helped with this book, most of them indirectly. I have known many women who were molested when they were children by their fathers, church leaders, family members, or trusted family friends. Though I didn't interview any of them for this book, I was inspired by their grace and strength. I did do a great deal of research of public stories of victims and the fear, shame, pain, and anger they experienced as they worked to overcome the emotional, physical, and spiritual damage they suffered. Although I was not a victim of child molestation, I did experience life-changing shame and trauma as a child. All this gave me a background I was able draw on to create *Robyn*.

I thank my wife, Chi*Ki, who gives me encouragement with all my writing. She read this manuscript as I wrote it and gave me many suggestions that helped focus the book. Writing this book stirred up unpleasant experiences of my childhood. Though they didn't rise to the level of child molestation as described in this book, they did impact me in ways that changed my life. As my best friend, Chi*Ki was always there to talk me through them and help me draw on them to build the emotion of this book.

INTRODUCTION

I started my first novel in the ninth grade. It went nowhere. Over thirty years would pass before I made another attempt. This time it was about the evil of child molestation prevalent in the 1990's news. I worked over three years. It was seven hundred pages, and I called it "Robin." No matter how I wrote and rewrote, I couldn't make it work.

My interest shifted to Jeffery Dahmer, Ted Bundy, John Wayne Gacy and other serial killers. There was a lot of data about how such men thought and acted. I read and studied over thirty books on writing fiction and took home study courses. Then I studied serial killers. "Dead Angels" was the result. I self-published it and went on to write and publish four more novels. I had each book professionally evaluated, and in the process, I learned a great deal about writing.

My new confidence caused me to go back to "Robin." I kept the basic premise and changed the name to "Robyn." What I wanted from this book required several different writing styles, and the story refused to follow a timeline.

I worked out a scene where a grown woman provides the details and trauma of the molestation of a child, but no child is in it. To make it work, I had to write the scene in second person—rare but not new.

In another instance, a victim is working with an analyst for several months. The words spoken in the sessions and poems written by the victim are the core. No descriptions, no tags, no quotation marks, no thoughts; just the spoken words and the words of the poems.

The story requires a major confrontation between the victims and perpetrator. In such a confrontation, the perpetrator will strongly defend himself. This would lead to a situation where things start to be about the perpetrator. "Dead Angels" was all about the perpetrator and his mind. "Robyn" is all about the victims and their growth. I was stymied.

Then, while reading a woman's description of her recovery, a period of my life came to me. My parents, to break me from bed wetting in the third grade, hired a professional. Her treatment was to shame me in powerful, sexual contexts. After a period of weeks without success, my parents stopped the treatment. But I was never the same.

As I relived that experience, the whole ending of "Robyn" changed. The confrontation changed, the people in the confrontation changed, the perpetrator's role in it changed, and the growth of the character who shapes the denouement sprang to life.

To create the flow of that character's change and growth, I used "stream of consciousness" mangled to fit my needs. Rather than a mental exercise, my character is speaking at another person, and moving around. I have a narrator move her, but he only speaks in verbs with prepositional phrases, (walks to door – sits on chair, etc.). The only punctuation I use is ellipses to create speaking cadence and allow the character to breath between thoughts.

I published "Robyn" in 2015. I have recently republished it and gave it a new cover and one more edit to correct some minor slipups.

PROLOGUE

July, 2012

Rain in July was definitely out of the ordinary. It fell softly, steadily, making the air warm and humid. Normally, Robyn Briggs liked rain, but things had already gone awry tonight and the unexpected rain was not helping. She was peeved at her husband, George, as he fiddled with the key to the front door. Naturally, she had not brought an umbrella. She held the flyer for the play over her head, but it did not provide much protection. On top of that, their plans were ruined. Her mother's father had given them tickets to the musical, *Chicago*, at the Majestic Theater on East Huston Street in downtown San Antonio for their anniversary. Joshua Godwin, Grandpa, had even volunteered to tend to Debbie, their three-year-old daughter. They planned to have an early dinner at the Lone Star restaurant on the San Antonio River Walk just a couple of blocks from the theater. They would be able to enjoy some quiet time together and feed ducks that gathered in the river before it was to time go to the theater. When they got to the restaurant, George discovered he forgot his wallet with his money and the theater tickets. They could not go home and come back in time to eat at the restaurant, so they decided to go home and grab a snack before returning for the play.

George had an Apollo face with blond hair and deep blue eyes. He had played wide receiver on the high school football team and small forward on the basketball team. Robyn's girlfriends were all jealous of her relationship with him. She didn't love George then. She didn't lust after him either. Robyn thought back to that night years ago. Making out in the car was exciting, but more than that wasn't in her plans. She could have said no, but she didn't. She knew it would hurt, and it did. It wasn't as if she had succumbed to temptation; she wasn't tempted at all. She lay awake all that night with a line from a song playing over and over in her mind. She couldn't remember any more of the song than that line. *I'm just a girl who cain't say no.* But she could say no to just about anything. She had a well-earned reputation of being a feminist in high school. She didn't like any kind of animated movie and easily refused to go with George to see *Avatar*. After what Jake Carter said to her about boys looking up girls' dresses on the monkey bars when she was in grade school, and the things the lady in the green dress said when she pulled Jake away from her, Robyn stopped wearing skirts and dresses except to church. She had no trouble saying no to her parents on that issue. She didn't like any kind of food from the sea and wouldn't put even a bite in her mouth. Why couldn't she say no to sex?

The pregnancy changed everything—a quick, unplanned marriage to George and an early end to Robyn's high school career. George was graduated from high school and was preparing to go on a two-year mission for the LDS Church, but the pregnancy and the wedding made him ineligible for a mission. They both had given up a great deal for that one-night blunder.

Her mother and grandfather wanted to know why she had "succumbed to temptation." She honestly couldn't say why. Grandpa said it must be the bad blood from his first wife, and he forgave her. No one ever talked about Grandpa's first wife, Robyn's maternal grandmother. That divorce occurred before Robyn was born. Her grandmother ran away with a man from California and was never heard from again.

George was caring and considerate. Over the past years, their high school infatuation had grown to a deep love. As George fumbled with the key, Robyn could see he was as disappointed as she. She gave him a peck on the cheek and said, "Don't worry; it'll be fine. We'll get back in time for the opening curtain."

Robyn walked into the entryway of the house they were renting. The entryway was six-feet by six-feet and led directly to the living room. To the right there was a hallway going to the two bedrooms and the bathroom. To the left was a dining area that joined with the kitchen. The kitchen was separated from the living room by a wall.

Robyn could see the back of Grandpa's head where he sat on a couch watching the *Little Mermaid* on their TV, located opposite the entryway. With the race between Obama and Romney heating up, Grandpa hardly ever watched anything but Fox News in the evening. Robyn took a second to take in the scene of him watching a Disney cartoon with Debbie as she waited for George to come in. It was so good of Grandpa to take his time to watch animated movies with Debbie, knowing it drove Robyn crazy to watch them, especially Disney cartoons.

Grandpa's head jerked around at the sound of the latch on the door when George closed it. Grandpa quickly put something aside, and as Robyn came around the couch, she could see him buttoning the top of his Levis. He jumped up and started to buckle his belt. "What the heck!" George shouted as he rushed past Robyn.

Grandpa said, "You don't understand. I can expla ..." As he stepped back, he tripped over the throw rug, falling back and banging his head with a hollow thud on the hardwood floor.

George was six feet three inches tall and 210 pounds, while Grandpa was five feet ten inches and 180 pounds. George turned around. With his hands held out from his hips, palms forward, he said, "I didn't touch him."

Debbie was sitting in the corner of the couch with her eyes and mouth wide open, looking at Grandpa in fear. Robyn followed Debbie's stare and saw Grandpa lying on the floor with a small pool of blood at the back of his head. As she looked at him, she could see the crotch of his pants begin to look darker as his bladder emptied. "Oh my God! Is he dead?"

George knelt beside him as Robyn rushed to pick up Debbie. "He's breathing, but he's unconscious. You better call nine-one-one."

When Robyn came back after making the call, Grandpa was sitting on the floor holding a towel on his head. "Grampuh hurt?" Debbie questioned.

"No," Robyn assured her. She looked at George questioningly.

"He woke up, and I got him a towel." George paced in front of the couch.

"What were you doing to Debbie?" Robyn asked.

"We were … I don't know … watching TV? What happened?"

"You had your pants down. What were you doing?" George's fists were doubled at his sides.

Grandpa cowered back, looking surprised at his wet Levis.

"You're frightening him," Robyn said. "Don't you see he's confused? Let me talk to him."

George looked at her. "You talk to him then." He stormed into the kitchen.

"Grandpa, how do you feel?" Robyn asked.

"Did you enjoy the show?" Grandpa looked around.

"What were you doing with Debbie?"

"I peed my pants. I don't know why I did that. Why am I on the floor?"

"You fell down."

"I did? Why? My head hurts."

"When we got home, your pants were undone."

"Because I was peeing?"

"No. That happened after you fell down."

"My head hurts." He pulled the towel down and looked at it. "I think I'm bleeding."

Robyn examined his head. There was a small split in the scalp that had begun to clot. "You hurt your head when you fell, but the bleeding has stopped."

"I don't feel so good." Grandpa leaned to the side and threw up on the floor.

Robyn wrapped the towel around his head and helped him to a chair. She called George to clean up the mess. He brought another towel to clean the floor.

"I think he has a concussion," Robyn said.

"I didn't touch him. He stepped back on his own and tripped."

"I know; I saw what happened."

"I'm sorry he's hurt, but he was doing something to Debbie … something with his pants down."

"I don't know … I mean I saw him … putting his pants on or something."

"I called the police. They're sending a detective over."

"What? We don't even know what happened."

"If nothing happened, the police can determine that."

An ambulance arrived shortly. The paramedics determined Grandpa needed to be taken to the hospital for a more detailed examination.

"Can I ride with him?" Robyn asked the paramedic.

The paramedic explained she couldn't ride in the ambulance, and it would take about an hour to go through the process of examining Grandpa to determine if he should be admitted. "You can use the time to notify his family," he concluded.

"He's my grandfather. His wife died a few years ago; he lives alone."

"Well, you should come to the hospital in about forty-five minutes."

After they left, Robyn told George she was going to call her mother.

"I don't think you should call her until after we talk to the police and find out how Grandpa is doing. Maybe this is nothing. Right now, it could be unnecessarily awkward." George stepped closer to Debbie. "Did Grandpa do something to you?" he asked her.

Debbie's eyes got watery. "Grampuh fall. Grampuh hurt?"

"Grandpa will be okay," Robyn said. She turned to George. "I don't think she's going to be able to tell us anything … at least not now. She's too upset by Grandpa's fall."

CHAPTER 1

1984 – Thursday Games; Karriane

"This is not the kind of thing I can talk about so easily, Bishop. It's embarrassing. It's not straightforward, that's for sure."

"Take your time. Tell it how it's easiest for you. Let's just see how it goes."

"Okay ... this goes back to the nineteen sixties when I was in grade school. It'll take a little to time work into the story ... just don't interrupt me." She sits forward in her chair and puts her hands, palms down, on his desk.

"Um ... people have days they hate. Some children hate the first day of school, because it is the end of summer freedom. Others hate the last day of school, because they will miss some of their school friends. There are other days they hate, but the day of the year I hated most was *every* Thursday.

"On Thursday, mother goes to Relief Society meetings. Usually my little brother is watching his favorite TV show, and baby sister is sleeping in her crib. Father wants me in the room, and I do not know what the game will be tonight. I can't remember when the games started. I do not remember a time wherein there were no games.

"Father locks the door and tells me to lie on the bed and pretend to be asleep. So, the game is to be Snow White. The first component of Snow White is me lying on the bed asleep, courtesy of the apple from the Wicked Witch. It's my favorite game ... well ... actually, I seriously do *not* want to experience it; I hate it, but it's not as bad as the other games.

"I lie quietly with my legs straight down, my knees touching each other, and my arms by my sides; my fists are clenched, waiting for the Prince's kiss to wake me up whereby he and I live happily ever after. But I'm trying to think about Disney's version of *Snow White*, wherein Grumpy is my favorite dwarf. I want to think about anything but his game. I feel the back of my neck getting tight, and I know this is going to precipitate the headache later.

"I'm not allowed to open my eyes ... not yet. I want to hide in the darkness behind them, but the darkness is not big enough ... and then I know he is there ... ..._

She pulls her hands from the desk and puts them in her lap. "Nope, I can't do this. I thought I could, but the feelings are coming too strong, and I don't know if you will be able to comprehend it anyway."

"Maybe you could write it down," the bishop suggests.

"No. I don't write with enough expertise for this. You can't know this as much as you must feel it. Let's try this. You think of a man you personally know ... one you trust and admire as a spiritual leader. Do you have one?"

"Yes, brother ..."

"No! I don't want to know who it is."

* * *

Imagine he has a drug that puts you *completely* in his power. The drug confuses you so you can't bring logic and experience to help you understand what transpires. When he drugs you, he does things to you that are based upon Walt Disney movies.

Now, you have been drugged and you're lying on the bed with your eyes closed ... and then you know he's there ... the Old Spice tells you that. You know he's naked ... experience tells you that, and all you want is to be someplace else, but the drugs will not let you escape from the game.

As the game unfolds, he gently pulls your pants down, running his hands along your thighs in the process. It is a universal mystery to you how his hands can always feel so cold, even on a hot summer night. He loops his fingers around the waistband of your underpants and gently pulls them off. Then he puts a hand under your left knee and takes your left ankle in his other hand, lifting your knee, he moves your foot up and to the side. He repeats the process with your right leg, rendering you in a vulnerable position, and you wish you didn't feel so embarrassed, like someday the whole world will see you like this.

You wonder why he wants this game, but you don't ask ... you are afraid to ask ... and you don't know why you are afraid because of the drugged confusion. Next, you feel the scratchy stubble of his face on your inner thighs, and his wet tongue and soft lips move over what should be private. While he's administering the wakeup kiss with his lips, his hands unbutton your shirt and his fingers lightly stroke your chest. The physical feeling is tingly all over and not unpleasant.

Your confusion deepens because this is very wrong for you, because you should not be with a man ... not like this. The irony of it all is ... you know something is wrong, but in your drugged confusion you cannot decide exactly what and you feel somehow you are responsible.

Still, it feels good, but it's so confusing because you feel so ashamed at the same time, and you wonder if you are secretly gay. And you feel guilty, but you can't say why.

He stops the kissing, and calling you Snow White; he tells you to wake up. You open your eyes, and he pulls off your shirt and does what he always does ... for this game he does it on your stomach. And your guilt and your confusion multiply.

He leads you to the bathroom and takes you in the shower with him. He gently washes you clean with warm water and soap, as if cleanliness is even possible at this point ... as if guilt can be washed from you in *this* water. He staunchly insists you must never tell anyone about the games. If you do, you will be abandoned ... not worthy to be his friend. And you feel this is a terrible responsibility you have to shoulder. You don't understand why you can't tell someone and put a stop to this. The drug wears off, and in the morning, it's back to work, back to normal ... whatever that is. And then comes the next time. There are different versions of the Disney stories that you must experience with him. Here are some versions by way of example:

Snow White: The aforementioned game.

Pinocchio: Pinocchio's nose hangs soft and limp. You must hold it until it grows hard and straight. Then you rub it with Vaseline until he's done, and you follow it, as always, with the shower and the eternal admonition to *never* tell anyone under any circumstance.

Cinderella: You must demonstrate affection for the Fairy Godmother's magic wand by rubbing it all over your body and holding it in your mouth at the final stage. Then you brush your teeth and gargle in the shower.

Thumper: The worst game. You hold Thumper and slap him against your body ... like Thumper pounding his foot on the ground. At the final curtain, your friend rolls you on your stomach and Thumper runs into his hidden burrow ... in you, and this *really* hurts, hurts, hurts! You feel like you are walking funny all the next day. And for you, it is this way because you are a man, but if you were a woman it would be different ... on your back ... a different burrow.

You are an adult with experience and maturity. Do you think you can understand the depth of pain a child would experience ... if the trusted person were the child's father?

* * *

"I'm sure it would be terrible. Fortunately, children are very resilient. With love and guidance, they ..."

"You don't get it at all! Think for a minute. This man ... your friend ... someone you idolize to some extent, took your power from you. He put in a position whereby you felt some level of physical stimulation in a decidedly perverted experience. Can you not imagine how that would raise doubts in your mind? Think of a child … don't you realize how the games would mess with her personality at a foundational level? Love and guidance? Are you kidding? No! The first thing is; *Don't let it happen.* Put aside the coping mechanisms you have developed as an adult. Try to look at it from this point of view … that you were powerless and that he violated you in a way that was a perversion of what you are. What do you think about your friend that you admire so much now?"

"To tell you the truth, I don't know. I know we each have people who have wronged us in one way or another. At some point we have to forgive them so we can mov …"

The woman slaps her hands on the bishop's desk and stands up. "You are sitting there thinking of Christ on the cross … 'forgive them Father, for they know not what they do?' I want you to get Christ off the cross! Think of him in the temple grounds chastening the money changers … think of him saying little children are the Kingdom of God … think of him hanging a millstone around the neck of one who would offend a child and of him casting that man with the millstone into the sea. I only gave you a sample of the trauma I had to experience at my dad's hands. Think again of this little girl trying to cope. There's more." She bends forward and leans on her hands on the desk.

* * *

Most Thursdays your friend does not force you to the room at all, and sometimes, when he takes you there, he just wants to vent his views. He tells you he is a proud Texan, born and raised. He hates Utah and when the time is appropriate, he is returning to Texas with the family whereby he will become filthy rich and live in great a mansion. He insists you are also a Texan … it's in your blood. He hates President Johnson because he gave part of El Paso to the lazy Mexicans. Sometimes he regales you with the evilness of stepfathers and Mexicans and Catholics and you imagine, on those nights, you are his special confidant. You do not know which Thursday he will require a game, so Thursday is always a day of eternal tension until you see how the evening unfolds.

Sometimes your friend brings his camera, and you hate, hate, hate that he takes photos. He prides himself on his quality photos in his quality albums ... albums of his family holidays and trips, and you lay awake many nights wondering about those quality photos of the aforementioned games, and that he may accidently deposit one in a quality family album whereby you will be exposed.

He is forever telling you versions of Walt Disney stories. Some are funny, some are scary.

Thursday nights are different. On *those* nights ... the game nights ... he staunchly insists you *act out* different versions of the stories ... the games you are not allowed to mention to *anyone*.

Your friend's sister regularly takes you aside to warn you that being gay is a sin. She tells you if anyone wants you to play gay, you must tell her about it, and she will help you put a stop to it, and you wonder about your friend and what his sister knows, and you wonder what she suspects. And you are drowning in questions.

Suppose now that you are a child and Sunday the class is on Jesus and sin, and you learn that Jesus had to suffer on the cross because of everyone's sins ... to pay the price. You feel wretched thinking about Jesus suffering on the cross, and you vow you will never add sins of your own doing to his suffering. The following Sunday, you are reminded about baptism and that it spiritually cleans sins, and Jesus takes them away so you will become a new and a sinless person. And all week you think about sins ... about your sins. You know you have lied and once you pilfered money from your mother's purse, so you know you have already caused Jesus to suffer, and you cry for him that night and for the part of his suffering you brought about with your sins.

The next Thursday, your friend requires you to accompany him to the bedroom. Later, you are standing in the shower with your friend, brushing your teeth and spitting, and you are suddenly engulfed in an epiphany that the games are evil, and at that moment your friend is giving you the time-honored admonition to never tell anyone, and you *know* you are *never* telling his sister anything about *this*.

Suppose you are a child, and your friend is your father. You lay awake all night thinking about the games and about sin, and you wonder how your father could be so good and hold positions in the Church and then lead you to sin on Thursdays, and you think it must be your fault ... you must be doing something that makes him do it, and you wonder tirelessly what it is. You feel your fingernails digging into your palms, and you know you cannot, you simply can*not* play the Thursday games any more ... for Jesus's sake. So that morning, you tell your mother about the games so she can intercede on your behalf ... because you trust her.

Everything seems normal in the house, and Thursday your father says nothing about the games. Well, there are a lot of Thursdays wherein he does not play them, so you are still in a mystery about whether your mother stopped him or not.

That Saturday is the day you are baptized, and you experience a cleanliness that defies description, and you think Jesus is smiling on you. Finally, you realize there is a kind of water that *can* wash all the slime and sin from Thursdays, and you think maybe the games are over.

Throughout the next week, your parents do not demonstrate any behavior that manifests a change caused by your talk with Mother, and you wonder why your mother does not tell you about the talk, and the mystery congeals. Thursday progresses in a normal way until about fifteen minutes after Mother departs for Relief Society, at which point, your father practically drags you to the room. He accuses you of divulging everything to your mother, and you flinch as if he is shouting, but it is not a shout ... it is a tone. Then he says he is going to teach you a lesson. And this time it is not a game.

It is violent and painful and deeper than ever before, and when it is done, he warns you that you better not tell your mother anything else, because she will inform him, and you will become the sorriest, ungrateful kid ever. He says if you do not want to play the games with him … fine. He does not even want to see you on Thursdays. You can go be with your friends or to the library for all he cares, but you just better not say another word to your mother or anyone else about this or there will be consequences.

He sends you to the shower alone where the water flowing down the inside of your legs is pink, and you have never been so alone and so in pain in your whole life. Your confusion is monumental. Your father and mother teach you the Gospel and take you to church. You father gives you special blessings and you should be pure and clean, and they should love you, and God should love you, and Jesus should love you. And then … there was tonight … and who was there to protect you tonight? Who really loves you? Your mother? God? Jesus? That is the unfathomable, eternal mystery of the Universe. The ones who are supposed to love you put you right in perdition. You experience a mountain of confusion. Your mind and spirit are paralyzed because you can't sort it out. You are ashamed, frightened, guilty, sore, and it's all mixed in a brew of pain and confusion that will not congeal into something you can understand. You are powerless to unwind the confusion. And that night you experience the dream for the first time but not the last by a long shot.

You are walking along a meandering, gravel pathway on a warm summer evening. A hummingbird is humming and dipping into a bright red feeder with four small perches and four yellow, plastic flowers wherein the nectar is waiting. Another hummingbird is on a twig in a nearby lilac bush preening, his bright red throat glistening in the sun. The aroma of the lilacs fills the air. On your left is a broad meadow covered in dark green grass. Dark purple irises with bright yellow trim line the border of the grass. The soil on your right forms a round-topped mound that meanders with the pathway. The aforementioned mound is decorated with patterns created with pansies of differing colors, roses, and varying shades of green herbs. The edge of the pathway is lined with tulips of many colors. There is a knocking sound, and your attention is drawn to the movement of a woodpecker banging on an old pine behind the mound. You feel this must be what Heaven is like, and God smiles on you and your world. As you walk, the pathway beckons you to a small grove of Christmas tree sized pines. The aroma of pine fills you as you crunch along the pathway. At the end there is a door.

You open the door and start to step in. Suddenly, you are pulled in by a mystic, magnetic force that holds you suspended in midair without any visible means of constraint. The door disappears and the walls are bare, and it is tight like a closet. Just as you begin to respond to the confinement, the walls suddenly expand away from you. At the same instant, you begin to shrink. In just seconds you are smaller than an atom, and the room is larger than a universe. You are petrified, and you want to scream, but you cannot, and you realize ... this is your descent into oblivion.

Just in the nick of time, you awaken and open your eyes. Your room is around you. In the dim glow of the nightlight you see the door, the dresser, the ceiling light fixture. Suddenly, the room accelerates away in all directions, and you shrivel in the bed. The unfathomable mystery here is that your eyes tell you nothing is changing, the door is still there, your feet hold the covers in an unmoving mound, but it is undeniably happening! You are aware of your arm and you know you could lift it if you wanted to, only you do not necessarily want to. Your heart is banging against your ribs like a frightened bird in a cage, and the room is fading into a darker darkness. A fear is expanding that the bird will escape the cage, and you will cease to live, and you will become a miniscule part of a damp fog over a stale swamp ... forever. You could stop this if you lift your arm, and you do not know why you do not do it. You see the string of beads you got at Mardi Gras two years ago hanging on the wall. You concentrate on them, and the room stops expanding, and you stop shrinking. You tip your head back and observe the headboard of your bed, and it is absolutely still and violently spinning at the same time, making you dizzy and almost sick to your stomach.

You become aware you are breathing very shallow and fast, and you cannot get enough air. You concentrate on breathing slowly ... deeply, and you focus on your fiercely beating heart, mentally tying it to the pace of the air you breathe. You breathe in and out againagainagain-again-again-again … again … … again … … again … … … again; and your breathing and the beating of your heart pace down together. The headboard stabilizes; the dizziness subsides. You look down, and your arm is floating about eight inches above your chest.

You remain motionless, looking at the beads. You are so tired. You close your eyes to go to sleep, but the instant you do, you are standing in the pines and the garden door bursts open. You fling up your eyelids so hard and wide you feel the skin on your forehead wrinkle and air moving across your bare eyeballs, but with your eyes open your panic subsides. You close them, and the pines and the door spring at you, and you open your eyes. You repeat this repeatedly all night; each closing of your eyes brings the pines and the door. Colors gradually fill in the shades of gray as dawn pushes darkness from the bedroom where you stare unflinchingly through scratchy, dry eyes at the beads … the purple beads.

You robotically dress yourself for school. Downstairs, the adults in the house are sitting at the table over eggs and toast. Your bottom is sore, and you worry more blood might trickle out. The female adult says you look terrible and should see a doctor, and you focus your eyes on the emblem on the front of the Meadow Gold milk carton. The male adult is having none of the doctor, and as he talks, you focus on the sound of the compressor in the fridge, and then it turns off, and the fridge shudders, and so do you, and the male insists you go to school. And you go.

* * *

She paces in front of the desk. "And that's the story of my dysfunctional family, Bishop. I thought it was only me … that my dad didn't inflict himself upon anyone else. But I've recently been apprised, after all these years, that he also molested my little sister … probably starting when he banned me from the house on Thursdays, whereby I would not be an observer of him disappearing into the bedroom with her."

"Your father is a spiritual leader in the ward. Are you absolutely sure your memory is accurate? I mean … well, sometimes memories from a younger age are … you know; they can get a bit garbled."

She sits down, folding her hands in her lap. "Are you asking if this is some newly formed repressed memory? No, it definitely is not that. This happened over a period of several years. I can't remember when it started, but my memories are and always have been very clear regarding the last years of this abomination and, especially, the violent night it ended."

"If you've had the memories all these years, how come you're just bringing them forward now?"

"Like I said, at first I thought it was only me. It would be me against him and my mother, and I would not come out of it favorably. Now, I find it happened to my sister when she was about my same age, and I know she's telling the truth because the details of the stories and rituals he inflicted upon her are the same as the ones I was forced to experience. My problem is, if he did it to me and my sister, well, I don't think guys like that change or stop repeating the behavior. So, what I'm concerned about is, if he's hurting someone else. I mean, it looks like he prefers prepubescent girls, and you know he can find little girls like that," snapping her fingers. "He can find them in the Church. So mainly, I don't know what to do."

"Unfortunately, those kinds of problems are all too common. In fact, good Mormons are not free of its impacts. Because of that, the Church occasionally has to deal with the perpetrators. I'll get with the stake president, and we'll work out a program to deal with your father."

"My sister and I confronted him about it, and he's denying everything."

"Of course, they start out with denial, but, believe me, *if he's guilty*, once the fear of God comes into his heart, he'll confess and mend his ways."

"How are you going to discover *if* he's guilty, and how is the fear of God going to be imparted into him?"

"You shouldn't worry about that. The Church and the priesthood can get to the bottom of this."

"Well *you* should worry about it. In a sense, you are the father of the ward. It's your duty to protect all the little girls in the ward."

"Your father is a High Priest, and so he has a firm foundation in the power of forgiveness and the need for confession to achieve it. Like I said, the Church has powerfully spiritual men who have also been trained in how to deal with these kinds of problems. You can trust this problem will be handled through the Church."

She folds her arms and leans back in her chair. "The fear of God didn't prevent him from molesting me; I seriously doubt it's going to get him to confess. But you go for it, and I wish you all the luck. I'm reporting this to the proper civil authorities. I don't know anything about the statute of limitations, but I will acquire the knowledge I need, and if it's possible, I'll have him arrested whereby he can atone for his crimes and be removed from the environs of temptation."

The bishop sits up straight in his chair. "You definitely should not do that. Once the police get involved, the victims have to come out and face public humiliation in court. If your father should go to prison, that's just a school for criminals to network and improve their skills. As far as atonement is concerned, that's a spiritual process. You'll find that seeking revenge will only lead you away from happiness."

She sits up straight in her chair, matching the bishop's posture. "It's not revenge I aspire to achieve. My monumental concern here is that he never reenacts his perversion on another child. Furthermore, I'm not afraid to confront him in court; in fact, I relish the idea of looking him in the eyes in a court of law."

"Do you have any idea of the recidivism of sexual offenders when they leave prison?"

"Pretty significant, I've heard. I've never heard of one molesting a child while he was confined in a penal institution."

"Nearly one hundred percent repeat their crimes shortly after leaving prison. If he's taken to court and he is molesting another young girl, she would be the key witness ... not you. You should give some consideration to that girl. For everyone concerned, victims and perpetrators, it's much better to leave this to the inspired church programs. Working through the Church, God will see that justice is done, victims are treated gently, and the crimes are not repeated. That's why you should leave it to the Church and to the men of God. You should focus on overcoming your pain. With patience and forgiveness, you will heal the pain you have."

She pushes her chair back from the desk and crosses her right leg over her left knee. "You talk of patience and forgiveness ... bully for you. When you can see that little girl shaking on the bed with her eyes closed, waiting for the game, and you rush to her with a righteous whip in your hands to save her, you will be a man of God in my eyes. You and the Church can handle him as best as you can, but I'm going to see if the police can put the fear of God in him." She stands up and walks out of the office.

Robyn – July, 2012

A few minutes after the ambulance left, Sergeant Floyd of the San Antonio Police Department arrived. Robyn's mother had worked for the police department when Robyn was young. Robyn had met Sergeant Floyd several times at parties her mother hosted. Her mother was a hero and received a medal for saving another policeman's life, but she had to kill a man to do it. She refused to go on patrol or carry a gun again. After a few years working behind a desk, she quit.

Sergeant Floyd was a tall, slim, black man who appeared to be in his late forties. He was dressed in a dark brown business suit with a white shirt and maroon tie. He offered his hand as he entered. "Hi Robyn, how're you doing?"

Robyn shook his hand. "I'm not sure right now."

"Have a seat, and let's discuss it."

Robyn recounted the story of how she and George had come home unexpectedly to catch her grandpa doing something to Debbie, how he fell, hurt his head, threw up, and was confused.

"So, you didn't actually see him do anything to Debbie?" Sergeant Floyd asked.

"Like I said, his pants were pretty much up by the time I saw him. He said something like, 'This isn't what it seems,' and that's when he stepped backward and fell."

"That how you saw it?" The sergeant directed the question to George.

"I was behind Robyn, but I could see over the couch. What I saw was … he was just finishing zipping his pants up, and then he started to pull his belt tight, and then he stepped back and tripped."

"Was Debbie dressed?" the sergeant asked Robyn.

"We put night panties on for her to sleep in because she occasionally has accidents. They're right there." Robyn pointed to the panties on the couch. "She was still wearing her daytime panties, so it looks like Grandpa was just getting ready to change them."

"Well, it would be easy to surmise that your grandfather was preparing to change Debbie's underwear, and before he took her day underwear off, he was pulling his pants down. That's the easy assumption, but if I get you right, he was about to offer an explanation before he fell."

"He seemed really surprised … the kind of surprise you have when you've been caught," Robyn said.

"What does Debbie say about it?"

"She is mostly upset about seeing her grandpa fall and bleed. She talks some, but she is just three, and to be honest, she is a little behind in learning to talk." Robyn answered

"What you saw, though very suspicious, does not make a good case. However, I recommend you have Debbie examined by a doctor, just in case."

"Why? I mean we got here before he could do anything," Robyn said

"You could have caught him before he did anything, or he could have been just finishing, or there might have been something done before and some evidence of it could be evident."

"Oh God," Robyn gasped.

"Really, I don't want to upset you. It's almost certain nothing happened. If you want to pursue it, I'll assign an unbiased detective to look for evidence in the house."

"What do you think we should do?" Robyn asked.

"I can't tell you what to do. I know your mother and grandfather too well to advise you."

"I don't know what to do. I just have this sense that something about what happened is missing. Do I have to make a decision right now?"

"No, tell you what … I'm going to give this to Detective Hanson and have him review it. Maybe you or George will remember something after you have time to get over the shock. In the meantime, I recommend you not do any cleanup tonight in case Detective Hanson wants to look around a little. Does that work for you?"

"What would he be looking for?" George asked.

"That's hard to say. Even though you partially cleaned up, there is still some mess. He would check that out and take photographs. When Mr. Godwin wakes, he may have an explanation, and the evidence here might corroborate or disprove it."

"Thanks. We'll do what you say and see where it goes," Robyn said.

* * *

After the sergeant left, Robyn and George took Debbie to the hospital for a cursory exam. Robyn was greatly relieved when there was no sign anything had happened to Debbie. George left the hospital to take Debbie to his sister's house, where they had made arrangements to spend the night. They had taken both of their cars so Robyn could wait at the hospital until Grandpa's exam was completed. Robyn sat in the waiting room trying to decide what to do. Since the examination showed nothing had happened to Debbie, Robyn wondered if she might have overreacted. But something seemed wrong. She went over and over what had happened, looking for anything that could explain the sensation she had. It wasn't just this night. Other times she had a similar nagging sentiment that Debbie was in some inexplicable danger. At those times, Robyn always felt she was an inadequate mother. She had talked to her mother about this. Her mother said it was normal for mothers to be overprotective of their children, but Robyn was sure what she was experiencing was stronger than normal. At least if Grandpa's explanation could clarify what Robyn had seen tonight, that could be cleared up.

Finally, the doctor came in. Grandpa had a minor concussion and would be held overnight for observation.

"Is he awake?" Robyn asked.

"Yes, but he's still a bit confused about what happened. He doesn't seem to remember."

"Do you think he will eventually remember?"

"It's hard to say. I've seen these things go both ways. But if there is memory loss, it should only be around the time of the accident. Other than that, his memory should be fine."

"Can he have visitors?"

"It should be okay, but I would keep it to a minimum. Did you want to see him?"

"Um … not right now, thanks," Robyn said.

Robyn called her mother and asked if she could come over to see her. She did not want to try to explain the accident over the phone.

CHAPTER 2

1958 – The Wedding; Dianne

Dianne Taylor pulled her jacket tightly around her body. Joshua Godwin put his arm around her. They had brought their warmest clothes from San Antonio, Texas, but they provided little protection from the January cold of Salt Lake City, Utah. Dianne tipped her head back to look up at the Gothic building soaring over two hundred feet to the golden statue of the Angel Moroni on top. "What did they say the temple is made of?" she asked Josh.

"Quartz monzonite, but it looks like gray granite."

Dianne had always been taught it was the house of the Lord. "I'm not sure I'm worthy to go into the temple."

"Of course, you are … your temple recommend says you are." All members of the LDS Church who wanted to enter the temple were interviewed by a bishop and a stake president. Then, if they were deemed worthy, they were issued a paper recommend allowing them entrance into the temple. In the LDS Church, a local parish was called a ward. The leader of the ward was called a bishop. A group of wards was organized into a stake, which was led by a stake president.

"What if I wasn't truthful when I was interviewed?" In the cold air, Dianne could see the small clouds her words made as they drifted up into Josh's face. He was six feet tall and thin. He had light brown hair and clear brown eyes. With his straight nose, full lips, and prominent cheekbones, he was one of the handsomest men she knew. She should feel lucky to get him. All the other girls in the ward were jealous of her.

"In what way?" Josh put his hands on her shoulders and turned her, so they were face to face.

Another couple walked by. Dianne waited until they were out of earshot. "I told them that I was morally clean."

"Are you saying you've been with another man?" Josh dropped his hands and took a step back.

"No, but we did a lot of petting and making out."

"Yes, but we didn't have sex."

"I know, but I was always taught that those things we did are wrong."

"Why? Because they lead to sex. Well, they didn't lead to anything with us." Josh pulled her close and wrapped his arms around her.

Dianne leaned into the warmth of Josh's body, but in spite of what she just said, her real doubts had nothing to do with worthiness. A marriage performed in the temple was not till-death-do-you-part; it was for time-and-all-eternity. She wasn't sure Josh was the man she wanted to be married to forever, but she was afraid to tell him.

They started walking around the temple as Josh explained the symbolism of the building. "The three towers on the east end represent the First Presidency of the Church. The twelve pinnacles represent the apostles."

Dianne first met Josh when he moved into the ward when she was eleven. He was a sophomore in high school at the time. He was handsome, popular, and a natural leader. The Church had many activities for the youth, and he was involved with all of them. He paid special attention to Dianne, and she felt he was the big brother she never had. When she was twelve and could participate in the Church Young Women's programs as a Beehive Girl, Josh spent even more time with her.

"Those circles at the bottom are called earth stones, and they represent the Earth," Josh continued.

After high school, Josh had gone on a mission to the Western States Mission, which was headquartered in Denver, Colorado, and covered Colorado and New Mexico. He was there for two years. He left a boy and came back a man. Dianne, at sixteen, thought of herself as a woman.

"The circles on top of the earth stones are called moonstones, and they represent progression from darkness to light."

As soon as he got home from his mission, Josh started dating Dianne. She went with him because she felt like a woman with him, but it was a little strange because a part of her still saw him as a brother. He had proposed last May, just two months after her seventeenth birthday. She told him no, explaining her parents wouldn't let her get married that young. Though she was certain they wouldn't, the real reason was she had no romantic attraction to Josh.

"The circles with rays coming out are sunstones, and they represent the celestial kingdom." In LDS doctrine that is the highest level of heaven.

Dianne's jaw dropped when her parents consented to the marriage. Now, because she hadn't told the truth to start with, she felt trapped. She could still back out, but that would cause an upset she didn't want to confront.

"Those stars at the top of the arches are star stones, and there are three kinds. The down pointing ones represent the sons on God. The up-pointing ones represent the governing power of the priesthood, and the small ones represent the saving power of the priesthood."

Josh wanted to get married right away, but Dianne wanted to wait until after her high school graduation. They had compromised on January 18, the middle of her junior year—tomorrow. During the past months, her feelings for Josh had matured some, but she was still not sure about him.

They walked to the west end of the temple. "Can you see the marks in the wall way up there?" Josh pointed.

"Yes."

"Can you see they look like the Big Dipper?"

"Oh yeah, I see it now."

"Well, travelers use the Big Dipper to find the North Star, which gives them the direction to travel. This Big Dipper symbolizes how the temple gives direction to reach eternal life in the celestial kingdom. That's what our marriage is all about."

In spite of her doubts about the marriage, Dianne was eagerly looking forward to going into the temple. She had no idea what would happen there; members who had gone were not allowed to talk about the ceremonies or the things they learned in the temple. They could talk about their feelings. Everyone she had talked to told her it was the most spiritual day of their life, and the spiritual lessons they had learned created closeness to God they had never imagined could be possible.

Dianne's parents had never been to the temple. They supported Dianne and were active in the Church but had never reached the level of worthiness necessary to enter the temple. They smoked, they liked their morning cup of coffee, and they did not pay a full tithing—all things that made them unworthy to go to the temple. They were trading their birthright for a bowl of porridge, the bishop lectured. And now, they were missing their daughter's wedding. The Church prided itself on its support of family, but parents deemed to be unworthy had to be excluded from their children's temple weddings—no exceptions.

* * *

After the wedding ceremony the next day, Dianne and Josh went outside for pictures. Dianne squinted into the painfully bright reflection of the sun off the dazzling white snow. The big doors on the east side of the temple served as backdrop for their post-wedding pictures. These doors were sealed until the second coming of Christ. Josh stood tall with his arm around her. Dianne leaned against him, nose running, eyes watering in the bright sun. They had to hold their breath while pictures were taken so their cloudy breath wouldn't ruin the pictures. *The picture is far from optimum anyway*, Dianne thought. There would be a small reception back in San Antonio. The pictures there would be better, but that missed the point. Several cameras clicked. The family, Josh's family, wanted more poses. Dianne was shaking in the crisp, cold Utah air.

"Don't you think that's enough, dear? I'm freezing," Robyn said.

"Of course, not … *dear*. This is the only time we have for pictures outside the temple. Let's not be stingy about it." Dianne sensed a note of sarcasm in the way Josh said "dear." "Besides, my mom still hasn't taken one with my camera." Josh had a secondhand Polaroid camera. When his mother finally took the picture, Josh ran to pull out the multiple layered film and tuck it under his jacket to keep it warm for sixty seconds while it developed. When it was done, he pulled the tab separating the picture from the chemicals. It was a very nice black and white photo.

Looking at her image with her faked smile, she realized this was all a mistake. If only she had known what was going to happen in the temple before she went in. She had so many questions. So many things in the temple she did not understand, some of which were really scary.

After the picture taking was over, they went to the Hotel Utah across the street, where Josh's stepfather, Mitchel, had reserved rooms for the whole family. Mitchel had arranged for them to meet him in the parking area after they changed their clothes. When they got there, Mitchel handed Josh a set of keys.

"What are these?" Josh asked.

Mitchel pointed to a bright red car like no car Dianne had ever seen. It was a beautiful full-sized, bright red, two-door convertible. Instead of the outlandish tail fins most big cars had, this one had the fins folded into the shape of the trunk. Josh's jaw dropped. "That's the new Chevy Impala," he gasped in obvious disbelief.

"Yes. I ordered it for you as soon as it was available, and she's the big one with all the add-ons. I'm talking the 348 series 1800 turbo-thrust V-8 with three speed turbo glide tranny; you'll get up to 315 horses out of her. She has power steering, power brakes, power windows, and power seats, along with dual exhaust, quad headlights, and the new triple taillights. There's no car like her."

Dianne was not really interested in cars, but Josh and his friends talked about them all the time. This was the first production year for the Impala. Dianne had never heard of an Impala before, but this was one of the prettiest cars she had ever seen. It was loaded with chrome trim, but not to the point of being gaudy.

"Well, what do you think of her?" Mitchel asked.

Dianne had never seen Josh so speechless. She knew he didn't like Mitchel, though Mitchel was always friendly and helpful. Mitchel had married Josh's mother while Josh was on his mission. Josh had not gotten along with his previous stepfather, and Dianne believed his negative feelings toward Mitchel were a carryover from his first stepfather.

"I can't believe it. You got this for me?"

"Yes, why don't you take her for a spin?"

Josh put his hand out and shook hands with Mitchel. "I don't even know how to thank you ... thank you so much."

Josh opened the driver's door and signaled Dianne with a wave of his hand to get in. Dianne sat behind the wheel and slid over to let Josh in. The car felt even bigger on the inside than it looked from the outside.

Josh turned on the engine and it roared to life but quieted down when it was in idle. Josh turned on the radio. It was set to KNAK 1280 on the dial. "At the Hop" had just started playing.

"Remember this," Josh said. "'At the Hop' is the number one song on the chart this week. All the car magazines say the Impala will be the number one car of the year. So, we just started our marriage with the number one car playing the number one song. This is a number one marriage."

They had planned to walk to Kelly's Café on Main Street a couple of blocks south of the Temple for an intimate brunch together. Instead, Josh carefully drove their new Impala, finding a diagonal parking space in front of the building next to Kelly's. Though Dianne was excited about the car, she was still thinking about the way Josh had treated her while they took pictures. Underneath it all, she was concerned about her negative feelings in the temple.

"You seem a bit lacking in enthusiasm," Josh said, as they looked at the menus.

"It's just that I was freezing all the time we were posing for pictures. I know my nose must have been as red as a beet, my eyes were all squinty, and my feet were numb. And on top of that, none of my family was here to celebrate with me."

"I wouldn't worry about that. I don't think you realize how beautiful you are even with a red nose. Besides, I wanted to get married last summer, when it was warm. And whose fault is it that your family isn't worthy to go to the temple?"

"If I had known what the temple was going to be like, I wouldn't have gone there either … at least not without a lot more preparation." There it was. Dianne hadn't intended to say anything negative, but it just escaped.

"What do you mean?"

Dianne had never seen the kind of anger that flashed in Josh's eyes. "It's not that I don't believe … it's just that … well, I don't think I was prepared for what happened."

"Specifically," Josh demanded.

"All that stuff about secret oaths and covenants … it all seemed too much like the secret combinations of the Gadianton Robbers. I just had a dark feeling about it." In the *Book of Mormon*, the Gadianton Robbers were a secret combination inspired by the devil.

"But the Gadianton Robbers were evil. This is different; it's not secret; the temple is sacred … there's a difference."

"Maybe, but this whole secret … or sacred stuff is new to me. I wasn't expecting anything like that."

"Oh that," Josh said dismissively. "I had a little of that on my first time when I was starting my mission. It's not uncommon. I talked to the mission president about it. He told me not to worry. It takes some people many visits to the temple to develop the full understanding. And he was right. When I got back from my mission, I spent several days in Salt Lake and went to the temple several times a day. When I was done, I got the big picture. The feeling of light comes to some people a little slower than others."

"I don't see us going to the temple very often when we're back in San Antonio. Isn't the Mesa temple in Phoenix the closest one? That's about a thousand miles from San Antonio."

"I've been thinking about our honeymoon and the Impala. Let's drive her down through Manti. We can go through the temple there, and then let's go on to Saint George. We can spend a day there and do three or four sessions in the Saint George temple. Then we can go down for a night in Vegas, and from there we can go to the Mesa temple before heading back to San Antonio."

Dianne could see he was serious! "Even if we didn't stop to do temple sessions, that's days out of our way home. We could never get back in time for the reception my family has planned."

"Well, you'll just have to tell them to postpone it. It was their choice not to come up to Salt Lake for the celebration here."

"They were supposed to drive all the way up here for your family's reception, and then stand out in the cold while the ceremony was done in the temple?"

"Mitchel offered to fly them up with the rest of us."

"I know, but that's kind of like accepting welfare that they don't need."

"That's their problem and their choice. You promised in the temple you would be obedient to me as I am obedient to the Lord. The choice here is whether we allow time to go through the temple and increase your knowledge of it or drive straight back to San Antonio. I think it's pretty clear my decision is in keeping with being obedient to the Lord. So, we'll do what I said. End of discussion."

Dianne was speechless. She had made the covenant to obey him as he obeyed the Lord. The narrator in the temple offered opportunities for anyone to pull out of the ceremony if they had any question about making the covenants, but she didn't know what they were until after she agreed to proceed. Perhaps she still could have refused. There were choices, and she had made hers. After the food came, Dianne said, "We could stay here another day and go through the temple a couple of times, and then go through the temple in Manti. That way we could go home from Manti and still get back in time for the reception."

"I guess you don't get it. End of discussion. Period."

"Why are you being so mean all of the sudden?"

"I'm not being mean. Look, when we were dating and talking about getting married, things were different. The relationship was based on a terrestrial footing. Now we're married. We're on a celestial footing … a foundation of the priesthood. It's my duty to lead and yours to follow."

"I don't get a say-so?"

"Of course, you do. You just had your say-so, but then someone has to make a decision. If no one makes a decision, we get nowhere. By the covenant of our marriage, I have to step up. You call your family after we eat and tell them we'll be another week or so."

Dianne ate very little of her meal.

When they arrived in San Antonio, after multiple temple sessions in four temples, Dianne had not understood the ceremonies any better.

* * *

Mitchel and Josh's mother lived in a large plantation-style mansion with a three-car detached garage. Josh lived in the mansion with Mitchel and his mother after he returned from his mission. Mitchel offered to let Josh and Dianne move in with them while Josh went to school. Josh wanted them to have their own place. Above the garage was a thirty-five by twenty-foot room with a pool table at the end of the room on the side opposite the door. Near the door was a game table that could seat six. Near the table were a couple of pinball machines. Along the wall facing out from the front of the garage were two small windows. On the opposite wall there were two doors; one led to a kitchen and the other led to a bathroom. Josh talked Mitchel into fixing up the area over the garage for them. Mitchel had purchased one of the new king-size beds when they came out a couple of years ago. He liked it so well that he built a frame around the pool table to accommodate a king-size bed for Josh and Dianne. The frame had to extend out both sides of the pool table because the bed was quite a bit wider. The bed was about eight inches shorter than the pool table. Mitchel had a cabinetmaker build a headboard that fit around and over the extra space. Steps were provided on both sides to make it easy to get in and out of the bed. Mitchel put a large armoire on the wall near the bed. He provided three slightly overlapping room dividers to separate the bedroom from the rest of the room. In the remaining part, near the door, he put a couch and left the game table to use as a dining table. He stored the pinball machines in the garage. Josh set all the rules in their living quarters, and since they were "righteous" rules, Dianne had to obey them.

In the LDS Church, the Young Women's Mutual Improvement Association (YWMIA) was organized to provide religious instruction and social activities for the young women of the Church. Dianne enjoyed her participation in those programs with her friends. The Church provided the Relief Society for grown women, "to prepare them for the blessings of eternal life by helping them increase their faith and personal righteousness, strengthen families and homes, and help those in need." After her marriage, Dianne was moved from the YWMIA, where she was counselor to the class president, to the Relief Society. In a way, it would have been easier for her if they had moved to another ward. The way it was, she was around her friends who were participating in the dances and other activities organized for the youth, while she had to go to Relief Society to learn about sewing, cooking, child care, and other activities to help her be a better wife and mother.

* * *

A couple of weeks after they got home from the honeymoon, Dianne had a subject she needed to discuss with Josh. After a nice dinner, she brought it up. "We haven't been doing anything to prevent me from getting pregnant."

"What are you talking about?" Josh demanded.

"Well, it's just that I'm only a junior in high school, and we agreed I would stay in school until I got my diploma. If I get pregnant, that will be very difficult."

"No, it won't be difficult at all. It will be impossible. You'll just have to drop out."

"But we agreed I could finish."

"You can … if you don't get pregnant."

"So that's what I mean. We need to do something to prevent that."

"Whoa! We never agreed to *that*." Josh's tone was dismissive.

"But when I told you I wanted to graduate, you completely agreed. You didn't say anything about me getting pregnant and dropping out."

"Well, I didn't think I'd have to tell you the obvious about the birds and the bees." Dianne was taken aback by the sarcasm in his voice.

"Why not?"

Josh stood up from the table. "Look, we can't have a kid if God doesn't send a spirit. You understand *that*, don't you?" He began to pace in front of her.

"Yes."

"So, it follows, if he sends a spirit, it's his will for us to have a child."

"What's your point?"

He stopped. "If we try to prevent you from getting pregnant, we could be standing in the way of God's will. We have to make it possible for God to send us a new spirit, and if he does, it's his will that you drop out of school to be a mother to the child he sent. See?"

"Yeah, I see all right. I wanted to graduate, and you told me if we married now, you would see to it that I could graduate. Now you're telling me you are not going to follow through with your promise."

Josh spun on his heels and walked toward the kitchen. He turned around, and Dianne could see the anger in his eyes. "Why in the heck do you think we got married in the first place ... just so we could have intercourse and live together? The marriage command is pretty clear. We must be fruitful to multiply and replenish the Earth. It's also clear your desire should be to me, and I should rule over you. That's in the scripture, and it's part of the covenant you made." He walked toward her, and with his finger in her face, he forcefully said, "Where do you think a stupid high school diploma fits in the scheme of eternal life?"

Dianne knew he wasn't shouting, but it seemed like he was screaming at the top of his lungs. She had to get away, so she ran past him to the bathroom and closed the door. In the mirror she could see tears streaming down her face.

There was a quiet knock on the door. "Come on honey, don't cry. Listen, I promise I'll make sure you can stay in school as long as you're not pregnant. You know, a lot of women take several years to get pregnant the first time. If it's God's will, you won't get pregnant until after graduation. It's all in his hands, after all."

"Leave me alone for a while, please." Why had she gotten married so young? That was her mistake. She was just beginning to get used to the idea, and now this.

"Okay, just one thing more and then I'm going down to my folks' place to watch Dragnet. A high school diploma is a good thing when it comes to getting a job ... other than that, it's superfluous ... in fact, it may be vainglorious. I promise I will always take care of you, so you'll *never* need to get a job. Come on down when you're ready."

After a few minutes, Dianne left the bathroom. She looked at the makeshift living room with its plain beige walls marked and gouged over the years when it was used as a recreation room for Mitchel and his two sons, both of whom were married now. The only thing on the walls was a copy of a photo of the Salt Lake Temple. If they wanted to watch TV, they had to go over to Mitchel's house. She wished she had at least a record player. *Vainglorious?* she thought as she sat on the edge of the bed. There were more changes in life as a result of the wedding than she had imagined. *What a mistake*!

* * *

Josh never seemed to care about whether Dianne enjoyed sex; it was all about him. In fact, a number of times he said for a woman to enjoy it was a sin. But after their discussion about contraception, Dianne not only failed to enjoy sex, she began to dread it. Each time she wondered if that would be the time to end her days in high school. And then, in March, she missed her period. When the doctor confirmed she was pregnant, Josh insisted she drop out of school immediately.

"But I'm not even showing yet," Dianne protested as they climbed the stairs to the door of their apartment.

"You need to be home taking it easy." Josh unlocked the door and held it open for her.

"I'm the top player on the girls' tennis team. They are counting on me." Dianne walked into the apartment.

"Tennis? You've got to be kidding. No way are you going to be on the tennis team."

"Why not? I mean, I asked the doctor about it, and he said it would be okay for a couple of months."

"I don't care what the doctor says, you can't be running around like that while you're carrying my son … that's one. But you especially are not going to run around in those skimpy tennis outfits anymore. That's for children; you're a woman now."

"There's nothing wrong with a tennis outfit."

"They expose your legs all the way up to your crotch. How can you wear your temple garments in a tennis outfit? Whatever you wear has to cover your knees."

"I don't see you wearing your garments while you're playing basketball on the Church team."

"Well, at least my basketball shorts don't expose my legs up to my crotch."

"A lot of women with temple recommends go swimming in swimming suits that are not as modest as a tennis outfit."

"Look, you're pregnant, so you're dropping out of school to stay home, and you're dressing modestly like a wife and mother should. That's the proper decision, and that's my decision, and you will obey. End of discussion."

Dianne's eyes brimming over. "End of discussion" was how most their discussions ended anymore. She went to the bathroom and closed the door so Josh wouldn't see her crying.

"I don't like it when you rush to the bathroom every time we have a disagreement," she heard Josh say from outside the door. His voice was conciliatory, but she knew that didn't mean he had changed his mind.

"Arguing makes my bladder explode," she lied. "What makes you think I'm carrying your son; it could be a girl, you know."

"If you were more in touch with the spirit, you could know these things too."

Dianne blew her nose and sat on the toilet seat with her face in her hands. She wondered why she had such a rebellious spirit, and if she would ever be spiritual enough to know things like that.

* * *

Dianne dropped out of high school before the end of her junior year. The tennis team barely missed qualifying for the State Tournament. She had let her friends down. Summer was hot even with the fans in their apartment running around the clock. In the autumn, her friends headed back to school for their senior year. Dianne stayed home with nothing to do. Maintaining the apartment and taking care of all her other duties left a lot of time for boredom. She liked to read novels, but Josh would only let her bring church books into the apartment. She looked forward to having the baby to take care of. At least it would give her something to do. She wanted a larger apartment so they could have a nursery for the baby, but Josh insisted they could make room for the baby so they could save their money to move later. He made that statement a week after he emptied their savings account to buy himself a new target rifle—he already had two. So, Dianne busied herself organizing things to make room for the baby. Josh insisted on using blue paint for the walls in the corner where the crib would be. They bought some little blue rompers along with diapers and baby bottles. Things were ready when Dianne's water broke, and they rushed her to the hospital.

Josh insisted Dianne have the baby without anesthesia because he believed natural childbirth helped bond the mother to the child. When they put the baby in her arms, she felt a flush of love. Though Josh was certain it would be a boy, somehow Dianne wasn't surprised at all to find it was a little girl. She was beautiful.

They cleaned the baby, and then took her to the nursery. It was a long time before Josh came in to see her. "Did you see our beautiful little girl?" Dianne asked.

"Yeah, I saw her all right."

"Aren't you excited? She's so perfect, so beautiful. Did you count her fingers and toes?"

"No, she was bundled up, but I suppose she has the required number."

"I know you were expecting a boy, but the most important thing is that she is healthy and perfect."

"Look, I expected our daughter would have a big brother to look out for her."

"But she'll have a great father to look out for her."

* * *

When they took the baby home three days later, Dianne found the corner of the room was painted pink, and there was a small wardrobe of pretty pink outfits folded on a small dresser Josh had purchased while she was in the hospital. "It's beautiful, thanks so much," Dianne said, though she was disappointed she hadn't been included in any of the preparations, especially shopping for baby clothes.

"It's not her fault she's a girl," Josh said.

Dianne didn't know exactly how to take that statement. "I know that we were going to name the baby Joshua Junior, but that won't do now. I was thinking that we could name her after my mother."

"I want to name all my daughters with names that end in *NE*, like their mother."

"Oh ... you mean something like Caroline."

"Yea, but I was thinking Karianne."

"I like that. It's not as common as Caroline."

"Okay then, Karianne it is. Her middle name can be my mother's name."

"Oh no. Our girls aren't having middle names."

"Why not?"

"When they get married, their middle name will be Godwin."

"But they can still ... "

"End of discussion."

For the first few weeks Josh seemed out of sorts. But Dianne knew he had accepted Karianne when he started calling her his little peach fuzz. Then he really jumped in with her; feeding her, changing her diapers, bathing her, getting up at night with her. As soon as he got home from work, he would spend time playing with her before dinner. He played peek-a-boo, blew bubbles on her stomach, and basically kept her laughing until it was time to eat. They were quite a couple, and Dianne was proud and happy Josh was such a great father.

When Kari was about six months old, Josh sat down at the table to have a discussion with Dianne. "I think it's time for us to start working on another baby."

"I was thinking of waiting until Kari is at least a year old."

"Look, I'm certain God's plan was for us to have a boy first. I have thought about it a great deal. I have come to the conclusion he sent a girl because you have been so difficult. I want you to increase your spirituality and stop giving me so many problems when I make decisions for the good of the family."

"You're thinking that Kari was sent as a punishment ... to me?" Kari leaned back in her chair.

"All I'm saying is, there are certain protocols in a family, and you seem to have a difficult time recognizing them and submitting to them. That weakens the family structure."

"I just want a fair part in making decisions like it is with my parents ... I mean ... my example is two people discussing pros and cons and coming to a mutually satisfying conclusion."

"Look, when choosing between black and white, gray is not an option. God doesn't work in gray tones. And your family isn't what I would call a good example of righteousness. I don't mind working toward a solution to a problem that fits both our needs, but many solutions are not ... it's just that gray doesn't work. But, okay ... let's try to ... I mean we'll work to incorporate our differences on some issues."

"Okay. You want to start working on having another baby, and I want to wait." Kari folded her arms. "I want us to get a bigger place, and we definitely can't live here with two babies." She leaned over the table with her hands on it. "So how about this; we start looking for a new place big enough for two children. When we have made that move, we start working to have another baby."

"We don't need to get a new place until the new baby arrives." Josh stood to the room dividers. "This place is plenty big enough for now."

"But, Josh, this is not a black and white decision like 'thou shalt not kill.' There is room for gray here."

Josh paced back and forth a couple of times. "This house, I mean where Mom lives, is going to be my house after they die. Mitchel is twelve years older than Mom. He's going to die first. As soon as he dies, I plan to move in with Mom to help her care for the house and to make sure she leaves it to me in her will. If I don't make sure I'm around, I could end up losing the house to one of Mitchel's sons." Josh sat down again.

"Well, he is their father, and that's the house they grew up in." Kari spread her arms with her hands turned up.

"I know that, but they're going to get major fortunes from his company. They both already have fantastic houses. It only makes sense that I should have this house."

"But you can't really think you are going to live over a garage and raise all the children you plan on having until Mitchel dies. We have to move someplace bigger."

"Okay, just so you remember that any place we move to is temporary."

Dianne stood and rushed to him. She leaned over and gave him a big hug. "Thank you so much. This really means a lot to me."

They found a new place and over the next few months, Josh was more amenable to letting Dianne participate in the decision making, though there were still many decisions he reserved for himself. Dianne found it much easier to bend to his will now that she was allowed some input.

Twenty months after Kari was born, Dianne gave birth to a beautiful baby boy. Josh named him Joshua Jace Godwin Junior, and he called him Junior. At the time, he praised Dianne, saying it was her righteous acceptance of her role in the family that brought God's blessing in the form of a son.

* * *

After Junior was born, Josh began to wake up in the night with nightmares. He wouldn't talk about them with Dianne. One night he woke up screaming.

"What is it Josh? Please tell me."

"It's my brother, Jace," Josh answered in a daze.

"Didn't he die when you were about eight or so?"

Josh turned away. "Come on Josh," Dianne pleaded. "We shouldn't have secrets."

"Okay … he was murdered." Josh sounded like a little boy.

Dianne sat up straight in the bed. "What do you mean?"

"Never mind, go back to sleep; I'll be fine." Josh turned away.

"Oh no, you can't drop something like that and then brush it off. You tell me. I'll find out from your mother."

"She doesn't know. In fact, I don't know for sure. There's no proof." Josh rolled to face Dianne.

Dianne turned on the lamp. "Why do you think he was murdered? Who did it?"

Josh told her when he was eight, his family worked on a farm as sharecroppers. His stepfather, Mel, made him work hard on the farm, but Josh's little brother, Jace, was too little to help. Mel wanted to ship him to Arkansas to his grandparents, but Josh's mother wouldn't hear of it. "I really loved Jace. But not Mel. To Mel he was just a moocher."

"The summer before Jace was going to start first grade, Mel brought him in from the fields. He was just limply hanging from Mel's big hands. Mel said Jace ran under the wheel of the tractor, and he hadn't seen him until it was too late."

Josh explained his mom went into shock. She cried and screamed for about an hour, and then she went into a trance for several days.

Mel put Jace in a large, cotton flour sack and buried him by the barn. When Josh's mother got her wits back, she demanded Mel give Jace a proper burial. Mel told her there was no money to get him buried properly and he was dead; the location of his body didn't matter. He said if they reported the accident now, days after it happened, the police would start nosing around.

Josh got out of bed and began pacing. "The way he used to slap that kid around, I think he hit him too hard out there in the field, and that killed him. I think he put his body under the tractor wheel and rolled over him to hide what he did, and he didn't want the police checking the body too closely, just in case they could see what really happened."

Josh said Mel told the school they had sent Jace to live with his grandparents in Arkansas. About eight months later, Josh's mom earned some money from a neighbor for helping them bottle fruit.

She took it to a local salvage yard and bought some used wood. When it was delivered, she told Mel to make a box and dig Jace up to give him a decent burial. Mel called it a waste of money. Josh's mother threatened to call the mortuary to help her if Mel didn't do something.

"Mel made the box, but he wouldn't dig up Jace. He made me do it. When I found him, the sack and his clothes were pretty much deteriorated. What flesh he had was rotten, and he smelled terrible. I had to dig him out piece by piece and put him in the box. It was horrible, because he didn't come out in one piece. There was no way I could even recognize him. His eyes were just holes in his skull, and his lips were gone, so his teeth just sat there."

Dianne pulled her knees up to her chest. "That's terrible. Your stepdad didn't help at all?" Dianne knew she sounded stupid, but she couldn't think what to say about a story like that.

Josh stopped pacing and stood beside Dianne's side of the bed. "Hell no! He left me there alone and told me to come get him when I was done. When he came, he pulled most of the mint out of the garden to put around Jace in the box to hide the smell. It didn't help much." There was anger in Josh's voice and his shoulders were shaking.

"After the box was nailed shut, we all got together behind the house and buried him. Mom said a prayer and put a wood cross on the grave. Anytime anyone asked about the cross, Mel told them it was a pet dog."

"Didn't you ever report it to the police?"

Josh walked to the window and looked out at the night. "I planned to report it when I turned eighteen, but the asshole died of a heart attack when I was sixteen."

Dianne knew Josh had a stepfather before Mitchel, though no one in the family talked about him. She didn't know he had died.

She got out of bed and stood beside Josh. "That was a terrible thing."

"I cried about it every time I thought about it for a couple of years. I had nightmares until I was in high school, but then they faded away. I think taking care of Junior has brought the memories back."

"You should talk to a therapist, Josh. That whole thing is ghastly."

"Therapy is for women. I don't know why I told you any of this. I'm certainly not going to reveal the whole thing to anyone else … especially a stranger. I handled it when I was kid; I'll handle it in my own way now." Josh walked back to the bed, pulled up the covers, and rolled over. Dianne heard him say, "End of discussion."

Though Dianne tried to bring it up a couple of times after, Josh let her know it was a closed subject. The nightmares ended soon after.

* * *

Robyn – San Antonio, July 2012

Robyn slammed on the brakes. The car came to a sliding stop about five feet into the intersection. She had been thinking about the night's events as she drove to her mother's house and didn't see the stop sign until it was almost too late. There were no cars coming, so she pulled through the intersection and stopped next to the curb. She put the car in park and leaned back. Her hands were shaking, and she could feel her heart racing. It wasn't just that she nearly ran the stop sign. She should be sitting in the theater watching *Chicago* with George. The feeling that something basic had changed in her life had grown as she drove, and she didn't know exactly what it was.

The soft rain continued falling straight down from a windless sky. The reflection of lights on the wet street and the tears that filled her eyes made driving difficult. The smell of the fresh, clean air seemed a mockery, but of what?

Robyn took a deep breath. She relaxed and let her mind wander. She thought about a Sunday school class on genealogy she had taken when she was twelve. For this particular class, the teacher had requested the students bring in genealogy sheets for four generations of their family tree. Her mother had reluctantly given her copies from the family genealogy book. Much to Robyn's surprise, she discovered that Grandma Mary was not her real grandmother, and she had two aunts she had never heard about.

As she sat in the car, she mentally reviewed the events of that day long ago. The genealogy sheets were confusing, so when she got home from Sunday school, she asked her mother about the missing family members.

Her mother explained that Dianne Taylor was married to Grandpa in the Salt Lake temple. Josh and Dianne had six children. Karianne was the first, and they called her Kari. Joshua was born after Kari and they called him Junior. The third was Darlene. Dar was her nickname. Robyn had never heard of Kari or Dar. Robyn had always thought Uncle Junior was the oldest and Marlene (Marli) was the second of the children. Joanne (Jo), and Lorianne (Lori) followed. Jo was Robyn's mother. After Lori was born, Grandpa and Dianne were divorced. Following the divorce, Grandpa married Mary and they had a son named Ronald (Ron). Ron had Down syndrome, so they decided not to have any more children. Robyn had never been told about the divorce, so she thought Mary was the mother of all the children.

According to Robyn's mother, Dar and Kari ran away to California. When they got pregnant out of wedlock, they returned to Salt Lake City where the family was living at that time.

Jo explained Dianne wanted to pursue her own dreams, so she left Grandpa. When the divorce was final, Grandpa was so upset it nearly killed him. Marli, Jo, and Lori were still living at home. Dianne got a big cash settlement and a fat alimony check, but she wasted all the money partying. She tried to force Grandpa into selling his house and cashing in his retirement savings to give her more money. When he refused, she convinced Kari and Dar to tell a monstrous lie about him to destroy him. It was then that Kari and Dar ran away the final time. Dianne ran with them to Southern California.

At the time of the accusations, the family still lived in Salt Lake City. The accusations had done so much damage to Grandpa's reputation he felt he had to leave Salt Lake and move back to San Antonio, Texas, where he had grown up and his family lived. "Good riddance to all of them," Jo said.

When Robyn pressured her mother for details about the divorce and the accusations Dianne and the girls made up, her mother told her she was too young to understand.

As Robyn sat in the car reminiscing about that conversation from so many years ago, she had a sensation that whatever happened with Dianne was linked to the feeling something in her life had changed. She wiped her eyes and put the car in gear. Her mother wasn't going to like it, but Robyn had to have the answers tonight.

CHAPTER 3

1984 – The Accusations; Darlene

Wednesday: March 28

Is there any reason why you think you may be responsible for your daughter's death?

I don't exactly know … I mean I can't fucking remember what happened, you know. I just want to remember, that's all. I just fucking need to know.

But you seem to have a prejudice to blame yourself. Can you think of a reason why?

I'm not fucking prejudiced about anyone. And what the fuck would that have to do with this? My daughter wasn't any kind of minority; she was just a tiny baby.

Right. What I mean is, is there any reason you think you may want to blame yourself?

I DON'T FUCKING WANT TO BLAME MYSELF! My dad thinks I'm all fucked up! Yeah, a lot of people think I'm pretty fucked up! But I for sure don't want to blame myself … FUCK THAT! Sorry.

Nothing to be sorry about. You can shout as much as you like while we're here. It's part of the process of letting the emotions out. Okay. I get you don't want to blame yourself, and I'm not here to blame you or upset you. I think it would help if I understood why your dad thinks you have a problem.

My fucking, end of discussion, dad blames it on the drugs. Ha! My sister thinks it's all because I'm a fucking whore. Little does she know! Mr. Falcone would say I'm a fucking slut. He's a fucking pervert. I ran away after Mr. Falcone fucking *raped* me. He was the first to take me like that, but when it was over, he told me I wasn't a virgin. What an asshole! How could I go to school after what that bastard did? I could make those fucking high school jerks feel good and be done before they ever got to actual ... what shall we call it here? Intercourse?

I suppose it is safe to say if he raped you, he had sexual intercourse with you.

Yeah, that's what he did all right. Okay, I wasn't perfect, but we'll just say I could make those other guys feel good without fucking intercoursing them. Why did I do it? Not for the fucking fun of it, I can tell you that for damn sure. It was 'cause I can get guys to do anything I damn well want for the pleasure I give. I'm in fucking control.

Who is Mr. Falcone and what happened with him?

It's kind of a long story.

I'm listening.

A boy in school, who shall remain nameless, stopped me behind the auto shop one day and asked if I wanted to see him with his fucking clothes off. I didn't actually ... but since he was asking, I said okay ... and, honestly, I wasn't really as impressed as he fucking thought I would be. So, he starts to show me how to touch him ... really fucking inappropriate, if you know what I mean. It's not as straightforward as you might think, either. With practice, I get good at it. So, he fucking tells *everyone*, and before you know it, I'm stroking some fucking guy almost every week. Then another guy, who shall also remain nameless, teaches me how to get the same result by using oral means. It fucking got to be almost every other day I'm behind the fucking auto shop with some horny guy.

What about Mr. Falcone?

He was the fucking geology teacher at high school. So, one day he fucking keeps me after school because he's heard about me … I have a fucking reputation. And he says I have to take care of some of his needs and he won't tell my fucking parents about my fucking reputation. As an added bonus, I won't have to worry about my fucking grades. So, he did what he did and it hurt but there was no blood, so Mr. Falcone said I already wasn't a virgin before he touched me. Like he fucking thought I cudda forgot something like that.

And you didn't like doing that?

Being raped by a schoolteacher? Jesus, no.

What about the things with the other boys?

… Fuck no!

You seem a little hesitant.

Sometimes … yeah, I got some enjoyment. I don't know … maybe it was that I liked the control, but mostly it was just a mess. The fucking novelty of it wore off pretty fast.

Why didn't you refuse?

That's a fucking good question. For some reason, I just didn't seem to be able to say no … well, fuck, I can *say* no, but when they push me, I just do it … while saying no … but all the time I'm pleasuring the bastards and sometimes, I'm just thinking about flying a kite or something while I'm doing it. I was some kind of a fucking *wimp*. If I charged money, I coulda made a fucking mint.

What about now?

You mean if some fucker wants *me* to make *him* happy?

Yes.

I can usually say no, but if he keeps pushing, I usually find myself falling into the same old pattern.

Why do you think that is?

Well, I wish I fucking knew the answer to *that* fucking question. But what I'm really here for is to find out about my daughter. What I'm thinking is, if someone could hypnotize me … that would *drag* the fucking memory to the surface.

What is it you want to remember?

All I remember is loading my daughter into the fucking car. We went about a half mile before the accident, and I don't fucking remember none of it. I know the fucker that T-boned us was drunk and ran a red light. There are plenty of witnesses to *that*. What I'm wondering is ... if I wasn't paying attention, and I fucking let it happen ... I mean the intersection is pretty open, so logic says I should've seen him coming in time to stop ... unless there was something like a fucking truck or a bus blocking my view.

I don't do hypnotism, but I have a colleague whom I work with. She has a lot of experience with memory issues. She is also a psychiatrist.

Isn't that a lot of money?

Yes, but if she can break the ice and get things started, I can work with you if you need more help after. I'll set up an appointment, if you like.

Okay, we'll see what happens.

Wednesday: April 04

I got the report from my colleague. I had a suspicion there might be something like this based upon your experience during high school and your difficulty in saying no.

I'm not sure I can *believe* those fucking memories the hypnotist got out. It's not even clear to me what happened at this point. Could a father really do something like that to his own fucking daughter? I mean, it seems so *perverted*. You know what I mean?

Unfortunately, it happens all too often.

What I mean ... oh God.

Are you all right?

Yepth.

Here's a napkin.

Sorry. I don't know why that pops up like that ... all of sudden. I hardly ever cry, but since my daughter ... it seems to pop up *often* for no fucking reason. I'm living with my mother ... me and my two boys. I told her about this ... the memories from the hypnotist. She was very tender, and we cried together, but she's no help.

How so?

She's sympathetic. She knows *something* happened, and she wants to help, but sh ... she ... she doesn't be ... believe me, and well ... ...

Here, take the whole box. Just let it out ... it's okay.

I don't usually get like this ... fucking snot and tears all flowing together ... you know.

Do you keep a journal?

No. There ain't nothing about my life I would put in a fucking journal.

You've never kept a journal ... even when you were young?

Why do you want to know that?

There's a type of therapy called "writing therapy" where the patient uses expressive writing through a journal, poems, or storytelling to get in touch with her feelings. We find that kind of thing often helps a person's memory. It also helps to deal with the emotions the truth brings up.

I used to write a little bit of poetry, but I'm no good at it.

It's not about being good. It's about the thought process one goes through as she works to define her feelings in order to put them on paper. Also, it gives a patient something to look back on as she progresses in her ability to handle the effects of the trauma.

But what I really *want* is to find out about my daughter.

It seems that's very tightly connected to the sexual abuse you suffered. My colleague and I feel the issue of your daughter will resolve itself as you work through the molestation.

So, you're giving me homework, like I'm back in fucking school?

No matter what kind of help you get, it will involve homework on your part. That's always a part of the process. So, for our next session, I would like you to start putting your thoughts on paper in a journal ... or in poems, if that suits you better.

Wednesday, April 11

How did the writing go?

I did a lot of writing ... starts of this and that ... fucking junk, but you were right, the more I worked at it, the more the fucking memories came out and the clearer they got.

And how are you feeling about it this week?

I can't *believe* what fucking hap ... I can't believe *any* of this, but the fucking memories are so *clear* now. It's like some fucking dam has been busted. I can't *believe* it, but I can't deny the fucking memories ... the goddamned, fucking, perverted, sick, disgusting, fucking memories! No one could fucking do that, especially a fucking father to his daughter! But the memories put a lot of things in perspective. A lot of shit that didn't make sense is suddenly clear. And *every* day some other piece of shit falls into place. God! I'm going to have to believe my fucking father FUCKED me. Shit! I fucking don't know how to even *look* at this. FUUUUCK!

Did you bring anything that you wrote?

I can't fucking write *this* away. Jesus! I wrote a stack of shit ... total shit. I tore it up ... some I burned, and watched the fire, and cried. I pissed in the ashes of some. So okay ... I brought *one* poem. Here it is.

I FOUND OUT TODAY

I was used,
I just found out today.
I was abused,
I just found out today.

And all my life I've failed,
And now I know why.
And all my hopes seemed jailed,
And now I know why.

> You used me for your needs,
> You Bastard!
> You used me as object of your deeds,
> You Bastard!
>
> I locked it as in a vault,
> I found out today.
> It was not at all my fault,
> I found out today.

Tell me about this poem.

Well, ain't much to fucking *tell*. It's like I was a *person*, but *he* didn't see me that way. It's like I was just a fucking *object* to him to use to get his fucking rocks off. I feel anger, but at the same time there's a disappointment … you know.

Disappointment about what?

That I thought I had … I mean my own fucking *father* didn't care a fucking *shit* about me. They said *I* was rebellious. Fuck! Who wants to follow a constant storm of fucking rules? My dad set the law, and we followed. It was fucking embarrassing sometimes. I didn't do *anything* bad; I just challenged the fucking rules. I'd get home from activities late, sluff school sometimes, I even fucking shoplifted a few times. I was *nothing* like my older sister. She fucking argued and back talked. She and my dad were *always* in one upset or another, and she *always* caused it.

She's always been okay to me though. She's four years older, and I looked up to her more than my fucking dad and mom. It was her who I turned to after I ran away from home and was lonely for family.

Okay, I'll admit that fucking stuff I started doing behind the auto shop was … more serious. I couldn't seem to say no when a guy wanted something. I probably would've fucked them if they insisted, but they were happy with what I did with my hand and mouth. It was that fucking *Falcone* that popped my cherry. I didn't believe him when he said he wasn't the first to fuck me. What? That fucker didn't think a girl would *remember* the first time? But now … FUCK! My own fucking FATHER! Jesus! What a fucked-up mess! I'm so angry. I could spit fucking horseshoes. I can't *stand* this.

You had a vision of your relationship with your father, and though it had its problems, the memories you are experiencing now are far worse than anything you imagined before. In a sense it's like a death.

You got *that* right.

When you suffer that kind of loss it's normal to grieve over it. The grief is a process that manifests in many ways as a person goes through the loss and puts it behind them. Not that they ever forget it, but they learn to go on with life without carrying the pain.

Well, I'm *not* grieving. I just want to fucking *destroy* the bastard.

As I said, grief manifests itself in a number of ways. Anger is an important part of grief. But let's look at your mother. She's faced with a big loss also. Imagine finding out your husband hurt your daughter.

Except she doesn't even fucking *believe* it.

Often, when a person first confronts a loss … and this is quite normal … the first response is denial. That is followed by anger, and then emotional pain manifested as what we normally call grief. This would include uncontrolled crying. It seems to me your mother may be experiencing denial but at the same time sharing your pain and tears.

So, what are you saying?

Namely, that your anger is normal, and your mother's denial is also normal. They are just different places on the continuum of recovery. You remember last week you weren't really sure the molestation had happened, but this week you seem pretty positive.

Yeah … well, the memories got too damn clear to fucking deny.

So, the denial phase was reasonably short for you. I want you to continue to write and be aware of the feelings that come up as you do.

Wednesday, April 18

So how are things going?
    I don't know, I'm still angry.
    Did you do some writing?
    Yeah … I brought one poem. Want to see it?
    Sure.

YOU WANTED ME??

You wanted me born - you forced Mom to have me,
And don't think I am ungrateful for the life you gave me.
    But Why?

You called me from my spiritual home above,
And I know you gave me shelter, food, and love.
    But Why?

You wanted to use my little body for your selfish reasons,
And I know you fucked up my life in all its seasons.
    Is That Why?

In this poem, I see the anger is still there, but now you're beginning to question and think about the reasons. This shows movement toward a step we call bargaining. That's where the grieving person searches for reasons and some power to protect herself from the pain.

So, does that mean I'm getting better?

It shows you're progressing, which is the path to recovery.

Well, I don't *want* to stay in this fucking mess. I think about a lot of things when I try to write, and some of them I fucking don't like.

That's a good sign. Do you want to talk about those feelings?

I feel so angry sometimes I think I could kill the bastard. It's all bottled up like it's going to fucking explode.

A couple of sessions ago you said you don't know how to look at this. Part of the process of letting the pressure out requires that you look at it. By that I mean to bring out the details of what happened when you were a child so you can evaluate them as an adult. Do you think you are ready to do that?

You mean remember what happened? That's what I've been fucking doing. That seems to be the whole fucking problem.

What I mean is to face the memories and talk about what happened and how you felt at the time.

The fucking details?

Exactly. Can you do that?

Well, what I remember are perverted Walt Disney games. For instance, the least perverted game was fucking Snow White. This is fucking sicko, but it's the least. It starts with me on the bed with my eyes closed … …

Wednesday: April 25

How did things go last week?

I had some fucking nightmares about those fucking games. I know the games were his perversion, not mine. I can see … actually feel at a gut level I was the victim. I got this sense of being a very innocent little girl. And then I was used. But it's not like a sudden new me appeared. I'm still angry, and Mom's still trying to work this out, so the bastard didn't do anything to me.

Did you get a chance to write something more?

Sure. Here.

BUTTERFLIES AND INNOCENCE;
WHERE DID THEY GO?

A little girl chases butterflies,
Running and jumping across the green grass.
Her red dress flows and her blonde hair flies,
Her innocence shining like polished brass.

Who would think to hurt or abuse,
This precious gift from God above?
What fiend would want to misuse,
This everlasting proof of His love?

HER DAD??!?!?!!??!

yep

sooo sad…

I can clearly see you grasping at your innocence. It may not seem important to you right now, but that is a major step. The fact that you still feel the anger doesn't concern me. It often happens that a person gets stuck in a step along the way as she progresses. We haven't been at this very long, so I wouldn't worry about some parts taking longer than others. It's all a process of healing, and the rate is different with each person.

Wednesday, May 2

How did this week go?

I don't know. I can't seem to get over the fucking anger. And now I'm feeling … I don't know … maybe the term is anxious or afraid, but I don't know of what. I just couldn't bring myself to write.

Sexual abuse is not just a mentally emotional experience. I believe there's a strong physical component that causes damage to your body.

Well, that's all healed up by now.

Yes, that's true. Sometimes physical healing leaves physical scars you can see. But I believe physical damage also leaves unseen scars that often express themselves through fear and anxiety. This is a blocked emotional energy that can be released by physical activity. Some therapists have their patients focus this activity in an aggressive way, such as hitting a pillow when they're angry. I have had good results with patients using almost any strenuous activity when they're feeling anger, fear, or anxiety. That could be running, playing tennis, riding a bicycle … anything that gets your heart rate up and leaves you out of breath.

So, you're saying I should go run around the block.

It's not a magic pill, but it helps, and over time you can get stable results.

What I'll get is a place on the fucking Olympic team.

Well, let's talk about some physical things you could do and how to apply physical work to your healing process.

Fine. … … …

Thursday, May 09

Did you have a good week?

I suppose I stayed out of trouble. I'm not getting any fucking closer to finding out about my baby, and I'm thinking … it's like maybe I'm not fucking good enough to know anything about that.

It's common for victims of child abuse to feel unworthy partly based on feelings of shame.

When I was young, I lived in a dark cloud of constant fucking shame, but I'm not feeling it now.

But you are feeling unworthy or undeserving of a better life.

Fuck yes.

That's generally based on a foundation of shame or guilt. It may be buried, but the consequences of it are impacting your progress now.

So, what do I do about that?

I believe the shame victims of abuse experience stems from spiritual wounds to the soul.

Well, this is where we part. I don't have any interest in fucking religions. I had a friend who was raped by a fucking preacher. She fucking died because of the emotional problems from that, and the fucking bastard is still a preacher … loved and adored by all. The fucking church I used to belong to protects perverts. No, I'm not getting involved with a fucking church. I'm fucking done with that forever.

I'm not talking about an organized religion. All the times your father molested you, he assaulted your body. He could do that because he was bigger and stronger than you. The natural consequence was physical fear and anxiety. Then he used his emotional power over you to force you to keep his secret. That results in emotional anger on your part. All the time he was molesting you, there was a part of you that knew what he was forcing you to participate in was fundamentally, morally wrong. Morally wrong actions lead a person to spiritual feelings of shame and unworthiness. When I talk about spiritual healing, I'm talking about steps to recover from damage to your spirit. You can call it your higher self, your higher consciousness, or your soul; whatever. This is not something that is healed in an organized religion at Sunday morning services. Though many who follow spiritual healing practices believe in God, others don't. But they do believe there is a higher self that serves as their moral guide. In any case, there are numerous kinds of meditative practices that can help you expand your self-awareness and help the deeper part of yourself heal from the underserved shame that was put on you.

This could fucking take years. I don't ... fuck ... why me?

It took years to get you in this mess. But we're not talking about years of therapy. What you need to learn is how to overcome the negativity of what happened. There are things that can help you. Would you be willing to try doing some meditations?

Fuck. I don't have the fucking time for that shit. I'm not into Hare Krishna chanting or whatever the fuck that Hindu, Buddha shit is.

I'm not talking about Eastern religions. The meditation I'm talking about is quiet time to let your mind move away from stress. Many of my patients have made good progress with just ten minutes of meditation a day. Would you like me to show you how it's done?

I guess I might as well. I don't know what the fuck else to do. ... ...

Wednesday, May 16

How has the meditation been working?

The running and meditations? I don't know. Sometimes I feel like I got something or I'm on the verge. I did write something this week, but mostly, as I work at it, everything is greyish. Here, read this.

WHY DAD?

What did I ever do to you?
I was just a baby
Did you know how it would hurt?
You didn't know? –
Maybe

> Did something happen to you?
> When you were just a baby
> Did you ever think of me?
> You didn't feel? –
> Maybe ... ...

How do you feel when you look at what you wrote there?

That was one of those on-the-verge things. I was feeling something, but as I look at it now, all I feel is fucking empty.

I see here an attempt to move out of your pain and to even think that your father may have some pain of his own. This is an important phase. This emptiness is normal, and it's something you need to experience. It's a time of reflection about what was lost and what it meant. It's quite normal to feel sadness, emptiness, and even despair. In a way, it's letting out the sadness of what happened. I wouldn't try to force you through this too quickly, because going through this will allow you to come to terms with the loss. It's not the end, but it's definitely progress.

Wednesday, May 23

How did last week go?

Maybe I've slipped back to anger. The more I thought about what my dad took from me, the madder I got. So, I just confronted him.

What happened?

He *fucking* denied it and got all angry with me. So, I told *everyone*; my siblings, his new wife, my mother. Holy fuck, the shit *really* hit the fan. Nobody believes me ... not *even* my own fucking mother ... I mean she's nice and sympathetic and all, but she still keeps telling me I need to think about it more, be more *sure* of myself. So now I'm fucking isolated. And to tell the truth, I'm angry as hell ... at my own *whole* goddamned, fucking, screwed-up family. Well, I haven't told my sister in California yet, but I suspect the news will get to her pretty fast. This is what I wrote.

WHAT'S THE POINT?

> Okay, the truth is out
> So why lie?
> Now it's what we all talk about
> So why lie?
> The truth from you could have made us well
> So why lie?
> If you keep hiding it, you will go to hell
> So why lie?

I think if you had asked me about this, I would have suggested you wait until you were further along before confronting him. But I'm not concerned about the anger you're going through at this point. I think it's different. What I mean is, this is focused on his denial rather than just on the abuse. Not that that is especially healthy by itself, but it shows you're taking a broader look at the whole thing. If you don't believe in God, what did you mean by hell?

I'm not thinking of some fucking kind of afterlife hell. I'm thinking of him being forced to deal with what he did here … in this life.

What would that look like?

First he would have to admit what he fucking did. Then he would have to make a stab at trying to fix it … maybe confess and do some jail time … …

Wednesday, May 30

Did you have a good Memorial Day?

Not exactly.

What happened?

Oh my God! After our last session I told my mother the *details* of exactly what the bastard did. What I mean is, I *started* to tell her the details of the games. I did Snow White and Cinderella, and then her eyes suddenly went *wild*, like she was watching a parade of ghosts. And then she *fell* on the fucking floor on her knees and started to *cry*.

And she is just sitting there on the fucking kitchen floor all snotty-nosed and tearful, and she's blubbering about how she should have *known*. And then she gets on the phone to my *sister* in California, and she's just bawling and blubbering to *her*. And I'm fucking not getting any of this. I mean I'm telling her about *my* problem and she's on the phone with my *sister*, like it's *her* fucking problem.

Well, come to find out, that bastard had *also* molested my sister, only she didn't forget like me. She told Mom about the games too … years ago … when it actually *happened* … when it would have meant something. Apparently, my mom thought the fucking bastard was just roughhousing too much, and so she told him to tone it down. She never fucking *suspected* what the bastard was *actually* doing. What do you think of something like that?

Often the mother knows what's going on but doesn't do anything about it because she's overly submissive to the husband and is afraid to break the family up. But there are also times when the mother really doesn't know.

Well … I mean the way she was crying and all. She looked so fucking surprised in a real bewildered way when it all dawned on her, it was like her fucking eyes were going to fall out. I think she was one of those who didn't know. Anyway, here's my poem for the week.

GROWING

> I came, and where I came from was the best
> My school, my family, were better than the rest
> My country and my God set the example
> Anyone who said otherwise, I would trample
>   But I was young;

> For my own good, the bastard used a belt
> And I was told I earned and deserved every welt
> For his own pleasure he used my clay
> And left my soul wounded from his play
>   But I was young;

> The world has grown to be a more complicated place
> Every person is important, each an individual face
> Where you came from or where you belong
> Are not so important as your own song
>   But now I see;
>
> I see more an evil, self-serving side
> The bastard, in anger, would hide
> To make me wrong and show himself right
> He has decided to ban me from his sight
>   But now I see.

So, your father doesn't want to see you anymore.

Well, the feeling is *mutual;* I can *assure* of you that.

This poem is very encouraging.

It is?

Yes, because it shows the signs of acceptance. That is a much healthier place to be.

Acceptance?

Not acceptance of the acts that were committed, but acceptance of the *fact* that they happened, and that you didn't deserve to have them happen to you. … Here, take a napkin.

I should learn to bring my own. You know, I'm thinking some of the meditation is working. I'm looking at a bigger picture now.

That shows in the last half of the poem.

Wednesday, June 06

How have things gone this week?

I spent a lot of time meditating about religion and God. It's like on this Earth the fucking bastard is really *tied* into church and everything. The people in the Church think he's a *fine* fellow, and … well … I've got this reputation, so when it comes to taking sides, of course, *his* friends in the Church all side with *him*, and the same with my fucking family too.

How does that make you feel about the Church?

Well, the Church is just an organization, you know. It's full of good people and bad people, same as the whole fucking world. I'm beginning to think there might a God, and in some sense, he is my father, but I also have my bastard on Earth. And, well, this is kind of what I'm feeling.

THEY BOTH LOVE ME, BUT ...

one abused me
ONE sent me so he could

one hurt me
ONE knew that he would

my FATHER there sent me to progress
my father here gave me stress

HE sent me here to play my part
he took advantage and broke my heart

did I agree with HIM before my birth
to be subject to him while here on Earth?

maybe I had an important lesson to learn
or perhaps a special blessing to earn

... MAYBE NOT

This shows a lot of development. It's been hard for you, but I see in this poem very strong indications of more acceptance that you didn't cause the abuse in any way. How do you feel about it?

Acceptance? Yeah ... I think that's it. I feel good about my feelings, if that makes any sense. I mean, for as long as I could remember there was almost nothing about me that I felt good about. What I really think is ... I can deal with it now. I know it.

Wednesday, June 13

Is there anything new to report this week?

Well, my sister came up from California. She *totally* backed me up and supported my story to the rest of the family. My brother and a couple of my sisters tried to convince me my memories were implanted by the hypnotist, and they had a *bunch* of stories about that sort of thing to prove it. But my sister from California never forgot ... I mean her memories of what my dad did were real ones she *always* had. They were not repressed, and she was *never* hypnotized. And the ga ... the games he played were so detailed ... we couldn't have just accidentally made them up to be exactly the same.

My brother and another sister are standing sort of on the fence, but the rest of the family is *totally* destroyed. Somehow this whole thing got involved with the Church, and my dad is planning to leave Salt Lake because he says *I* have ruined *his* fuc ... his reputation. So now, there is all the hoopla about who's going where, and my dad has told *everyone* not to talk to me or my sister ... or my mother, for that matter. And so now we are the outcasts. *He* has set the limits.

How do you feel about that?

It's pretty sad ... really. But, on the other hand, I can't back down. I warned my siblings to keep their children away from him. I don't know what else I can do. Here, I did this poem about everything.

MY DREAMS

I had such high hopes for me and my children
To see them grow up with the love of a complete family
You were in many ways such a good father
I thought they would learn as you taught me

I miss you and the very special times we had
And sometimes I think I can understand
What it was that caused my dreams to disappear
To dry and blow away like sifting sand

My expectation was marred by your actions
And then destroyed by your denial of reality
I have struggled over the years to restore
My life, my self-esteem, and my spirituality

Once I desperately needed your approval
Another time just the truth at last
These were the things you could never give me
So, without your help, I cleaned my past

I miss you now, and oh how it surprises me
I thought I would hate and never forgive
It was beneath the dignity of your own spirit
There is a time to suffer, overcome, then forgive

I FINALLY FORGIVE YOU

I am so proud of you. It takes a great deal to reach the point where you can forgive.

Don't misunderstand me. I do miss some things, but I don't want to be around him. I'm fine with being separated from him, and in fact, if I could, I'd see him sent to prison, but it wouldn't be to get even with him or punish him. I think it's just better all-around if he's kept away from society, especially little girls. I don't think those perverts ever change. I sent him a letter basically telling him what he did to me, how I feel, and challenging him to come clean and make things right. So far, I haven't heard back, and I don't really expect to, but writing it was the most healing of all the things I've done.

You have come such a long way in a relatively short time. You get to a place where life is manageable, but unfortunately, it can never be like it didn't happen. Most victims of this kind of abuse learn to live happy productive lives, but there is always something there. You know, even your language has improved. Yeah … I always was a bit of a potty mouth.

It's not just that. Your grammar and use of language have also improved. It's not that you didn't know or understand good grammar;

your poetry shows better language than you spoke. Sometimes when a person is dealing with emotional trauma, they take on a different valence. In a way they become someone else ... not to the extent of a split personality. They begin to talk and act like their friends.

I know I feel so much better. I'm glad it shows.

It's unfortunate your father won't accept responsibility for the things he did. That usually makes the healing process that much more complete.

I suppose so. But, hey, I've got plans and a future I could never see before. I'm going to complete my education and get a career, so I can provide stability for my sons ... and for me.

December 6, 1984

Dr. Ruth Schroeder:

I can't express how grateful I am to you for your help last spring and summer. It was a vicious, trying time for me. Though we never got to the question of what happened just before the accident that took Cindy from me, I learned a lot that makes it possible to face my life. I stayed with my mom after our sessions were done. Joshua and Mary left Salt Lake as planned. They took my sisters Jo and Lori because they are minors and still live with them. They all moved back to San Antonio—his hometown. Junior and his family are staying in Salt Lake. My sister Marli got married and is also staying in Salt Lake. Mom is going to move to Southern California. She and Kari have formed a strong relationship since the truth was told. I am planning to move with them. Mom has convinced me to get an education and will help me do it.

I realize I am far from healed, but I learned a lot, and the tools you taught me are a great help for me when things get rough. I never go a day without meditating. What a help that is! I wrote a short poem about my journey with you—summarized a great deal. Love and anger are such strong emotions, but at the same time, totally opposite. So, I actually wrote two poems and printed them side by side. They are constructed the same, but the words show how opposite they are. They can be read back and forth or separately down the columns.

Love always,
Darlene

ANGER IS GOOD	LOVE IS BETTER
Anger is:	Love is:
the justified emotion	the uncontrolled emotion
disgorged from the mind	expressed from the heart
to the one who messed up your life	to the one who put meaning in your life
Anger is:	Love is:
the fire of hell	the peace of Heaven
disgorged from the soul	expressed from the soul
to the one who caused your strife	to the one who released your strife
Anger is:	Love is:
the first glimmer of life	the bright light of life
that propels the heart	that supports the heart
from the depths of despair	against trials and despair
Anger is:	Love is:
the internal motivation	the spiritual motivation
that propels the soul	that supports the soul
into sun and fresh air	on plains of light and air
I am full of anger - therefore I exist.	I am full of Love – Therefore I Live

Sincerely,
Darlene Godwin

* * *

Robyn – July 14, 2012

Robyn parked the car in front of her mother's house in a middle-class neighborhood. It was a two-bedroom stucco house built in the 1960s. The yard was kept in immaculate condition. The front yard had a beautiful rose garden surrounded by flower beds where Robyn's mother planted colorful varieties of annuals. This way she changed the appearance of the house each year by planting different flowers. As Robyn turned the engine off, she glanced at the clock on the dash; a bright green 9:37 PM stared back. Just a little more than four hours since she and George had left to go out to dinner. So much had changed in that short time.

Robyn's mother, Joanne Charles, was considered pretty by those who knew her, but she was critical of her straight hair and long nose. She had dark eyes many considered captivating. She and Robyn looked so much alike they were often mistaken for sisters. Joanne, or Jo as she was called, was forty-eight, but she looked young for her age. Now that she was a grandmother, she enjoyed the effect it had on strangers when they discovered she had a grandchild.

Robyn's father died when she was two years old; she had no memories of him. Jo never remarried or even had a boyfriend. After Jo's husband died, Jo and Robyn moved in with Grandpa for a couple of years, until Jo was able to get on her feet.

Robyn rang the doorbell. When Jo opened the door, she looked surprised. Usually when Robyn came to see her, she would just walk in the door as she had done when she lived there. Robyn was sure the redness of her eyes was also apparent.

"Come in. Shouldn't you be at the theater? What's happened? You look terrible." Jo's expression was one of concern and confusion.

"Mom, I need to ask you some questions. I'll tell you what happened after you answer them. This is hard for me, so I need your help. Please let me ask my questions first ... then I'll answer yours."

"I don't understand but come in and sit down. I'll try to do what I can. Why can't you just tell me what's going on? Is Debbie all right?"

Robyn walked into the living room and sat on the chair by the window. The room was done in Queen Anne style. It looked beautiful, as did all her mother's things. The living room was not used very often. Like Jo, it was formal and not comfortable. That suited Robyn fine for the conversation they were about to have.

Jo was dressed in a silk bathrobe with a flower design. Robyn realized her mother's whole life was stiff and formal.

"Debbie is fine. Mother, there are some things I need to know about Dianne, Karianne, and Darlene." Robyn purposefully made the statement in a flat, determined tone.

Jo's face turned hard. "I have told you before, and I will repeat it now; those women have nothing to do with our lives, and I do *not* intend to discuss them as long as I live!" There was the kind of finality in her manner that always put Robyn off. She had expected this. Her heart was beginning to speed up as she geared herself for the confrontation she anticipated.

"Mom, I really do need to get answers to my questions. If you won't talk to me, I'll call Aunt Marli in California and get Dianne's phone number." Robyn knew the family members in California were in contact with her grandmother and aunts.

"Why are you threatening me? You've never done that before. Tell me what has happened." Jo's voice was anxious, and Robyn could discern fear in her eyes.

"Why won't you tell me about them? It seems like everyone else in the family knows."

"Where are George and Debbie?"

"Goodbye," Robyn responded in a tired monotone as she stood up and walked toward the door. The action surprised her. It was not how she had planned to handle the situation. It was almost as if some other power were moving her.

"All right, what is the question? It's better you get the truth from your mother than to start chasing after other people and their lies."

Robyn sensed resignation in her mother's response, and that gave her courage. "You told me Dianne didn't have time for you. I want to know if she ever told you, face to face, that she didn't have time for you."

"No, she was such a hypocrite that she could never face me with the truth herself. She always made my father be the bearer of bad news. And she left him to deal with the pain her rejection caused. It was so hard on him to endure her rejection, and then to have to sooth and comfort me and the other girls also."

Robyn could see water gathering in her mother's eyes. "Did she ever tell you why she abandoned you?"

"At first she had a story. She said my father kicked her out. But if that were true, why didn't she fight for me? Why did my father cry real tears after she left? Why did she apostatize from the Church? Why did she move hundreds of miles away from me? Why wouldn't she come to see me?" Jo's voice began to break, and tears were on her cheeks. Robyn reconsidered bringing all this old hurt back. But she really needed to know the answers.

"Did you ask her those questions?"

"I tried at first. Either she couldn't answer them, or her answers didn't make sense. She tried to blame my father for everything. She said terrible things about him. You know what a spiritual man he is. He wouldn't be capable of the things she accused him of."

"What sort of things?"

"That he had kicked her out of the house, and that he was lying about her, that he cheated her in the divorce, and other things." Jo wiped the tears with the palms of her hands and sat straight in her chair. "I prayed about it as we are instructed in the scriptures. It says when you ask God if a thing is true that he will cause a burning sensation and a good feeling to grow inside you if it's true, and that if it's false, you will feel confusion about the thing. I prayed with my father about these things. He took me to the mountains where we could be close to God, and we knelt together to ask God. I felt very good about the things that my father told me and very confused about the junk that my mother told me. I had the assurance of the Holy Ghost about what was true and false. Grandpa is a very spiritual man who never misses going to the temple at least once a month. He has always held high positions in the Church and has always stayed close to God.

"I loved my mother, and I really missed her. Those feelings were not mutual. At first my father had to be both father and mother to me. It was so hard, because he was also suffering from the loss of his wife. Marli, Lori, and I were the only ones still living at home. Marli was involved with cheerleading at school and Lori was only around eleven years old, so I was the only one who could see and understand how much he suffered."

Jo stood and walked to the fireplace. "My father and I shed a lot of tears together. Finally, he married Mary, and she stepped in to be my mother. She filled a large void in my life at a time when I really needed it."

Robyn took a breath. "What was the evil story they made up about Grandpa?"

Jo's composure left her as she angrily responded, "That was the dirtiest, most lowdown, despicable thing that anyone ever pulled! The only reason that they could possibly have done such a contemptible thing was to defame a righteous priesthood holder. If there was ever any doubt that they were in the power of Satan and doing his work, it was that assault on the priesthood, the Church, and my father. It's sad to know that someone you loved has given themselves over so completely to that worker of iniquity. SOMETIME THEY WILL BE BROUGHT TO THEIR KNEES, AND THEY WILL CRY THE WAY THAT THEY MADE MY FATHER CRY!" Jo shouted the final words.

Robyn had never seen her so angry, but she had to persist. "Exactly what did they say he did?"

Jo returned to her chair and sat down. She dropped the level of her voice. "It doesn't matter; it was all lies … repugnant, devil-inspired lies. This was all discussed with the stake president, and we all prayed together about it." A stake president presided over several wards in the LDS Church. "We all got the assurance of the Holy Ghost that they were telling a lie and that my father was telling the truth. If you could have seen how he tried to fight back the tears, you would know what terrible suffering he went through because of those women and their evilness. You could just feel the darkness around them." Jo's voice began to quiver as she finished. The hurt was evident, but there was also unmistakable hatred. Robyn had never felt hate from her like this.

For the first time, Robyn began to understand why Jo considered her mother to be dead, and why she would not even allow her to be mentioned. Robyn could not allow this to deter her. "Mom, I need to know exactly what they accused him of doing." Robyn put more understanding and empathy in her voice, but she maintained the firmness intended to let Jo know she would not be put off.

Jo looked at Robyn. Her eyes seemed to soften. "Okay, if you insist. They accused him of filthy sexual games with them when they were just children and …"

Though Robyn was expecting something like that, hearing it caused her to audibly suck air into her lungs.

Jo knelt in front of her and took her in her arms. "It's okay dear. It happened a long time ago. I'm sorry I told you. I should have kept my mouth shut. I hope that now you can see why you shouldn't have anything to do with those women. They're no longer part of this family. God will repay them for the pain and suffering their that lies caused."

Robyn gently pushed her mother back. The whole pathetic mess seemed just too funny. Robyn began a humorless laugh.

Jo seemed confused. "You said that you would tell me why you needed to know about this. What has happened?"

"This is going to be hard, Mother." She intentionally used Mother instead of Mom to help her regain her composure and to send a message to her mother that she wasn't kidding about what she was about to say. Robyn began to explain what happened, but when she got to the part about Grandpa pulling his pants up, Jo interrupted her.

"STOP!" Jo stood up as she shouted. "I don't want to hear anymore lies about my father! You've been talking with those devil worshippers, and they put you up to this! I THOUGHT THEY WERE OUT OF MY LIFE!" Jo began to pace. She seemed to be talking to someone else. "This time they will not get away with it.

I'll sue them. I'll charge them with slander. We'll see how they like being in jail.

"First it was my sisters, now she has perverted my own daughter. I cannot stand this. I wish God would strike her dead!"

Before tonight, Robyn would have been afraid to see he mother in such a rage. Tonight, she felt outside the situation. She sat calmly until her mother had expelled all her anger. Jo screamed at Robyn and the devil and condemned her mother and sisters to everlasting hell. She threatened Robyn with all the dominions of hell and being cast into outer darkness for eternity if she didn't stop her questions. "My father has been through too much already over those lies! I simply will not have this brought up again. Where is he? What did you say to him?"

Robyn explained about the accident and that Grandpa was in the hospital. She also told her George had called the police, and they had talked to Detective Floyd about it.

"Why are you lying about him? What hospital is he in? If George hurt him, I'll see him in jail."

"Grandpa has a concussion. The doctor said he's awake, but I haven't talked to him. George and Debbie are staying with his sister, Jean, for a couple of days. I will be staying there too … just until the police have checked the house out and collected whatever evidence they need."

"Well, there's obviously a mistake here. You didn't actually see him molesting Debbie. You said he was trying to explain what happened when he fell. We'll just have to wait to see what he remembers when his head clears up. Have you made any formal charges against him?"

"No, not yet. We'll meet with another detective tomorrow after he examines the house. We'll see where this all goes from there."

Jo was calm and businesslike. "All I ask is that you don't charge him until after we hear his explanation. And for God's sake do not let this get back to any of the family until we have cleared it up. I'm sure that once we have time to check out Grandpa's story, you'll see that this is all just a big mistake."

"I'll wait, but if the evidence proves … you know … well, if he did something inappropriate, I don't think I have a choice."

"Well, it's late. We can talk in the morning. I'm going to call the hospital."

Robyn waited while her mother made the call.

Jo hung up the phone. "He's awake but still seems confused. I'm going to the hospital to see how he's doing. I'm sure we can straighten this all out in the morning."

CHAPTER 4

1980 – The Divorce; Dianne

"**G**od damn you for being a damn MEXICAN!" Josh's eyes flashed with a hatred Dianne had never seen as he stood in front of her with his hands at his sides clenched into tight fists. She had felt a lot of things with Josh over the years, but the fear that filled her now was new.

"I don't know what you're talking about," she answered as she backed away from him.

"You lying bitch, I'm talking about your great-grandfather, Luis Sandoval."

Dianne's face was hot. She had never heard Josh use that kind of language with anyone. "I've never heard that name. Which great-grandfather?"

"No use playing dumb with me. It's all out in your genealogy." Josh had backed her to the living room couch. She sat down. "Your father's mother's father ... Luis Sandoval," he said, wagging his finger in her face.

Dianne tried to remember her genealogy. Genealogy was a very important part of being a member of the LDS Church. The research on her family went back to the seventeenth century on some lines.

"My dad's mother was Carol Hayes, and her father was ... um ... John ... that's right, John Hayes."

Josh picked up the briefcase he had set on the floor when he came in the house. He pulled out a piece of paper and shoved it in front of her. It was a family pedigree sheet going back four generations on her father's side. It showed her father's mother, Carol Hayes, was the daughter of Janice Cooper and Luis Sandoval. Luis died and later, Janice married John Hayes and had two sons. Apparently, she had legally changed Carol's last name to Hayes. "Where did you get this? I've never seen this before."

"I got it from the genealogy library. But that's not the point. You lied to me."

"First, I never lied to you. I never said that I wasn't Mexican. But the fact is, this is the first I've ever seen this. You've seen my sheets before. This is something new." She thrust the paper back at him.

"There is such a thing as lying by omission. When we were dating, you knew I can't stand those lazy money-grubbing Mexicans, and you failed to tell me you're one of them."

"I can't tell you what I don't know. Are you accusing me of being lazy?"

"I'm saying this proves you are Mex...i...can," he pronounced the word slowly and disdainfully. His face was pulled into a snarl.

"But you've seen the sheets I have," Dianne weakly answered as she backed away. "They don't show that. That must come from later research. But so what? I'm not lazy or money-grubbing, and all people are God's children. The Church even gives the priesthood to blacks now." Some of her fear was being replaced by anger. She stood her ground.

"I'm not even going to argue about that. I can't stand Mexicans, and now I'm married to one."

"Yeah ... well then, your children are Mexicans also." There was a shadow of defiance in her voice.

"THAT'S THE WHOLE GODDAMNED PROBLEM RIGHT THERE!" Josh walked over and knocked the table lamp into the middle of the living room floor. The fear rose like bile in Dianne's mouth. Josh turned and put his right finger in the air. "Wait a minute. Thomas Jefferson had black kids. He said that when the black blood got to one thirty-second, the person would be white again. So, your grandmother was half-Mexican. That makes your father one-fourth and you one-eighth. So, our kids are down to one-sixteenth, and since they started from a brown race instead of black, you could say that they are all white now."

"You could say that … if it makes things better for you." Dianne tried to sound strong, but her mouth was suddenly dry as she looked at the lamp on the floor.

Josh stepped in front of her, and his finger came down to about an inch from her nose. "I'll tell you what makes me feel better. You go to the bedroom, take your clothes off, and get into bed. I'll be right behind you."

Dianne opened her eyes as wide as she could. "NO! No, no, no. You're not using me like that. That's supposed to be an act of love, not hate. No. Never again … at least not until your attitude about Mexicans changes drastically." To use sex like this was another side of Josh she had never seen. She was angry now.

"You're refusing me my marital rights?"

"For as long as you refuse my human rights."

"THIS ISN'T OVER … NOT BY A DAMN SIGHT," Josh shouted as he walked out the front door, slamming it behind him.

Dianne was shaking from a cocktail of surprise, anger, and fear. Just this Wednesday Del had called from Santa Barbara to announce Kari had delivered a daughter they were naming Frances. Everything seemed so good just three days ago. Kari and Del had moved to Santa Barbara where Del got a good job managing a grocery store. She and Josh had talked about planning a trip to California to see them. But that was Thursday; today was Saturday. Tomorrow the family was supposed to be in church. How could she go there with this hanging over her head? How could she live in a house where she would be hated for something that was not her fault, and something she could not change? It was not something she even wanted to change. Dianne could see no solution. Josh would have to be the one to change this time, and change did not come easily for him. *God laid a big one on him this time*, Dianne thought.

* * *

Josh returned late that night and slept in the room Dar had used when she lived at home. He had nothing to say all day Sunday. It wasn't until Tuesday that he was willing to talk to Dianne again. Marli was doing homework at a friend's house and the younger girls, Jo and Lori, were at a school activity with their friends.

"I don't see us living our lives like this," Josh began.

"What do you mean?"

"Not sharing a bedroom."

"Well, I'm not going to stop being part Mexican. I think we should see a marriage counselor."

"No. I'm not having a stranger prying into our private lives. We're going to have to work this out together; meaning you are going to have to be willing to take care of my needs as is your duty."

Not this time, Dianne thought. She knew she was right, and she was strong enough to stand her ground on this no matter what he would try. "You always tell me you are obeying the Lord, and as long as you do that, I am bound by my covenant to obey you. Okay … I've gone along with that all our married life. This time you are judging a whole group of people based solely on race. Mexicans are *completely* accepted by the Church. That means the Lord accepts them. We should love everybody regardless of race. I'm proud to be part Mexican. I want my children to be proud of their heritage also." Josh visibly flinched. "Your attitude is not in keeping with the Lord's commandments. This time you are not obeying the Lord, so I'm not bound by covenant to obey you."

"You are *not* allowed to judge me."

"Nevertheless."

"So, you plan on denying me my marital rights from now on?"

"That's entirely up to you."

Josh paced slowly. Finally, he stopped in front of her and turned. "Oaky, let's say we do see a counselor; I don't see us living together until after we work things out. It would be like you flaunting yourself but withholding from me. Someone is going to have to move out ... at least temporarily."

"Someone? That would be you, wouldn't it?"

"Well, I'm in the Bishopric, so I have to stay in the ward boundaries in order to fulfill my calling. Your only calling is President of the girls MIA program. That's not nearly as important as my calling, so you should be the one to move."

Dianne recognized he was bargaining this time instead of throwing "End of discussion" at her. "My calling is as important to me as your calling is to you."

"But as far as the ward is concerned, you are over twenty to thirty girls. I'm over everyone in the ward, including all the girls. If you really want to work things out, you're the one who has to move."

"It'll be pretty expensive to rent a place big enough for me, Marli, Jo, and Lori."

"Look, the girls have their friends in the ward, their classes, and everything. It would be too disruptive to move them away from all that."

"We could move someplace in the ward."

"That would be like not moving at all. We would be involved in all the ward activities, and it would be just too weird with all our friends around. They would get enmeshed in the process of us working things out."

"I don't like moving out and leaving the girls behind." Dianne couldn't think of a strong argument to counter what he said.

"It wouldn't be like that. It's just temporary and you could see them any time. They could have sleepovers at your place on weekends ... or you could just move back into my bedroom and submit to me like a righteous woman would."

Josh was using words and a tone that left Dianne no way out. She didn't want to move, but the conditions Josh was placing on her to stay were impossible, and she could tell he knew it. A marriage counselor was the only way to save the marriage. She would have to do whatever was necessary in order to get Josh into counselling with her. It would take a professional to get him to see the barriers he had placed. She was trapped.

* * *

In April, Dianne gave up her calling in the MIA and moved into a basement apartment in Sugar House, a neighborhood of Salt Lake City located about seven miles from the house where Josh and Dianne had lived. Josh located it and moved the furniture from Dar's room to it for her. It was the basement of a house near Twenty-First South and Ninth East. The house was a brick house about eighty or ninety years old. It had a large, covered porch across the front and a side door near the back of the house. Dianne's entry was through the side door. Inside the door was a landing. The stairs went straight up from the landing to the house and down to her right to the basement. At the bottom of the stairs was a room with a furnace and hot water heater. There was a storage room to her left. The basement had a moldy earth smell. Straight ahead was a wall showing the studs on this side and the back of dry wall that was nailed to the other side. Straight ahead an old quilt hung from the ceiling. Behind the quilt curtain was an opening through the wall into the basement unit where she would live. After pushing the quilt aside, she stepped into a room that went across the basement left to right. It looked like it was about twenty-five feet long and fifteen feet wide. The floor in front of her was concrete painted dark chocolate going from the wall on her right to about fifteen feet to her left. From there to the left wall of the basement, the floor was linoleum. In the area with the linoleum, there were a sink in a Formica countertop, an electric stove, a refrigerator, some white metal cabinets, and a small table with two chairs. In the middle of the floor in front of her there was a dark blue shag rug covering about three-fourths of the floor. There were a beige couch and two matching over-stuffed chairs, all of which were old, worn, and stained. Straight ahead, across the room, was another blanket hanging from the wall. Behind that blanket was the opening to a bedroom about ten feet wide and fifteen feet long. The concrete floor was painted light blue. There was a small, dark blue rug in the middle. The room was furnished with a bed, a dresser with a mirror, and a dressing table with a nightstand and a chair, all of which came from Dar's room. The clothes from Dianne's drawers were piled in the middle of the bed. On the wall to her left was the only real door in the apartment. Behind it was a bathroom with a toilet, a sink, and a metal shower along the back wall. Next to the wall to her right was a commercial clothes rack like the ones found in inexpensive clothing stores. All her hanging clothes were hung there. The rack had more space than her clothes required. There were also some metal cabinets along the wall to her left. The bathroom floor was covered with a different color and pattern of linoleum than the kitchen. Essentially there were four rooms; the living room, fifteen feet by fifteen feet; a kitchen, ten by fifteen; a bedroom, fifteen by fifteen; and a bathroom, five by ten. Each room had a two-foot high by four-foot long window near the ceiling looking out of a window well below the outside ground level. They let light in but provided no view.

 Josh had a Ford Falcon and the old Impala his stepfather had given him, but Dianne couldn't drive either because Josh would not let her get a driver's license. He gave her the address and called a cab to take her there. He told her he was too busy to take her, but after seeing the apartment, she realized he didn't want to have to confront her with this. After the landlady left her alone, she sat at the kitchen table with her face in her hands and silently cried. The place was dreary, and she could see no way to brighten it up. She could not imagine how she could bring the three girls here for a sleepover. There were no hookups for a phone or television. She did not even have a radio. She wanted to call a cab to take her back, but she didn't feel up to asking the landlady to loan her a phone.

When she had talked to the bishop about giving up her calling with the Young Women, he had requested she hand in her temple recommend until the problems between her and Josh were resolved. It seemed the whole world had crashed down on her, and the only way out was impossible for her.

Finally, she did borrow the landlady's phone and had a taxi take her home. When she got back home, she told Josh the apartment was unacceptable, but he insisted it was only temporary until they could meet with a marriage counselor; besides the rent was already paid a month and was not refundable. The apartment was ideally located so she could meet all her needs without a car.

Josh drove her back the next day with the rest of her personal things. He drove her around the neighborhood. He was right, everything was convenient. She got him to promise to pay to have a phone line put in for her.

Each time Dianne talked to Josh about starting their marriage counseling, she had to walk over a half mile to the Snelgrove's ice cream store on Twenty-First South to use their pay phone, and each time he put her off. After two weeks of living in the basement, it became clear he had no intention of meeting with a counselor. She decided to have it out with him once and for all. She arranged a meeting at Fairmont Park, close to her apartment. It was an auspicious day; she heard on the news on the cheap radio she bought that the U.S. Olympic hockey team had beaten the Russian team in Lake Placid. It was touted as a miracle victory, leaving the U.S. team only one game away from the gold medal.

* * *

Fairmont Park was a little less than a mile from where Dianne lived, so she walked to the Sugarmont Drive entrance. Josh's car was in the parking lot, and he was sitting at a nearby picnic table. "You said if I moved out, you would go to counseling with me. Why are you stalling about the counseling?" Dianne began.

"Before we can even think about counseling, you're going to have to admit to the bishop you're having an affair with Brother Addison and get that all cleared up."

"What in the *hell* are you talking about?"

"There's no need for you to use that kind of language … it's completely unbecoming. You know exactly what I'm talking about." His tone sounded like it was a widely known fact.

"No, I do not. There's nothing at all going on between me and Brother Addison."

"You don't think I noticed how the two of you get together at church at every opportunity?"

"I was president of the Young Women's Association, and he's president of the Young Men's Association, so we had to coordinate activities between the two groups. But that's all there was to it. I haven't talked to him at all since I was released from the MIA calling."

"I don't know how you think you can prove you two don't have anything going on between you."

"Of course, we can't prove that there's nothing going on between us. But the point is, you're the one who's making the accusation, and therefore you're the one who needs to provide the proof. I would like to see you make that accusation to him face to face."

"What I'm telling you is; you have to resolve this issue between yourself, the bishop, and Brother Addison before we can even begin to resolve the problem between us. You're the one having the affair, and so you're the one who has to clear it up." Now he was downright smug. Dianne realized it was all made up and he didn't care if she knew it.

"The only problem that has to be cleaned up is the one that we're having because you're a bigot. You're making this whole Addison thing up to cover your bigotry. Why don't you just admit you're trying to get rid of me because I'm Mexican? What are you thinking … that you can get rid of me and marry someone who can give you acceptable kids?"

"If that's going to be your attitude, this conversation is over, and our relationship is over until you get these problems resolved. End of discussion." Josh got up from the bench and walked back to his car.

Dianne sat at the table watching him drive away. She realized her marriage with Josh was over. End of discussion. He was intentionally making it impossible to proceed with any kind of help or reconciliation. Three days later she was presented with divorce papers. She allowed Josh and his attorney to convince her to let Josh continue to live in the house and have full custody of the minor children so they could also continue to live in the house. She was given half the current appraisal of the house minus the current mortgage, the money to be paid to her whenever the house was sold. She traded her interest in Josh's retirement in order to avoid having to pay child support. Josh listed all the furniture in the house and assigned a value to it. Dianne got half of the value in a cash settlement. She got one year of alimony to allow her time to get job training and find a job to support herself. The alimony barely paid her rent. All her other expenses had to be paid from the cash settlement. Too late, she realized Josh's estimate of the value of the things in the house was about one-fourth of the real market value.

She also fell for Josh's argument that he should have full custody of the children because they needed to live with him in the ward, and he would be providing for their expenses. She quickly regretted she had not consulted an attorney to look out for her interests.

* * *

As Dianne looked for a job, she was handicapped by not having a high school diploma or a car. She thought about the day Josh made her withdraw from high school and his promise to take care of her so she would never have to support herself. She thought about the times she spoke to her friends with pride that she didn't have a driver's license because—because why? It seemed simple then, but now all she could do was shake her head at how stupid she had been from the beginning. Josh met her when she was a child. She had felt special for the attention he had given her, and she had swallowed all the crap dressed in false church doctrine that he fed her. He always treated her like a child—someone who needed his constant guidance in every part of her life.

After five weeks of searching unsuccessfully for a job, Brother Addison offered her a job as a clerk in his clothing store. Though she hated to take it because it added to Josh's narrative about an affair, she was desperate and had to accept it. She had to transfer buses twice on the way to work. It took her an hour and fifteen minutes to get to work and the same time to get home. Though Brother Addison offered take her to work and back she refused.

Kari and Dar were both in California. Junior was on a mission for the LDS Church in Canada. Marli, fifteen years old; Jo, twelve years old; and Lori, eleven years old, all lived at home with Josh. When the divorce was final, Dianne realized her life would have to change drastically. She couldn't afford a better place to live, so she moved the bed into the living room, bought a full-size box spring and mattress from the Deseret Industries secondhand store and set them up on the floor in the bedroom for the girls to use when they visited. She had a phone line installed in her apartment—Josh had no memory of offering to provide her with a phone.

When she met with the bishop of her new ward and told him she enjoyed working in the Young Women's organization he gently informed her that, as a divorced woman, she was not considered a good example for the young women; in fact, there were no callings in the Church she was qualified to hold. She had no friends in the ward, and so she became inactive. This was just another excuse for Josh to discourage a relationship between her and the girls. Josh set very strict rules about Dianne's visits. Soon, she noticed all three of the girls were becoming quite cool toward her. She got a sense part of the problem was her continued connection to Brother Addison. A couple of weeks later an opening came at the Snelgrove's ice cream parlor. She quit her job and took the lower-paying job. It had the advantage that it only took her about fifteen minutes to walk to work.

Dianne started correspondence courses from her high school in San Antonio in order to get her high school diploma, which she got in March of 1981. In May of 1981 Josh married Mary Mortensen, a widow who had no children of her own. In June Dianne started taking classes at Westminster College near Sugar House in preparation to register for a degree program in Business Administration. The college was about the same distance from her home as Snelgrove's, but it was east while Snelgrove's was southwest. There was a big grocery store on 1700 South, about a quarter mile away. The landlady let her use her washer and dryer for an additional ten dollars per month. Though the apartment was dismal, everything Dianne needed was within walking distance, so she didn't need to get a driver's license or buy a car, which she couldn't afford anyway.

In early July, Dar called to say she was pregnant again and wanted to move back to Salt Lake City. Dianne wasn't allowed to have a baby in the apartment and was on a tight budget that would not allow her to move. Ultimately, Dar moved in with Josh and Mary. Dianne felt it would be a good thing for Dar because Josh set strict rules. On October 22, 1981, Dar's second son, Chas, was born at the LDS hospital in Salt Lake City.

* * *

Robyn – July 15, 2012

The morning after Grandpa fell, Jo called Robyn at George's parents' house to tell her there was a perfectly clear explanation of what had happened, and she invited Robyn and George to come to her house for breakfast so she could explain.

On the way over, they stopped at their house to pick up some clothes. When they had left it the night before, it was a mess, but now it was all cleaned up and smelled of cleaners. At first, they couldn't figure out what had happened. The police weren't due until later in the morning, and they wouldn't have cleaned up anyway. George remembered during their move to the house, they had given Jo a spare key. George was enraged and wanted to go directly to the police station to formally file charges against Joshua for child molestation and against Jo for evidence tampering.

Robyn sat on the chair. There was no way she could explain what had happened. Her mother had never done anything so blatant before; it was impossible for Robyn to explain what she was looking at. She insisted they talk to Jo before running to the police with accusations. Surely, she knew that cleaning up a potential crime scene was a crime. It made no sense to Robyn at all, but her mother must have some explanation. She asked George to cool it and let her be the one to talk to her.

Jo greeted them at the door with a carefree smile. The house had the friendly smell of fresh-cooked sausage and eggs. Jo was dressed in a bright floral jumpsuit with an elastic waist and a high U neckline that flattered her figure. Her hair was curled and combed out. It was short on the sides and cut back from her ears. The top was long enough to be permed and had a full look. Her hair was dark brown, almost black. Jo plucked her eyebrows to a peak above each eye.

The preliminaries were perfunctory and short. They all sat in the living room—George and Robyn on the couch, and Jo in a chair at a ninety-degree angle to the couch. Robyn was closest to her mother.

"I had a long conversation with the doctor," Jo said. "Your grandpa is doing okay. However, these kinds of injuries sometimes create small blood clots that can lead to an epileptic fit or even a major stroke, either of which can be fatal. It seems that the critical period is about thirty days or so after the first event. That means that Grandpa has to be watched closely for about a month. I plan to move into his house to watch him and be close in case something does happen."

"What are the chances of something like that?" Robyn asked.

"They say everything looks pretty good, so most likely everything will be fine. I want to be close just in case the unlikely does happen."

"We hope everything will be okay. If there's anything we can do to help, let us know," Robyn said.

"Thanks, and I'm sure Grandpa will appreciate your concern."

"We stopped by the house on the way over. Someone has cleaned up all the evidence. Do you know anything about that?" Robyn asked.

Jo responded in a matter-of-fact tone, "After I talked to your grandpa last night, I was too keyed up to go to sleep. He said that he threw up and he thought that the house had been left in a mess, so I decided that the least I could do would be to clean it up for you."

"How could you do that? You knew the police were going to be looking for evidence!" Robyn raised her voice.

"Because after I talked to Grandpa, I realized that there is no need for evidence. It was all a misunderstanding. Besides, the police would have …"

"What do you mean a misunderstanding? I told you what I saw!" Robyn was adamant.

"Just calm down and I'll explain it. Your grandpa was about to change Debbie's pants for bed. He was picking up Debbie when she spit up on his pants. He put Debbie on the couch beside him and was pulling his pants down to wipe them off when Debbie wiggled and started to fall. Just as he picked her up, you and George came in. He set her back on the couch to pull up his pants, and before he could explain, you both hit the ceiling, and in the confusion, he tripped and fell. It was as simple as that."

"When he threw up after he fell, he was leaning to the side, so all the vomit went on the floor and rug and not on his pants, so the only thing on his pants besides his urine should be Debbie's spit up, and that will support his story," George commented.

"They took his clothes off at the hospital when they admitted him and put them in a plastic bag. I took the bag to the laundromat and dumped all his clothes in a washer."

"Why did you take them to the laundromat instead of bringing them home?" Robyn asked.

"Because Debbie threw up on his pants, and I didn't want the vomit in my washing machine."

"Did you see the spit up when you emptied his pockets?" Robyn asked.

"They already emptied his pockets at the hospital. I just dumped his clothes in so that I wouldn't get the mess on my hands … plus he said he that had wet his pants when he was on the floor. And that's true, because I saw the stain on the rug."

"There wasn't any spit up on Debbie's clothes when I got her ready for bed," George said.

"That's because she spit up on his pants," Jo said.

"I got a pretty good look at Grandpa's pants when he was on the floor. I saw them getting wet when his bladder gave way. I didn't see any sign of spit up, and apparently, you didn't even look," Robyn said.

Jo stood up and answered in a very friendly, almost too-sweet voice. "Well, you were pretty upset. It would have been easy for you to miss that. What you think you saw doesn't make any sense at all. You know what a religious man your grandfather is." She began to pace as she continued with her answer. "He loves all his family and wouldn't hurt any of them for the world. What he told me explains everything that happened, and it's the only explanation that makes sense. You only got a short glimpse of what was happening, and I'm sure that if you think about it, you'll come to the same conclusion. He wouldn't do anything like that. George, what do you think?"

George stammered back, "I came in behind Robyn, so I didn't see as much as she did. I can't imagine Joshua would molest a child, but at the same time, the story you just told is just as crazy. I'm pretty sure there was no spit up on his pants. I don't know what to think, but I'm going with Robyn on this. She saw something, and I trust her. It's just too bad we don't have the pants … that would certainly clarify a very important part of the story."

"Wow," Jo said. "I just never thought that it would be an issue after I heard Grandpa's explanation. I'm so sorry that I washed those pants. That was stupid of me." She turned to Robyn. "I just never thought that *you* would question his explanation. That *you* would require him to prove himself innocent. I'm sure that when you have had time to consider the kind of man that Grandpa is, you'll see that he couldn't do what you thought he did. He just would never do such a horrible thing. The whole thing rests with you and what you *thought* you saw in that split second. I'm sure you realize that there are several interpretations."

Robyn looked at her mother. This was so stupid, and what her mother said didn't make sense. For some reason, her mother had acted in a way that went against the basic protocols she had learned as a police officer. Someone else could give that excuse, but not her mother. "Mom, I just don't think I was mistaken."

"The truth is plain for anyone who wants to look at the person and not rely on emotional interpretations of things that were not clearly seen."

"I don't want to believe he could have done such a thing, but I can't go just by what I want to believe. I at least have to talk to Detective Hanson about this."

"I understand," Jo said.

Robyn let it go at that. Challenging her about tampering with the evidence would do no good and would more likely create a rift that would make everything so much more difficult. She left with George to pick up Debbie and take her home, and then she went alone to her appointment with Detective Hanson.

CHAPTER 5

1985 – The Goodbye; Darlene

Darlene heard the crunch of the tires on the gravel as her mother pulled the car away from the shoulder onto the narrow asphalt strip, but she didn't turn back to see her drive away. Not far away, the grass had recently been watered, and it sparkled in the early morning sun. A robin hopped rapidly four hops, stopped, and cocked its head—searching. Suddenly, it slashed its beak into the soft ground and pulled out a worm.

Darlene walked up the low slope from the road, laid the roses on the ground beside her, pulled open the canvas director's chair, and sat down. She laid her arms on the flat, wooden arms of the chair and grabbed the ends with her hands, tipping her head back. A lone cloud hung in the southwestern sky approximately over the Utah State Prison in Draper. She stared at the cloud wondering if she could see the face of God, or Jesus, or Joseph Smith. Seeing nothing but the cloud, she closed her eyes. The cloud would soon change but not the stone at her feet. With her eyes closed, she leaned forward out of the chair onto her knees and stretched her hand out to the stone; it was cold and smooth, like glass. A hot pain seared in her left hip joint—another reminder of the accident. She curled her fingers and dragged them across the stone into the engraving. She didn't have to feel it or see it to know what it said:

Cindy Godwin
Beloved Daughter and Granddaughter
Born November 6, 1983 - Died February 9, 1984

More than a year had passed since the terrible accident. So much had changed. Through therapy, Darlene discovered the dark family secret that was ripping the family apart. She didn't bring a camera—a photograph of the marker would be as cold as the stone. She would make a mental picture, wrapped with her feelings of love and lost hopes; one that would last the rest of her life. It would include the memory of tiny, pink fingers wrapped around her finger and the smell of fresh roses and Cindy's sweet, milk breath, the contented cooing of her little voice after nourishing herself from her mother's body, and her sore nipples she so hated then but longed for now.

Her father had paid for the stone. She knew that if he could, he would have added a postscript, "Killed by a Drunken Mexican." Fernando was illegal, didn't have a driver's license, didn't have insurance, and was drunk when he ran the red light, but he was not a Mexican. He had come up from Argentina to earn money for his family. To her father, all Spanish-speaking Latinos were Mexicans, and he had no use for Mexicans. Fernando was not injured in the accident. He was arrested, released, and then ran away before he could be deported. She never met Fernando. At first, she hated him as much as her father did, but now, she realized nothing could undo this stone or what lay beneath it; she would never again feel the warm breath of her baby girl on her cheek.

She heard the faint call of wild geese in flight. Above her, their V formation headed north to their summer nesting grounds, the west leg several geese longer than the east leg. *Everything changes*, she thought, and then she wondered if her winter would ever welcome spring. Her mind drifted back in time.

She ran away the first time in 1977 when she was fifteen. Derek had taught her how use her hands to make him feel good a year earlier. Other boys taught her other things, and she learned she could get anything with that knowledge. Then Mr. Falcone kept her after school. He knew her reputation. What he demanded, she had never given, and she told him so. He only became more insistent, and when he was done, he said she was already not a virgin before he touched her. Of course, that was a lie—she had thought.

After Mr. Falcone, she ran away; away from stupid rules at home, away from religion crammed down her throat. Or was it away from Mr. Falcone? It was winter, so she hitchhiked south down the I-15. She didn't see Provo when she passed with her head in the lap of the man in the station wagon, doing what he wanted her to and listening to "Dancing Queen" by ABBA on his radio. She silently cried as the lyrics accused her of being a teaser who turns men on and leaves them burning and all she really wanted was to be young and sweet and dance and jive and have the time of her life, but it just wasn't that simple.

Much later she watched the empty desert fly by from high on the seat of an eighteen-wheeler driven by a man who didn't ask for services in return for the ride; he only wanted to help. She mailed a letter home at the truck stop in Barstow, California, just to let her family know she was all right.

The trucker dropped her off at the truck stop in Ontario, California. She thought she might look for a job there. Then she met Judy. Judy was five foot three inches tall and about a hundred pounds, but she was bubbly and energetic; energy she found from the pills she took. Judy was on her way to San Francisco where she had friends.

"Dar? What a funny handle," she said when they met.

"My dad doesn't call anyone by their name; everyone has a nickname."

"You ran away from that scene. So? What's your name?"

"Darlene?"

"Darlene … well then, Darlene … you should seriously come with me."

The name Darlene sounded strange to her, a new start. She would no longer be Dar. She would be Darlene; Darlene from San Francisco. She wrote a letter home, talking about her new job in

Rancho Cucamonga, California, and mailed it from the truck stop before getting in the eighteen-wheeler headed for San Francisco. Judy shared her ride to San Francisco, and she shared her drugs, and she shared her story about Pastor Bowden:

Judy's story

When I started to get my boobs, I thought I was bitchin' awesome. I was a top student, and figured I'd go to college and get into the medical field. At that same time, I had a crush on the pastor at our church. Of course, he was a married church dude, so nothing between us could be kosher. Still, I guess I was scoping him out in my fantasies, and maybe he was getting my vibes. I liked to be around him, so I stayed after to help clean up at a church social. I wanted … I'm not even sure *what* … but for sure, I wasn't thinking about actually getting it on with him. But that's what he was thinking. He first touched me on my thigh, and I was freakin' about that. He told me it was nothing … we were just friends. But he just stayed focused and led me right down the garden path. We ended up boinkin' before that night was over. I didn't know if it was my fault or his. I was really freaked out about the whole thing. The next day I told him we should, like, tell someone or repent or something. He wasn't cool with that. He said it was all my fault for leading him on to start with.

That's when I began to get into trouble. I skipped school and hung out with what my parents called the "disreputables." They were totally cool with me. They taught me about drugs. The drugs were rockin'. Sure, I started having sex too. It was plastic, not like with his holiness. I was mondo cool with my new mellow friends. My grades went in the toilet. Well, I could see I was just getting deeper into the shit. I knew better than to give the lowdown about Pastor Bowden … he was a minister … no one would believe me. So, I decided the only thing to do was split the scene. I ran away to San Fran. I found more drugs. I earned my moolah on my back and on my knees … if you get my drift.

I started scarfin' the food down and getting fat up in San Fran. I need to be able to see a space between my legs at the crotch when my knees are together. The boys like that. My goal was to stay below a hundred pounds. I realized all that eating was nowhere. I trimmed it back. By the time the fuzz arrested me, I was in perfect shape.

They sent me home to Riverside, Cal, and crapola, my mother cried and got all bent out of shape when she saw me. They told me I had to eat, but they couldn't force me. They wanted to make me into a pig, so I'd have to stay home. The doctor said I had anorexia nervosa. What a stupid name! I knew I was on the verge of getting fat. I had to control my life.

The prying shrink guessed I'd been raped before this all started. The prying shrink told her suspicions to my family and my pastor. What a lame brain she turned out to be. She was hoping that, as a minister, Pastor Bowden could help. When I found out she spilled the beans, I told her to stop drinking my Kool-Aid and refused to see her anymore. But the cat was out of the bag with Pastor Bowden. He talked to me, and he begged me to forgive him, begged me to keep his sucky secret ... for his sweet wife's sake ... for his darling children's sake. He had no interest in what would be good for my sake. There was no way out for me. So, I made like a chicken and flew the coop. And they're not taking me back there again. I'll die first."

* * *

Darlene stood up, watching another robin join the first in his search for worms. Back in the San Francisco days, Darlene's life was a dark tunnel without choice, but she didn't realize it at the time. She followed Judy and that tunnel because that's where it led her; to men, and drugs, and loneliness. Life was a party of songs, flowers, drugs, and men. She lived where the Flower Children had settled a decade before. And the men gave her what she wanted, and she gave them what they wanted. She controlled them and thought that would bring her satisfaction—it didn't.

She created a fanciful story of her life and put it in a letter to her sister. It was sent by a circuitous route so her family wouldn't know where she was. There was no satisfaction in that, so she made arrangements to talk to Karianne on the phone. Karianne was the rebellious one in the family. She was the oldest, then came Junior, and Darlene was the third.

Karianne was nineteen, so it could hardly be said she ran away from home when she left to go to Darlene. She told Darlene she was shocked she was using drugs and men and tried to talk her out of it. Karianne got a job, met Delmar, and moved in with him. She got pregnant, and Delmar ran out on her. She tried to talk Darlene into going home, but Darlene was firm about staying away from Salt Lake at all costs. Karianne left for home alone—to have her baby.

After missing two periods, Darlene confirmed she was pregnant. Judy asked if she knew who the father was—that was a joke, of course she knew. The father was legion.

Judy took her to a place where the little intruder could be extracted. Clean, white, sterile. The people there were kind, helpful, and somehow detached. Darlene felt the life within her, and at the last minute, she changed her mind.

Judy took her to a shelter for unmarried mothers and Colin was born June 25, 1978. A couple of months later, she left the shelter and returned to Judy and her friends. Judy was gone, and she was never coming back. An eating disorder took her forever. Her friends told how Judy's family came to get the body, and they were sad and sorry; so was Pastor Bowden, and no one would ever know why Judy had suddenly changed for no reason.

* * *

Darlene sat on the director's chair looking out over the valley—the spire of the West Jordan Temple stood out. Another memory came to her. It was in San Francisco and two-year-old Colin was playing with a truck in a corner of the apartment she shared with friends.

He was such a good baby, but he was living a terrible, neglected life. In times like these, when the fog of drugs lifted, Darlene felt guilty about her life. She still shared the three-room apartment with a parade of people moving in and out almost weekly.

Karianne had moved back to California, married Delmar, and they lived in Santa Barbara. In desperation Darlene had called Karianne.

"Look, I need to get out of this fucking mess I'm in."

"I've been trying to convey that to you for years," Karianne answered.

"I need to come live with you while I get my act together."

"No. Del and I are in a very small apartment. We can't accommodate another person."

"Fuck that. I'm your sister."

"I mean it, Darlene, we don't have space."

"Look, I'm fucking pregnant. You'll just have to fucking make room."

"You're pregnant? Again?"

"That's what I just fucking said. Look, we can get a bigger place. I'll get a fucking regular job and help with the expenses."

"You're not going to appreciate this, but your most favorable solution is to go back to Salt Lake whereby Dad and Mary would take you in, or maybe Mother could assist."

"Fuck that and fuck you." She slammed the phone. She sat by the phone waiting for Karianne to call back to apologize, to invite her to move to Santa Barbara, to help her. She waited five minutes—ten—nothing. "FUCK!" she shouted at the wall. Colin started to cry.

Darlene remembered the day she carried Colin in her right arm and a small, beat-up suitcase in her left hand as she walked nervously down the steps from the bus. She spied her father walking toward her with a strange woman walking self-assuredly beside him, his brand-new wife, Mary. She had shoulder-length blonde hair and bright blue eyes. She was wearing a short-sleeve, yellow dress that hung just below her knees. She was a couple of inches shorter than Darlene's father.

Darlene set Colin on the ground; he clung to her leg. "This is Mary," her father said.

"Hi Mary. I'm Dad's wild kid, Darlene."

Mary put her arms around Darlene's shoulders. "I'm so happy to meet you."

"Me too," Darlene said. She was uncomfortable and at a loss for words. When she ran away, she thought her parents were happily married, and now they were divorced and here was this new woman with her father—a stranger with her arms around her.

The first few days were uncomfortable for Darlene, as she tried to get used to a situation that couldn't be more unlike the way things had been before she ran away. Her father had a new wife, Darlene had a new son, and she was pregnant. But one thing was the same; her father immediately began laying down rules.

* * *

Darlene watched as a car slowly pulled into the cemetery. It was Joshua Junior's car. Her brother got out and walked toward her. He was six foot two inches tall. His black hair was combed back, but the natural waves held it up. He had a long face with a straight nose, thin lips, and brown eyes. His coloring was similar to Grandma Taylor, but his face looked remarkably like Grandpa Taylor. There seemed to be nothing of his father's family in his appearance.

"Mom said you'd be here." He walked up to her and put his arms around her. Of all her siblings, he was the one who had been closest to her.

"You don't think I'm the devil like everyone else?" she asked.

Junior dropped his hands and stood back. "You know I don't. Dad is still in that mode of thought. I don't think he had to move back to San Antonio, but there was no talking him out of it. He still thinks this is all about forcing him to sell the house to pay off Mom."

"This had nothing to do with the house, and I'm sorry for Jo and Lori ... I mean that they're having to move. What about you? Are you going to San Antonio when you graduate?"

"No. I'm going to finish school at the U, and then I'll see what opportunities there are. I'll look for a job in Salt Lake first. This is where I want to spend my life."

"You and Marli will be the only ones left in Salt Lake, and everybody blames me. I don't know who gave my story to the bishop, but I admit I talked to the police … I had to, but there was nothing they could do. I had to make sure everyone was aware."

"I believe you."

"Do you believe what I said about Joshua?"

"I can't say I believe you about that, but I don't think you're lying."

"What do you mean?"

"I'm not sold on repressed memories. Dad has a lot of faults. I know he treated Mom like chattel."

"What do you mean by that?"

"He treated her like property … something he owned. And he misused church doctrine to enforce that on her. I went to the same general priesthood meetings at conferences, and I know we were constantly told not to treat our wives the way he treated her. But on the other hand, he always treated children very well … with love and respect."

"So, you don't think he could ever molest a child?"

"It's hard for me to see that. But I can't dismiss it out of hand because of my own experiences."

"What are you talking about? Did he ever try to molest you?"

"It's kind of complicated."

"I got time."

Junior turned and started walking toward the gravestone. He put his arm around Darlene as she walked with him. "I don't remember any kind of molestation against me or anyone else. I don't want you to repeat this to anyone, because this is just my observation as a child."

"It's between you and me … promise."

They stopped at Cindy's marker. "I'm sorry you had to go through this. She was such a beautiful little girl."

"I don't think I can ever get over this, Junior. I don't want to sound like a cliché, but I think everything happens for a reason. I don't fully know why this happened, but Dr. Schroeder has put me on the right track. You were saying something about your experiences."

"My earliest memories of life start before I started kindergarten. Kari was already in elementary school, and you were a toddler. Kari was always conning me into running away with her. We lived on Sixth East, about two blocks north of Liberty Park, and that's where we always ran to. We would make lunches and stow them in her doll buggy, and when Mom was busy with you, we would run away."

"Did you ever wonder why she wanted to run away?"

"She always had reasons … to see the world … to have adventures. She never looked past Liberty Park. There were plenty of fun things to do there. As she got older, Kari seemed to always push Dad's buttons. I would have been afraid to push them as hard as she did, and yet she seemed to get away with it. I'm sure as you got older, you must have noticed that."

"Yeah, I would never have done things she did."

"There was something else I noticed later. Eventually I started having memories of you. I remember you changed a lot … I'm not sure when, but sometime after you started school. You were … I mean, you began to get morose and not so carefree.

"So, what I'm saying is, while I can't believe Dad did what you say, I'm personally in a quandary about the whole situation. I wonder if there was something … something that a small child could misinterpret as molesting. For instance, I know Dad told some pretty horrendous stories about cartoon characters. Maybe those stories had a deeper impact on you and Kari, and maybe you put a sexual connotation to them that seems real to you now. So, I guess what I'm saying is, I can't not believe what you feel."

Darlene felt tears filling her eyes, so she tried to lighten the conversation. "Dude, that's the weirdest use of a double negative I've ever heard. You better not let Joshua hear you talk like that."

"Look, I don't believe what you say happened exactly as you remember. I'm sure *something* happened … something that had a deep impact. I'm just not sure the details of your memories at that age are accurate."

"I get it, and thanks. That's a lot more than anyone else in the family will give me … except Mom and Karianne."

"I'm sorry you've had such a crappy time the last few years."

"In a sense, I can't blame anybody but me. I fought Joshua and Mary on everything after they let me move in. I should have given Mary a little more slack. After Chas was born and they kicked me out, I moved in with Daryl, but I was just using him, and he soon got that message and kicked me out … same thing with Robert. Mom helped me get government food stamps and Medicaid, and she helped me out with some money. I was very messed up, and then I got pregnant again, and again I didn't know who the father was.

"But there was something totally different about my feelings when Cindy was born. I had a closer understanding with her. And I couldn't stand seeing her in Joshua's arms. I couldn't put a reason for that feeling … it was like I knew she wasn't safe, but that was counter to all I knew about his feelings for children. I had no idea what had happened to me, but at a deeper level, it was all there. When I was with Cindy … intimately … nursing her or bathing her, I started getting crazy flashes of Joshua acting inappropriately with me. My fear of him for Cindy's sake was becoming unmanageable. I couldn't stand to see him hold her, and you *know* how he is; he wanted to tend her, change her, give her baths, and all the time something inside me was screaming out, *stop it*!

"Then the accident happened, and she was gone forever. I had not protected her, and I just couldn't stand it. I couldn't breathe. My insurance only paid two thousand dollars. When I let Joshua know I was going to use it to get some emotional help, he practically split his head, and it wasn't just the lousy money; he was upset that I was getting *outside* help. He wanted to handle it through the family and the Church.

"Then I started getting serious flashbacks, and I recognized that it was Joshua, and he was using me, but it was a cloud. I started seeing Dr. Schroeder and she sent me to a hypnotist, and with that everything started to get perfectly clear, and I finally knew what he had done."

"Well, that's where I start to have a problem," Junior said. "It's easy for a hypnotist to implant a false memory that really seems real. And it's not that they do it on purpose; it can be totally accidental."

"I know that happens. But I was having the flashbacks before the hypnotism. It was the whole process of having a baby girl and being responsible for her safety. Cindy was the trigger that opened the door, not hypnotism. On top of that, Karianne had the same details of the molestation, and her memories were not repressed."

"Perhaps her interpretations of the stories from Dad are the same as yours. I don't know the answer. You could be right, but it's hard to believe that of Dad. Especially that he would try to prevent you from getting help just to protect himself and his reputation. I know Dad used those Disney movies as a springboard to make up his own stories. I remember Dad had a whole story about Thumper digging his own magic burrow and protecting Bambi from the hunters and the fires."

"Yeah, well, his story about Thumper's burrow was drastically different for me, but my memory of the details was exactly the same for Karianne."

"I didn't come to argue with you. I'm really going to miss you and Kari. She was like my constant mentor. And with you it was just the opposite; you were my constant student. I was so much closer to you and her than I was to the other girls. Dad always put me in a role of being your big brother protector. And somehow I didn't do a very good job."

"You did as good as anyone could have. My problems in life have been self-inflicted in spite of anything Joshua did or didn't do. But now, I really believe I am on the right path for me. I have Colin and Chas to take care of. I'll have good support from Mom and

Karianne, but *I'm* going to work this out, and I just know my life will be better ... I *have* to. I owe that to Cindy."

"Well, I just wanted to see you before you left. And I wanted to let you know I really do love you. And if you need anything, I will do whatever I can to help you. I wanted you to know that. No matter what Dad says or wants, you are always my little sister. He has demanded that everyone shun you three, but I told him that wouldn't work for me. Marli is on my side on this. I don't know how it will be with Lori and Jo."

"Thanks. I can't tell you how much I needed that. You were my mentor. I always looked up to you."

Darlene walked back to Junior's car with him. She hugged Junior and kissed him on the lips.

Junior turned to get into the car and looked back. "I'll be down for a visit once you get settled in."

"I'll be looking forward to that."

Junior got into the car and waved out the window as he drove away.

After Junior's car disappeared, Darlene arranged the roses around the gravestone, folded up the director's chair, and walked down to the road to wait for her mother to pick her up. Her goodbyes were over. She turned from the gravestone and didn't look back. Cindy was firmly situated in her heart.

* * *

Robyn – July 15, 2012 – San Antonio

After meeting with her mother, Robyn and George went to Jean's house to get Debbie and take her home. Debbie asked about Grampuh again. She was mostly concerned about his hurt head and that the "doctor people" had taken him away. Nothing else about last night was bothering her as far as Robyn could tell. In the cold light of day, it was hard to believe anything else had happened. Robyn seriously considered calling Sergeant Hanson and canceling her appointment, but there was still an unformed question in her mind.

Robyn took the Interstate to the San Antonio Police Department Prue Substation. As she parked the car, she was more confused than ever. She was sure her mother wouldn't intentionally destroy evidence if she felt there were any chance a crime could have been committed. On the other hand, things that happened in the family before Robyn was born had a greater impact on her mother than Robyn had imagined. Was it enough to blind her from truth—to cause her to protect Grandpa if there was a chance he could be what the others had said? How could her mother be so sure?

Robyn walked through the front doors into the building looking straight ahead. *This must be how criminals feel*, she thought. The receptionist called Sergeant Hanson to the front desk. Sergeant Hanson was dressed in a dark brown business suit with a white shirt and maroon tie. He was a hard-looking man with deep-set blue eyes accentuated by thick, busy eyebrows. His brown hair was buzz cut. He offered his hand. "Hi Robyn, how're you doing today?"

Robyn shook his hand. "I'm not sure right now."

He led her to his office. It was orderly and professional, except for the San Antonio Spurs memorabilia that covered a shelf on one of his two cherry bookcases. Pictures of his family were on the credenza behind the desk. There was a four-drawer file cabinet with several closed file folders on top. The work area of his desk was clear except for an open file with only a couple of sheets of paper in it. Robyn assumed it was Grandpa's file.

"Would you like to sit here?" He indicated a chair in front of his desk.

Robyn sat down.

"I understand you were going to schedule an appointment for our forensic team this morning." Sergeant Hanson walked around his desk and sat down.

"Well, it seems my mother, in a state of insomnia, stopped by my house on the way home from visiting my grandfather in the hospital and cleaned up everything. There's no evidence to gather at this point."

Sergeant Hanson raised his eyebrows. "Did she know we were going to check for evidence?"

"Yes."

"I don't know where to start. Cleaning a potential crime scene is highly irregular to say the least."

"My grandpa told my mom Debbie threw up on his pants, and he was just pulling them down to clean the mess. To her, that made perfect sense, so she didn't think anyone needed to check for evidence."

"That story agrees with the statement he gave us."

"The evidence that would support Grandpa's story would be Debbie's spit up on his pants, but my mom washed his pants. George wiped the urine, blood, and vomit up where Grandpa fell, but there may have been traces of spit up from Debbie near the couch, but Mom cleaned up the floor also and washed everything, so now we can't check on anything."

"That's unfortunate. Did your mom give any explanation for why she cleaned everything up?"

"Just that the story Grandpa gave explained everything, and she didn't want me to have to deal with mess."

"Do you think your mother is covering up for Joshua?"

"I don't know. It's just that now there's no proof to back up Grandpa's story."

"Well, your mother shouldn't have touched the evidence. I'll look into that."

"I don't want to cause any trouble for my mom."

"I'll bear that in mind. I haven't ever met her, but she has an incredible history here. Now that you've had some time to process what happened, tell me exactly what you remember and give as much detail as you can."

Robyn repeated the story as she told it to Sergeant Floyd.

"So, the evidence in the house might have supported his story and exonerated him," Sargent Hanson said.

"It would if the spit up was discovered, but if it wasn't, that would swing things the other way. There's still something about what happened that bothers me. I can't put my finger on it. It has something to do with the way he moved, or something he did, or something else I can't explain."

"In my opinion, there's not enough evidence to pursue this case further. It looks like it boils down to a case of 'he said, she said,' and you don't seem to be very sure about what happened."

"So, you're saying I should just drop this whole thing right now?"

"No. Personally … and I've seen a lot of cases like this … I just don't see much of a case as things stand right now. However, if you want, you can file a complaint, and I will look into it more. The bottom line is that unless you remember something more definite or we find evidence, I don't see a real case here. What do you want to do?"

"I don't know what to do. I just have this sense that something is missing. Do I have to make a decision right now?"

"No. I'll tell you what … I'll leave it open, and I'll talk to your mother and grandfather. In the meantime, you can think about it. Maybe you or George will remember something more. If you come up with something else, call me. Let's touch base again next week to see where we stand. Does that work for you?"

"Thanks. I feel much better about it now. We'll do what you say and see where it goes."

* * *

George was waiting when Robyn got home. After what Jo had done, he was all for filing a formal complaint to get Grandpa Joshua arrested and put away. It was easy for him; after all, it was not his family that would be ripped apart. "We could file the complaint, but they won't arrest him without evidence we don't have," Robyn argued. "What if he's innocent and I put him through a bunch of crap for nothing?"

"And what if he's guilty and he rapes some other baby just because we don't prosecute him? What then?"

"You don't understand, George. The whole thing rests with me. You can't add anything to what I have. If only I were sure about what I saw, I would go after it wholeheartedly, even if I would lose in the end. The problem is, I'm just not that sure … his story could be what happened. I don't want to tear the family apart based upon supposition. Filing a complaint right now would do nothing. There's no evidence, so he can't be arrested, let alone prosecuted."

"Well, all I can say is it appears your family is already torn apart, and from what your mother told you, it was torn apart over the same issue."

Robyn realized what she had to do. "You're right George. You're absolutely right. Before I decide what to do, I'm going to have to meet those people and find out all about them and what happened when the family split. I've wondered about the rest of the family ever since I looked at those genealogy papers. I'm going to have to go to California to meet them. Can we swing that?"

"If it will help you figure this out … yeah … we can make that work."

"My mother is going to pitch a fit. I have a luncheon with her day after tomorrow. I'll tell her then."

CHAPTER 6

1977 – The Runaway; Karianne

Dear Karianne,

Well I guess everybody is looking for me in Rancho Cuc. I'm not there. I found a good friend, and we left Rancho. I can't tell you where we are, so I went to a lot of trouble to get this letter to you. I'm doing fine, couldn't be better. I live with my friend, Judy, and some of her friends. I couldn't stay in Salt Lake any longer—too many rules. I'm not one who can be forced into a jar of school or church. It's just not my bag. Anyway, I'm doing fine, so don't worry about me. Maybe when I get better settled, I'll let you know where I am. But I don't want anyone to come after me. I'm having a good life, and I can take care of myself.

Love Darlene – oh yeah – I don't like nicknames.

Kari put the letter on the bench beside her. It came in an envelope with just her name on the outside. Someone had pushed it through the vent in her locker at the Deseret Gym where she went to swim three times a week. Since she used a different locker each time, someone must have been watching when she changed to swim. She tried to remember who was in the locker room but couldn't remember anyone she knew. She had been worried sick about Dar since she ran away six weeks ago. The family had gotten two letters from her—one from Barstow, California, and one from Ontario, California. The last letter said she had a job as a waitress in the adjoining town, Rancho Cucamonga. Her parents had contacted the Ontario and Rancho Cucamonga police departments, but neither had any luck locating her. Her dad had planned a trip to Southern California to look for her. He was to leave in three days. This letter would prevent a wasted trip.

Kari had been completely surprised when Dar ran away. She often thought about running away herself, but here she was, a nineteen-year-old high school graduate, still living at home.

Kari gave the letter to her mother and father as soon as she got home. Her father read the letter out loud. "Where did you get this?"

"I found it in my locker at the gym. The arrangement for delivery was set up whereby I can't figure out who dropped it off. I only know that someone sneaked into the locker room while I was swimming and pushed it through the vents. It must have been one of Dar's friends."

"Or maybe Dar is back here in Salt Lake somewhere," Kari's mother interjected.

"I'm going to need a list of all her friends," her father said.

"I only know a couple," Kari said.

"Who are they?"

"What are you going to do with the names if I provide them?"

"I'll ask them where Dar is."

"Whoever did this was rendering a favor to Dar. It's pretty clear that person is not going to comply with your request for information."

"Then I'll call the police."

"But only one of her friends is involved, so which one are you going to call the police on?"

"All of them if I have to. Give me the names."

"At this point, it would do no good. How about I try to buddy up to them ... they know Dar and I are pretty close. Whoever it is might freely share some information with me."

"And how long will that take? You give me the names now."

"No."

"While you're living under my roof, you'll do as I say." Her father had raised his voice.

"So, go ahead, kick me out."

"I don't understand why it is that you two are always at each other's throats. Why does it always have to be a confrontation?" Kari's mother pleaded.

"What I just said makes sense, but he never listens to me." Kari left the room.

"You come back here; I'm not finished with you yet."

"*I'm* finished. End of discussion." Kari stepped into her bedroom and slammed the door. She knew one thing; she had to find Dar, and she intended to do it before her father did.

* * *

Kari talked to Dar's friends and told them to tell Dar she wanted to talk to her. After several days one of the friends made arrangements to call Dar and let Kari talk to her.

"Dar, I'm so glad to talk to you. How are you doing?"

"I'm doing just great. I got a lot of friends, and they're helping me."

"Do you have a job?"

"Nope. But I help around the apartment and stuff while I'm looking, and that way it's fair."

"Where are you?"

"Um … I'd rather not say. I don't want fucking Dad showing up on my fucking doorstep someday."

"Things are really getting hot around the house. Dad and I are in confrontation on a daily basis. He wants a list of your friends' names. I stupidly mentioned that I might know a couple, but I have staunchly refused to provide them, and so he is threatening to kick me out. I want to run away before he goes forward with his threat, but I don't want to experience complete loneliness. I was just thinking that if circumstances unfolded favorably, we could live near each other."

"Well ... if I tell you where I am, and fucking Dad shows up, I'll just fucking run away again first chance, and then you'll *never* fucking hear from me again."

"I know that."

"Give me a couple of days. I need to fucking think about this. I mean if you come, you can't fucking tell me what to do or how to live my life."

"I understand."

"Okay. I'm not saying I'm gonna give you info on where I am. I'm just gonna think about it. I'll send the address and etcetera if I decide to tell you. But if you fucking mess me up, it'll be quits for us forever."

* * *

Two weeks later Kari found another envelope in her locker. Inside was a piece of paper with an address in San Francisco. It was written in an unfamiliar hand, and there was nothing else on it. She took several days making arrangements to leave. She bought her bus ticket, withdrew most of the money from her savings account, and quit her job the morning she left. She left from the Greyhound station at 1:15 p.m. headed for Portland, Oregon, without telling anyone she was going. From there she sent a letter home and got a ticket to Sacramento, California. The day after she left Salt Lake City, she arrived in San Francisco. A taxi driver took her to the address on the paper. It was an apartment south of the Golden Gate Park.

It was 5:30 p.m. when Kari knocked on the apartment door. A very thin girl answered the door. "Hi, my name is Kari. I'm looking for my sister Dar. I have an address that says she lives here."

The girl looked her over for a couple of seconds. "Hey, Darlene ... it looks like Karianne is here."

Kari heard a familiar scream, and suddenly Dar was running through the living room. "Karianne, I didn't think you would really show up." She threw her arms around her and kissed her on the lips.

"I don't think I've ever been addressed by that name," Kari said.

"I hope you don't mind. I just don't like fucking nicknames. This is my friend, Judy." Kari said hi and the girl smiled and nodded back.

"How was your trip? You've got to tell me all about it. What did Dad say about you leaving? You sure he doesn't know where you are?"

"You are a bundle of questions, aren't you?"

Kari told her all about her trip and that she hadn't told anyone she was going. "I sent them a letter from Portland saying I was going to find you. And I plan to keep them informed about how I'm faring on a weekly basis. I just need to find a way to accomplish that without leaving a postmark from San Francisco."

"I know a truck driver that has a weekly run from L.A. to Seattle. We could drive everyone fucking crazy having him mail the letters from all along the coast."

"I don't want to drive them crazy. But since I sent them a letter from Portland, it'd be perfect if your driver wouldn't mind mailing my letters from Seattle. I'll tell them I have a temporary job near Seattle

"Mom cries a lot over you, but I think it'll be better for her if I can elaborate on how we are doing whereby she's not in the dark. I'm hoping that sometime our circumstances will unfold favorably for a return to Salt Lake."

"I'm never going back to that fucking hellhole."

"Maybe not to live, but perhaps to visit sometimes."

"Not till I'm fucking twenty-one years old. I don't want no cops thinking I'm a fucking minor and forcing me back to that fucking prison."

"Well, I need to find a place to stay until I can get a job."

"You can stay here. There are always people moving in and out."

Kari had never smelled marijuana, but she was sure the sweet smell she was picking up was marijuana. She took a quick look around. There were two couches in the room; both had mussed-up bedding spread over them. One was dark blue and the other was forest green. The chairs sat on a large shag rug that looked like a remnant of a carpet. It was a mixture of yellow and yellowish orange. Kari was sure it hadn't seen a vacuum in a millennium. There were two soft-covered orange chairs and a navy-blue recliner. They all faced the wall to her left as she came in, where a twenty-four-inch TV with rabbit ears sat on an old wooden table. The table, TV, and everything else in the room were covered in dust. The place smelled of old furniture and scented candles. Judy was sitting cross-legged on the bedding of one of the couches wearing a long flowery skirt and a tie-dyed T-shirt. Kari would not be comfortable living in this environment, but a short stay to get on her feet would have to be okay.

* * *

After two weeks, Kari found a job as an office aide in an engineering firm. On her second day, she was asked to accept an order of office supplies. The man delivering the order was named Delmar Salisbury. He was wearing rust brown, flare bottom pants and a sage green shirt with an over-sized pointed collar. He was quite tall in his platform shoes. "You're new here," he said as she began matching the items in the delivery to the order form.

"Yeah, I just started yesterday." Without the shoes he was probably about five-feet nine-inches and weighed about 170 pounds. He wasn't exactly movie-star handsome, but there was something attractive about his face. He had broad shoulders and carried himself with an air of confidence. Kari was immediately attracted to the mischievous look in his gray eyes.

"You live around here?" he asked.

"I just moved to San Francisco from Utah. I'm staying with friends until I encounter a place of my own."

They talked for about ten minutes—long enough for him to tell her his friends called him Del and that he had moved up from Santa Barbara a couple of months ago.

"Well, you better get back to work," Del said when they were done. "Um … people say I'm a fast mover … but would you think I'm too forward if I ask you out for a date?"

"No. Are you going to ask me out?"

"How about dinner on Friday night?"

"Yeah, that sounds great."

"I know a real nice place down at Fishermen's Wharf."

"That will be fun; wait a sec and I'll provide you my address."

* * *

Kari found she really liked Del. They dated for a couple of weeks, and then he asked her to move in with him. Kari was not ready for that kind of a relationship.

A week later, when she got home from work, she found Darlene stoned on drugs. "What are you doing?" she asked Darlene.

"You should try it." Darlene offered her a smoking joint.

"You must be crazy. How do you afford drugs and everything else? You don't even have a job."

"Don't you worry about that, I can fucking take care of myself."

"Yeah, I think *fucking* take care of yourself is the operative statement here."

"What the fuck do you mean?"

"I get the feeling you're a prostitute."

"I ain't no fucking prostitute. I ain't got no fucking pimp. I know one thing for sure though; I can get anything I want from a man; alls I got to do is know how to treat 'em. And I *fucking* know how to do that." Dar was defiant. Her words were slurred and she was babbling double negatives, which wasn't like her.

"But you're selling yourself."

"Fuck that. I own every one of those bastards. I'm not fucking selling myself. I'm taking control. And I told you up front not to fucking judge me. If that is too hard, there's the fucking door.

"Where're you going?" Darlene demanded.

"I'm packing my things whereby I can get out of this bordello. It was a mistake for me to come here."

"You can't just walk out without no place to go. What will you do?"

"Don't you worry about me; I can take care of myself, and I'm not stunting my opportunities by indulging in drugs or having sex with just any man that comes along in order to do it, either."

"You're not going to tell fucking Dad where I am, are you?"

"I should. Someone needs to take you out this mess."

"You fucking promised!"

Kari went the bedroom and started packing her suitcase. Darlene followed her. "Listen Karianne, maybe I need to lighten up some with the weed and all, but you can't tell Dad. So, I give a little to some guys I know, and they help me out. It's not like being a prostitute, but I swear, I'll go out on the fucking street if I have to, but I'm not fucking going back to Salt Lake."

Kari closed her suitcase. "Okay, I'm not telling Dad. I'll find a place whereby I can live in San Francisco, and we can still be friends. I just can't live in this clutter."

"Where will you go?"

"I'll be in touch." Kari walked out the door. In the lobby she gave Del a call from the pay phone. There was a Mormon Church a block away. She waited there for about twenty minutes. Del picked her up and took her to his apartment.

* * *

A couple of months later, Del and Kari went to see *Annie Hall* starring Woody Allen and Diane Keaton. They stopped at a Kentucky Fried Chicken on the way home. "On Tuesday I got confirmation of something important," Kari started. It was so simple, but she didn't know how to approach the subject.

"What about?" Del asked.

"Well, it's just that … um, I guess there's nothing to do but divulge the problem. I'm pregnant."

Del's eyes popped open. He slowly put down his chicken leg and swallowed. "You're absolutely sure?"

"Absolutely."

"Well, I don't actually know … I think there's a … I think it's called Planned Parenthood, and they can help us find a doctor to … you know … abort it."

"Abort it! Are you insane? I'm not doing away with my baby!"

"Well, I'm not ready to be a father either."

"I thought you loved me. How can you just …"

"This isn't about how I feel about you. I'm just not ready to be a father. I'm just starting my career. My God, I'm a delivery boy. I can't be a father … no way!"

"Then we're in a fine conundrum, because I'm not going to submit to an abortion. A baby is a major component of my dreams."

"I want a baby too, Kari, just not now. Not until I'm prepared to take care of it."

They talked and argued for an hour and a half. In the end, Del gave her an ultimatum. The next day, Kari bought a bus ticket to Salt Lake with money Del gave her. He took her and her things to the station and wished her good luck as he put her on the bus. Kari silently cried most of the way home. It had been a bad choice to tell Del about the baby after seeing *Annie Hall*. When she wasn't crying about herself, she was crying about Alvy reminiscing about the lost love with Annie.

Back in Salt Lake, her father wanted her to agree to let him adopt the baby as a condition of moving back home. Her mother supported Kari's decision to keep the baby herself and ultimately, they prevailed with her father.

* * *

Robyn – July 17, 2012

Two days after Robyn's meeting with Sergeant Hanson, she had the luncheon meeting with her mother. She had talked to her mother on the phone twice, and they had argued both times. Jo was upset by Robyn's indecision about her grandpa. He had been released from the hospital, but Robyn refused to meet with him. Robyn didn't know what to say to him. She was pretty sure he hadn't done anything to Debbie, but she still had that nagging feeling. Perhaps it was more related to the secrets in the family, and she still had not mentioned her plans to try to meet the other members of the family.

Jo had been exhorting her to get with her and Grandpa to pray. Robyn believed getting with Grandpa to pray about something he might have done was a formula for deception.

Robyn chose to wear a plain blue business dress to meet with her mother rather than the pants she usually wore. This meeting had an aura of formality to it, so she dressed accordingly. She knew her mother was well aware she hardly ever wore dresses, but Robyn wanted to emphasize the spontaneity of their relationship was temporarily on hold—not so much because of what might or might not have happened between Grandpa and Debbie, but because of the way her mother had interfered with the possible evidence at her house.

When Robyn walked in the door, she saw her mother seated at a table for two near a side window. She was wearing a flowery dress along with a green, wide-brimmed straw hat with a wide, silk floral band. Seeing her brought a faded memory or feeling of something that had happened in her past, but she couldn't quite place it. It had something to do with the hat.

The greeting was uncomfortable and perfunctory. Jo ordered a club sandwich with a glass of milk. Robyn ordered a tuna sandwich with iced tea. She wasn't a tea drinker because it was contrary to Mormon doctrine to drink alcohol, coffee, or tea. Jo raised her eyebrows. It was the effect Robyn was aiming for.

"Since when did you start drinking tea?" Jo asked.

"Since now."

Jo nodded her head but didn't let that sidetrack her. "Thanks for coming to lunch with me today. I just wanted to talk to you face to face. Grandpa probably should have gone to the bathroom to clean up that night, but Debbie throwing up caught him by surprise, and he just reacted. I don't know why you are making such a fuss about it."

"I'm not sure where we're going with this. I wish there were some evidence that Debbie even threw up at all. We aren't going to get anywhere with this; we can't even agree on a basis for discussion."

"Okay, as a basis of discussion, let's talk about whether you're going to make formal charges against your grandfather. I talked to Detective Hanson, and he said you left him up in the air on that."

"Right now, I don't have any immediate intentions to do anything like that. I need more time to think about it."

"You know that's one of the reasons that we have been given prayer. Whenever we are confused about something, we can go to our Heavenly Father in prayer to get an answer. That's one of the reasons that I've made sure that we have kept God and the Church so much a part of our lives. I have prayed about this, and I'm sure that Grandpa is telling the truth. Have you prayed about it?"

"It's great prayer works so well for you. I don't get the same results." Robyn had felt the strength of her mother's faith on many occasions. "I wish my faith could be as strong as yours. I think I'm afraid to pray as you do."

"But why would you be afraid to pray? Haven't we prayed together many times over the years? You're not making sense."

"We are taught when we pray about something, we should start with a strong desire to believe in the thing we are praying about. Then if it's true, the feeling about it will grow, but if it isn't true, there will be a stupor of thought and confusion. I'm afraid if I truly want to believe something, it will prejudice how I feel about the answer. I prayed about Santa Claus with faith. I felt very good about him, and then it turned out to be a lie. I just don't have your faith and understanding."

"When you prayed about Santa Claus you were a child; you thought as a child. You're are an adult now, and you should be able to think like an adult. Don't you understand that faith is not a perfect knowledge, but it's the hope of things that are not seen but are true? Can't you at least hope that Grandpa didn't do this terrible thing?"

"If my starting point is hoping what I saw was not true … wouldn't that would be a level of denial? We are taught that before we pray about something, we need to study it out in our mind. I need to do a lot more studying before I pray."

Jo's face brightened. "You are absolutely right. I think that you need to take stock of the kind of man that your grandfather really is. There are a lot of things about him that you have never known. I know him better than any living person. That's why, when I pray about him, I get my answers very fast with undeniable conviction. You need to spend some time with him and get to know what he stands for from the center of the soul."

"I've spent plenty of time with him … I grew up with him. I'm not ready to see him yet. My feelings are still too strong."

"You're going to have to know something more about him than you do now, or you won't be able to make an intelligent choice. To start with, let me just tell you some of the important things about him that you may not be aware of. Would that be all right?"

"If you think that might help, but I already know a lot about him."

"Of course, but just hear me out. He was born in Austin in 1935. His father died when he was only two." Jo told Robyn that Joshua's father served a two-year mission for the Mormon Church. He was killed in a boating accident before Joshua started school. Joshua's mother raised him, his younger brother, Jace, and his older sister, Ruth. When Joshua was six years old, his mother married Mel. A year later, Joshua's half-sister, Janice, was born. When Joshua was eight, Jace was killed in a farm accident. His stepfather died when he was in his teens. Joshua went on a mission, and while he was there, his mother married Mitchel, a rich oil man.

Joshua's dream was to get into the newspaper business. He refused an offer from Mitchel to join his oil company with a high salary. He moved to Salt Lake to get away from the pressure Mitchel was putting on him. He was fascinated with the newspaper business, so he worked for a local newspaper. Joshua did everything for the paper. As a teenager in San Antonio, he had a paper route. Then in Salt Lake, he worked as a reporter, photographer, accountant, ad salesman, and editor. After he moved back to San Antonio, he won many awards in the newspaper business.

"Dianne was a stay-at-home mom," Jo said. "She was never satisfied with how much money Grandpa made and always wanted more than he could give. She constantly tried to get him to move back to Texas and work in Mitchel's oil company."

Jo explained Dianne's family was dirt poor, and though Joshua wasn't rich, Dianne was much better off with him than before they married.

The waitress brought their orders and Robyn started to eat. Jo took a bite of her sandwich and then continued.

She described their four-bedroom house with a three-car garage and a giant fireplace in Kerns, Utah. "After Lori was born, Dianne had a hysterectomy without informing Grandpa about it before it was done. She never got a job herself, but just took care of the kids. At the time of the divorce, she was having an affair, so I guess she was thinking that guy would take better care of her. When that relationship didn't work out after the divorce, she was on her own, and she found out that she couldn't support herself."

"I don't remember you saying she was having an affair." Robyn had heard a lot of what her mother was telling her before, but there were some new things.

"A lot of things happened at that time. To make it worse, Dianne started partying all around town. She didn't have time to spend with her daughters.

"Grandpa had moved on and married Mary. Dianne tried to force him to sell the house so she could get the money from her half. She succeeded in doing that ... I can vouch for that."

"What do you mean?"

"Well, you might as well know it all." Jo told her Dianne couldn't support her lifestyle on her own salary. After getting the other girls to make the accusations of child molestation, she talked to Joshua's bishop and a police detective hoping to get him excommunicated and arrested. "I suppose she thought she could separate him from his friends and cause him to lose his job. By destroying him, she hoped to force him to sell the house so she would get half of the proceeds." Jo explained that the local church leaders were worried about how things would look to the world outside the Church so his opportunities for service in the Church were curtailed. Joshua and Mary had to sell the house and move back to San Antonio so he could get a new start and they would be near Joshua's family.

"I don't know how that would help him. I mean the Church records follow members wherever they go," Robyn said.

"His records were clean, because he hadn't *done* anything. The problem was personal between him and the local leaders who felt that they needed to protect the Church from the false accusations that a local leader was a child molester. So, you see, the whole thing about those terrible accusations was just so that Dianne could get more party money. I hope that it made her happy ... no I don't ... I hope that she choked on it."

"Wow, that's pretty strong."

"Well, it's not just how she treated my dad; she never cared a thing about me either."

"How can you be so sure?"

"It's something ... I can't tell. Oh, what the heck ... you want everything, so here it is. A couple of months after the divorce, a high school senior took me to his house one night and tried rape me."

"I never heard that!"

Jo explained that no one was home and the boy started making out with her. She was kind of excited about making out, but when he started trying to have sex, she told him to stop. When he tried to force her, she screamed so loud he threw her out of the house.

"When I got home, my dad was waiting, and he could tell something was not right. I ended up having to tell him ... and that was pretty hard, because he was a man, and what I really wanted was to talk to my mom about the whole thing."

"Why didn't you talk to her about it?"

Jo explained Joshua had to arrange all her communications with Dianne because he had custody. When Joshua told Dianne, she told him to handle it himself and it was entirely Jo's fault because she had snuck out of the house to run around with that type of boy. She also blamed Joshua because she decided he wasn't setting good rules for Jo.

"Did things improve between you and your mother as time went by?"

"She was busy with her life and I became busy with mine. She usually made time for my school activities, but personal, one on one time was almost nonexistent. I think things were improving, but then came the accusations. The family split up and spread all around the country, and we drifted further apart."

According to Jo, it was good they moved back to Texas. Joshua's mother had cancer, and she died shortly after the family moved to San Antonio. They all moved in with her for a while, so it gave Joshua a chance to be very close to her during those last months. Joshua's half-sister, Janice, died of tuberculosis shortly after they moved back. It was good Joshua was in San Antonio to help the rest of the family through both of those deaths. He had to make all the arrangements to set up the funerals.

"How old was his sister?"

"She was in her early forties, I guess. She had lived a very troubled life with promiscuity and a lot of drugs. She was a lot like my sister Dar."

"What about Dar?"

Jo told her Dar was a whore and had a very bad reputation at school when she ran away from home. Kari followed her to San Francisco, and they both came home pregnant and on drugs. At one point, Dar moved in with Josh and Mary, and then proceeded to cause them continuous heartache. She tried to live with several other boys and ended up pregnant again.

"When the baby was just a few months old, Dar got in a car accident and the baby was killed. Shortly after that is when she started with the so-called repressed memories. She tried to put the blame on Grandpa for all her personal troubles. Dianne took advantage of this and pushed the lie. You should be clear on this ... my dad *never* lost his temple recommend. Dianne lost hers. That's a pretty clear indication of who was honorable and who was a big liar.

"It was kind of a blessing in disguise when we moved back to Texas," Jo said. Joshua was bishop for many years, and the people in his ward loved and cherished him. They had a big party for him when he was released.

"The Church has always been a haven for him and his source of strength," Jo said. "He has always loved children and wanted to have as many of his own as he could."

Jo talked about the birth of Ronald and how much Josh cared for him. Even though Ronald was a real handful, Josh wouldn't put him in an institution until Mary's health started to deteriorate. "Now, since Mary has passed on, he goes to see Ronald at least once a month, and spends the whole day with him each visit."

Even after Joshua retired from the paper, he took full responsibility for the annual fundraiser for battered children that his paper sponsored. He helped raise millions of dollars over the years.

"There is just no way that he could do what you think that you saw him do. I want you to come to my house tomorrow night. I will have some other things there for you to see. Will you come tomorrow?"

Robyn was aware of a lot of the things her mother had just told her, but in the excitement of the past days, she had not thought of them. The new things she had learned about the family secrets would give her a great deal to think about. "Okay, I'll come over."

* * *

Robyn was getting tired of the whole mess, but when she got home, George was ready to continue the discussion.

"How did your lunch go?"

"It was okay. I had a tuna sandwich and iced tea. By the way, iced tea is a pretty good drink."

"So, does that mean this episode has turned you off on the idea of a temple marriage?" No one who drank tea could go to the temple.

"I don't think any of this has helped at all, but I really don't think it has hurt either. I just ordered the tea to see how it would affect my mother. I only took a couple small sips, just for effect."

Robyn confided, "The more I think of this, the more I think I must have been mistaken. I think if I just sit back and listen to my mother, all the doubt will evaporate. That's why I have to go to California soon. I want to talk to my real grandmother before time causes me to get apathetic about it, but I'm sure Mom and Grandpa both will think that would be putting me in the power of the devil."

"I know you have doubts about the temple and all that, but I don't think your grandmother can put you in the power of the devil. I trust you, and if you really need this, I support you. If those people are evil, I expect you will sense it. I don't believe in some magical power that can trap someone who was just looking for the truth."

"I need to go to California as soon as possible. I can stay with Aunt Marli, and I could take Debbie with me. Do you think it would be a problem if we stayed for a week or so?"

"It would be the first time we've been apart. Why so long?"

"I don't know exactly how to approach them about the subject. I don't want them to know about my suspicions about Grandpa. If it turns out he didn't do anything, it would be unfair to bring up all this with them. I want to find out what I can about the family's past from their point of view. From there, I just want to play it by ear, so I don't want to be pressed for time. Are you sure we can afford a round-trip plane ticket?"

"We can come up with the money ... it'll be okay. Just get this thing resolved, and maybe you might even find some answers about the temple while you're there."

Robyn knew George was anxious about resolving the question of the temple. Almost everything in the Church revolved around the temple and "sealed" families. Robyn felt the members of the ward loved and accepted her, but something was missing in her relationship with members who had been through the temple. For one thing, only those who had been to the temple held important leadership positions. For another thing, ceremonies in the temple were secret, so those who had gone through the temple knew something about creation and God's plan the rest of the members couldn't know. This created a caste system in the Church. George and Robyn were among the outsiders, and this was becoming a problem for George. His priesthood leaders constantly pushed and challenged him to resolve the holdup with Robyn.

Arrangements were made to fly to California the following Wednesday. Aunt Marli would pick up Robyn at the Burbank Airport.

CHAPTER 7

1998 – The Hat; Robyn

Robyn and her friend, Carol, arrived at the school around noon. They had about two hours to play. Later this afternoon, Carol's older sister was taking them to see *The Parent Trap* at the theater. It always seemed strange when she came to the school grounds to play on Saturdays, because all the noise and commotion of the other children were absent. Carol climbed to the top of the playground apparatus they called the "jungle gym" or sometimes the "monkey bars." It was a large open-air cube divided by smaller cubes made from steel pipes. This one was five cubes by five cubes and four cubes high, with a three by three set of cubes centered on the top. The children would climb on the pipes around and through the cubes.

Robyn climbed up and sat beside Carol on the top set of cubes. It seemed like they were on top of the world. As they sat talking about one of their girlfriends, Jake Carter appeared and called up to them, "Hey, what do you think you're doing on the monkey bars?"

Jake was in the grade above Robyn and Carol. Robyn didn't know him personally, but she had seen him bullying a number of boys on the playground. "You leave us alone, Jake Carter," Carol shouted down.

"First you come down from there."

"Why should we?" Carol replied.

"Girls shouldn't be allowed on the monkey bars."

"I never heard of that before. Why?"

"Cause girls wear dresses, and guys can look up at their underwear."

Robyn could see Jake's nasty smirk.

"Well, if you don't want to see their underwear, don't look. Besides we aren't wearing dresses," Carol said.

"Girls are weaklings, and they could get hurt playing that high off the ground. You should stick with hopscotch."

"You want to race to see who can climb up and back the fastest?" Carol challenged.

"I don't race girls."

"Of course, you don't. You're afraid to lose," Robyn interjected.

"Fraidy cat, fraidy cat," Carol chanted.

"You want me to come up there and knock your block off?"

"Come on up and try it, if you think you can catch us," Robyn said.

"You better get down here right now, if you know what's good for you."

"Come on up and get us," Carol said.

"I don't want to, because I might knock you off and you could break your leg. Come down if you're not afraid."

Carol started down. "Don't go down there, Carol. He's a lot bigger than you," Robyn warned.

"He's not going to do anything. He'd be in trouble with everyone if he hit a girl."

Robyn started down with her.

When Carol got down, Jake walked up to her. "So, who do you think you are, Mulan?"

"Who do you think you are, Shan Yu?" Carol responded.

"You shouldn't mix up silly cartoons with real life." Jake put a foot behind Carol's feet and shoved her shoulders hard with both hands. She screamed and fell backward with a dusty thud on the playground. Robyn shouted, "Hey!" and made a move toward him. Just then a lady in a green dress came from nowhere and grabbed Jake by the ear. He kicked and shouted at the lady. She gave his ear a twist and he settled down.

The lady looked like she was dressed for dinner. She wore a long, green dress and a wide-brimmed green hat low over her forehead. Under it she was wearing dark sunglasses. The little that showed of her face was pretty.

The boy started screaming like a smashed cat. In a few seconds his father came running across the street. He was a burly man a full head taller than the lady. He wore faded jeans and a sweat-stained T-shirt. "What the fuck is going on here? You let go o' my son!"

The lady immediately let Jake go, and he dodged away toward the man. "Why certainly. And I won't ever touch him again if you teach him not to attack girls that are littler than he is."

"Nobody pushes my son around and gets away with it." The man took a step toward the woman.

The lady took a half step to meet him and they stood face to face, her eyes coming even with his Adam's apple. She stared up into his eyes and said just as serious as possible, "Really? No one?"

"Don't get smart with me."

"Or what?" She didn't give ground.

"Or you could find your fucking block knocked off."

"Like son, like father." The lady stood a little taller.

"I don't know what you're talking about, bitch."

"I ... am ... just ... sure." Each word was emphasized as if it were a separate sentence. "You didn't see him push this little girl down? Pretty strange, because as soon as I pulled him back, you were right over here."

"Don't get smart with me, bitch."

The lady turned her back to the man, took a couple of steps toward Robyn, and then turned deliberately back. "I can see where your son gets it."

"Gets what?" the man demanded.

"Why, his courage to push a little girl down, of course." Her voice was cold and defiant.

Robyn could see the man double his fists. He was shaking angrily. "Fuck you."

The lady looked at his fists. She took off her sunglasses. "You even try to lay a finger on me, and one of two things will happen. Either you will get a painful lesson in the use of Kung Fu as a defense ... in front of your son ... or number two, I will own your house, your boat, your car, and your pension, but most probably both of the above." Her eyes went threateningly dark with power Robyn had never seen. She spoke with such force; Robyn immediately knew she could make her threats happen.

Apparently, the man got the same feeling. He looked at her for several seconds as his hands opened up. She didn't flinch or say another word. "I don't hit women ... not even bitches."

She slowly nodded her head. "It'd be a fine thing if you could teach that to your son."

He looked at her, and his eyes narrowed. Robyn couldn't imagine what was going to happen. The lady's eyes got even darker. The man grabbed his son and started back across the street.

The lady relaxed, but she didn't take her eyes off the man until he was across the street. "What's your name?" she asked Carol. Carol told her and the lady looked at Robyn. "And yours?"

"Robyn Godwin," Robyn answered.

The lady's face was relaxed, and her eyes were soft and friendly. She put her sunglasses back on, and still looking at Robyn she asked, "Why was that boy pushing you girls around?"

"He said we couldn't play on the monkey bars because we're girls," Robyn answered.

"He did?"

Both girls nodded.

"Do you think you can't do something you want to just because you're girls?"

"Some things ... I guess," Carol answered.

"Like what?"

"Play in the NFL."

"Is that fair?"

"What do you mean?" Robyn asked.

"What if you could play as good as a man and you wanted to play? Should you be allowed to?"

"I guess it's not fair, but there's nothing we can do about it," Carol said.

"People used to say that women couldn't vote, but we do now. They used to say that women couldn't be on the police force, but we are now. They used to say that women couldn't succeed in business, but we do now. They used to say that women couldn't be in the military, but we are now. They even used to say that women couldn't be doctors. All those things changed. Do you know why?"

"No," Carol answered.

"Because women have fought to make those things possible. And not just women … many strong men have fought with them. If someone tells you that you can't do something just because you're a girl, remember you can do whatever you are willing to work for. Perhaps someday you will fight to open opportunities for women that haven't been opened yet … maybe even get into the NFL." The lady smiled and walked away.

"Where did that lady come from?" Carol asked.

"Out of nowhere. But there's something no amount of fighting can make happen, and I wouldn't want it anyway."

"What's that?" Carol asked.

"To be a father." They both laughed as Robyn ran to the swings and Carol followed, but as Robyn sat on the swings, she thought about the things the woman said. She wondered if someday she would fight for others.

* * *

Robyn – July 18, 2012; The Journals

The day after the luncheon with her mother, Robyn arrived at her mother's house in the evening. Jo had a couple of boxes of journals. Grandpa had written in his journal all his adult life, as the Church encouraged. Although not every day was accounted for, every major event in the family was in the journals. When Robyn looked at the huge set of books, she felt overpowered. "Mom, I agreed to get to know Grandpa better, but this is a bit much."

"I don't intend that you read everything. Grandpa made these journals available to me ever since the time your father died. They have been a great help to me through some very hard times. I marked a few passages for you to read, and then you can read whatever else you want. I just want you to see what his thoughts were about some of the things that have happened to him over the years and some examples that show what kind of man he is. I picked these up from his house last night, and I spent most of the day finding passages that you should read. You'll see that your grandpa is innocent of any abuse of children."

Robyn took a couple of the journals to the family room and opened the first one to the first marked passage. Jo came with her to answer questions.

Jan 18, 1958, (Saturday): *Today I take pen in hand to write the history of my family. This is to be the authentic, systematic recitation of the important events in this family. It will be recorded in ink in a bound book. Although I have a typewriter, I choose to do it in my own hand. I will record the things that are important to the development and spiritual growth of the family and its individual members.*

Today, the most important event in the creation of any family occurred. Dianne and I were married in the Salt Lake Temple. The marriage is SANCTIFIED by God through His Priesthood in His Temple. That means, all the children born through the two of us will be SEALED to us throughout "ALL TIME AND ETERNITY." This is such a special blessing; only a very few of the MOST ELITE of God's children will ever get such an opportunity.

I am exceedingly blessed by the hand of the Lord today. The sacredness and sanctity of the Temple constrain me from describing the ceremony in that holiest of all places. After going through the experience, there can be NO DOUBT as to who is Lord and Master of this family. I face this awesome responsibility with mixed feelings of humility and anticipation.

"The Church teaches the man is the head of the household, but lord and master seems rather strong to me," Robyn said. "Did Grandpa act like a lord and master?"

"He was a very strong leader, but I never thought of him as a lord and master. He was probably a little carried away on the day he wrote that. What I want you to see here is that from the very beginning, the Church and family were the most important things in his world."

Feb 26, 1958, Wednesday: Dianne and I had our first clash of wills. She has forgotten the PURPOSE of marriage and demanded that I do something to prevent her from getting pregnant. She wanted to finish high school and maybe even develop a trade before having children. She is planning on my EARLY DEMISE and wants to prepare to take care of herself in that unlikely event. She was OBSTINATE about refusing to recognize the fact that when she accepts her calling as a MOTHER IN ZION, she will never have to worry. As long as she is faithful, even if I should die leaving her nothing, the Church would vouchsafe my children and their mother all the necessities of life. That is one of the LEGACIES OF RIGHTEOUS LIVING.

We have prayed about this, and I have PERSONAL WITNESS from the Holy Ghost that now is the time to start our family. Because of her LACK OF FAITH, she is not able to get that same confirmation.

Children are a blessing from the Lord, and I intend to have my quiver full. There are spirits in heaven who are assigned to me, and I will create bodies for them. Dianne will have to come to an understanding of that light and the righteousness of it.

To be a Mormon at this season in the history of the world, when the most VALIANT of spirit children of God are being sent to FAITHFUL PARENTS in the Church is the greatest opportunity in eternity. Dianne is all for missing this opportunity. RAISING SONS TO THE LORD—that is our calling and obligation in the Last Days.

From her knowledge of church teachings about the family, Robyn was sure Grandpa was over the line in these entries. She decided not to push this subject with her mother, so she went on to the next marked entry.

<u>March 23, 1958</u>, *Sunday: We have confirmation that Dianne is PREGNANT. One of the GREATEST days of our life is spoiled because somehow Dianne thinks it would be possible for her to complete high school. She has a STUPID NOTION that the members of our family will take care of OUR child while she goes to school. There is no way I would allow that to happen. It is time for her to GROW UP and accept the responsibilities of being a wife and mother.*

"Grandpa was intent upon taking away Dianne's childhood," Robyn commented.

"That seems true, dear, but you must remember that times were different back then. What I want you to see from the pages of his diary is how powerfully he was guided by his belief in the Church, even when that belief called upon him to take a strong hand with Dianne. He was a righteous leader of the family and insisted that his children have a mother in the home. He would never harm his children or violate the trust God put in him when God committed them to his care. Meanwhile, Dianne constantly rebelled against those principles, thinking only of herself."

December 19, 1958 Friday: *The long-awaited day is FINALLY here – at 12:35 pm my first child arrived from the spirit world—a very pretty, 8 lb. 1 oz. girl. Even though I prayed ardently that my first child would be a boy, I feel no resentment or lack of love for this little girl. My main hope was that the oldest would hold the Priesthood and be a guide to the other children in the family. It is lamentable that this little girl will not have a big brother to look up to and protect her. I suspect God sent us a girl to punish Dianne for her STUBBORN SPIRIT and her lack of enthusiasm in accepting her calling as a mother in Zion.*

The doctor said Dianne had a rough time. This was probably part of God's judgment on her. She is young and strong and will recover speedily. I gave her a blessing, and I FELT THE POWER OF GOD work through me. She will recover rapidly, and I just hope she learned something from this experience.

Dianne's old friends are still involved with childish pursuits of high school. They spend their time in bumptious activities of the immature—laughing and giggling about boys and worrying about high school proms, while Dianne has already taken the loftiest calling that a woman can aspire to—that of being a mother. Not just any mother, but a mother in an eternal family. While they play at growing up, she has accepted her calling and is on the first SOLID STEPS along the road to her eternal salvation and glory. She has been sealed to her husband and now is a mother under that COVENANT. Most of that she owes to me and the persistence and faith I have shown. I hope she comes to realize, to the extent she follows my lead, she will share in eternal blessings.

Robyn thought back many years ago to a lady who helped her at the schoolyard. She often thought about the things that lady had said. She wondered what she would say about these journal entries. "Mom, doesn't it seem to you Grandpa used the priesthood in order to control rather than lead the family?"

"He was always a strong leader for the family. He had to be, because Dianne was weak. She needed to be told what to do in almost every circumstance. You also have to remember that these things happened long before there was a women's liberation movement of the type we have seen in the past few decades. The main thing that these entries show is that Grandpa has always been a very spiritual person who has always tried his best to follow the counsel of the prophets in the Church, while Dianne has always been rebellious. He has made some honest mistakes about certain things because he's human, but I hope that are you beginning to see that he could never do the things that he has been accused of. He has always kept in communication with the Lord through daily prayer and by living a life that is exemplary in its spirituality. It's inconceivable that he could have done anything against children, especially his own. Don't you see how he reveres them as special gifts from God?"

Jo opened the journal to the next marked page. "Here, read this. You'll see what I mean about him."

December 28, 1958 Sunday: This evening in sacrament meeting, I took my first child, KARIANNE GODWIN, in a circle of fellow Priesthood Holders where I officially gave her a name and a blessing by the power and authority of the Priesthood of God. What a BLESSING TO ME as a father, to be able to perform this ordinance and to know it will be RECORDED FOR ETERNITY! Karianne is now started on the road to her personal salvation. I pledge I will make every opportunity available to her for her spiritual growth, and I WILL SHIELD her from the slings and arrows of this earth as long as she is in my protection. NOTHING IS MORE PRICELESS to me than this fresh spirit from heaven. I also know the time will come in the hereafter when she will remember every word I spoke in the blessing I gave her. If she is faithful, those blessings are SEALED UPON HER head by the power of God. The mother gives the gift of life, but the father gives the GIFT OF ETERNITY if he is true to his obligations in the gospel. What a blessed calling and responsibility! Feeling the weight of that responsibility just makes it that much easier for me to walk the "straight and narrow path."

It was hard for Robyn to contemplate that the man who had written those words about his daughter could have engaged in the disgusting act of molesting her.

"I think this entry clearly demonstrates how he felt about his daughters and what a blessing they were to him," Jo said. "In it, he dedicates himself to protecting Kari from all the slings and arrows of this life. It's impossible for me to believe that he could have molested her knowing that God was watching and that one day he would surely have to pay the price for his sin. He is very clear here that all the spiritual blessings that he gives his children are based upon his faithfulness. If he ever violated that faithfulness in the way Dianne accused him, all those blessings would be lost. It would crush him to do that. There's one more entry that I have for you to read. It's from a time when he was part of a bishop's court for a woman who had committed adultery, and it shows what he thought about sexual sins."

March 8, 1968, Saturday: Today I sat in on a Church Court for Sister X. Because of the confidentiality requirements, it would be inappropriate to discuss the particulars of this case, but it was a pity to see the results of failing to keep the RIGHTEOUS COMMANDMENTS of the Lord. It was a very tearful time when she was informed, she was to be EXCOMMUNICATED from the Church for adultery. There was an outpouring of love to her as the sentence was passed and her membership in the fellowship of Christ was REVOKED. Such a court is a COURT OF LOVE. All the leaders are prepared to assist her through the steps of repentance that must now be taken to bring her back into the fold. It is a very humbling thing to think about. It gives me renewed desire and strength to hold to the IRON ROD of the WORD OF GOD. It is only by staying close to the Church that one can protect himself from making those kinds of serious mistakes. The greater obligation is to LEAD MY FAMILY in such a way that none of them will ever face such a court. Sometimes I feel they all take the teachings of the Church too lightly.

Robyn closed the journal and set it on the table.

"So now I hope that you can see that Grandpa would never do anything like he was accused of because he would certainly lose his membership. And that is not even to mention what the scriptures say about a person that offends a child. And I hope you get a grasp of the kind of woman Dianne was that led her to create false stories about him"

"Well, the journals are interesting, and they helped me understand Grandpa better than I did. The thing is, people who know a thing is bad sometimes do the bad thing anyway. I would guess most child molesters understand what they're doing is wrong, and the punishment is great, but for some reason they still do it. Do you mind if I just skim through the journals for a while?"

"Take as much time as you like. I'm sure that the better picture you get of the type of person that Grandpa is, the more you will realize that he could not have done the things that he's been accused of."

Robyn sat at the kitchen table perusing the journals as Jo went to fix some sandwiches for lunch. Robyn read a few entries and then looked up what Grandpa wrote when Joshua Junior was born.

August 22 1960, Monday: Today, the first of my MANY SONS was born. He will be a GREAT BLESSING to the family, and after I have passed on, he will be the Priesthood Leader of this family. I look forward to the many activities he and I will share along with his brothers. It will be UP TO ME to work with each of them in order to develop their faith and leadership abilities so they can take their places in guiding other members on their paths to salvation. THEY WILL BY MY LEGACY.

As Jo put the sandwiches on the table, Robyn asked, "Grandpa expected to have many sons. It must've been quite a disappointment to him to have so many daughters with only two sons. How did he handle that?"

"He loved all of his daughters and sacrificed for them. Even after their treacherous behavior to him, he is still ready to forgive and forget ... all they have to do is admit that they lied about him and ask for forgiveness. I really believe that left on their own, they would have done it by now. It is only Dianne who keeps the fire of the lies alive. I truly believe that after she dies, they will soon come back to the fold. I only hope it will happen before Grandpa has passed. Junior has been a great son and priesthood leader. In the hereafter, even Ronald will be made whole and take his eternal place in the family as a priesthood leader. My dad is very proud of both his sons, but he is also proud of his daughters who have stayed active in the Church and loyal to him."

Robyn continued to thumb through the journals, looking for some of the major events the family had passed through.

Jan 8, 1967: At 1:22 pm, after having baptized Kari yesterday, I confirmed her to be a member of the Church and gave her the gift of the Holy Ghost. Now, because of the PRIESTHOOD I HOLD and MY FAITHFULNESS in the Gospel, Kari will be able to benefit from the constant companionship of the Holy Ghost, provided she keeps herself worthy. It is such a privilege for me to have the opportunity to use the power and inspiration GOD HAS GIVEN ME to bless my own family. Today saw the first of my children become a full member of God's Church. I felt the inspiration of the Holy Ghost move upon me as I pronounced the blessings upon her head. Brother Saunders even commented that HE COULD FEEL THE POWER OF GOD in the building as I performed this most blessed responsibility.

Kari has begun to show signs of a REBELLIOUS NATURE. I hope the power of this blessing will lead Kari to the will of God and her proper place as an obedient child in this eternal family.

My mother and my brother and his family came all the way from Texas just for this event. It was almost a SANCTIFICATION of the whole proceeding to have them here. They plan to stay for two weeks in this area to sightsee, do some genealogy research, and visit the Temple while they are here. They will stay with us most of that time.

Robyn thought back to the day Grandpa confirmed her to be a member of the Church and gave her the gift of the Holy Ghost. It was a very special day, but Robyn also remembered something made her uneasy about that day—something she couldn't put her finger on. "In this entry about her baptism, Grandpa says Kari is beginning to show signs of rebellion," Robyn commented to her mother.

"Kari was so much older that I didn't ever get to really know her. I know that there was a lot of friction between Kari and Dad in the years before she ran away. Her rebelliousness was a family legend. I think she just came from the preexistence that way. I'm sure part of her experience in this life is to overcome that. Unfortunately, Dianne has too much influence over her."

"But Grandpa says she *started* to show the rebellion about the time of her baptism."

"That was before I was born, but I don't recall anyone saying it began then. I don't know what Grandpa means by that statement. It's just sort of common knowledge she has always been rebellious. Maybe that is when it was beginning to be a problem."

The family always talked about the day they had moved into their house in Kerns as an important family event. Robyn thumbed through 1968 until she found an entry at the end of April.

April 1968: Now our peripatetic attempts at raising our children have COME TO AN END. This month we completed the move into our new home in Kerns, Utah. We have worked assiduously every day for the past six months to get the house ready to move into. The house will become the apotheosis of home as we DEDICATE OUR LIVES to the Lord. It will be the anchor of our family until we move into our proper home.

Now that we have this family home, the Lord will bless us with many more children, including BOYS, to fill it. We are both still young and have many more years to produce children unto the Lord. Dianne has shown that all the doctors who said she shouldn't have more children were WRONG. The Lord has selected her to be the mother of a multitude of children who will have our grandchildren, and so forth, until the time of the Second Coming. When all those children stand up to bless her in the last days, SHE WILL BE THANKFUL for my perseverance in convincing her to be productive. Which of her children would she send back to the Lord?

"It appears Grandpa intended the house in Kerns to be temporary until they moved into their proper home. What proper home?"

"What do you mean? He was very upset when he had to sell it. He said that he planned to have his grandchildren come there to visit in his old age."

"It says here he was looking forward to moving into a proper home."

"Let me see that. … Well, I suppose it's because he planned on having many more children and a four-bedroom would get crowded. But Dianne had that hysterectomy about a year later. I guess that put the kibosh on needing a bigger house."

"Why did the doctors say Dianne shouldn't have more children?" Robyn asked as she pointed to the sentence in the journal.

"I think that she used to bleed more than normal."

"It doesn't seem like Grandpa cared much about how many children Dianne wanted to have."

"He most certainly did. It just took him a while to convince her, but in the end, she always agreed to get pregnant. He never forced her against her will."

Robyn looked up the time of Lori's birthday. She found an entry a few days after the birth.

May 22, 1969; Thursday: *Today the doctors took Dianne in for emergency removal of all that MAKES HER A WOMAN. They have now "FIXED" it so she will not have any more children. They did this WITHOUT GETTING MY APPROVAL. I am sure this is NOT the will of the Lord, and they will have to pay for this ABOMINATION in the Final Judgment. THEY HAVE PLUNDERED me of my posterity. Lorianne is to be our last child. They have taken away any chance of having more male heirs to carry my name. It all ends here, with this DAMNABLE operation.*

"I just read about Dianne's emergency operation after Lori was born. Apparently, it was the hysterectomy, and they didn't notify Grandpa it was being done."

"They said that she was bleeding a lot, so they decided to do the operation. Grandpa was out on a story for his paper. He never believed that the emergency was so big that they couldn't have waited until they contacted him. Like I said, it was normal for her to bleed more than average. Dianne signed the papers for the operation, and Grandpa always suspected that she did it so that she would not have to have any more children."

"What do you believe?"

"Grandpa wouldn't lie in his journal because it's a bound, written record."

Robyn was interested in what happened when Dar and Kari ran away. She wasn't sure about the date, but she was able to find when Kari came back.

Nov 3, 1977; Thursday: KARI CALLED TODAY. This was the first time we have been able to talk to her since she ran away. She ran to California, which seems to be the center of the devil's kingdom on earth. She called to say SHE IS PREGNANT and she wants to COME HOME to have the baby. She has been so consumed in her own PERSONAL HUBRIS that she cannot identify with the simple truths of the Gospel. We told her to come home, but when she gets here, I am going to LEGALLY ADOPT the baby to be my own. That is the only way I can assume the responsibility of raising it. I am sure it is going to end up being MY RESPONSIBILITY to take care of her and her baby. It breaks my heart to see her so messed up. Thank the Lord for repentance and the redemption of Christ's blood. Perhaps this is His way of GIVING ME A SON Dianne is unable to give. In a way, if it turns out to be a boy, he will be my actual son, because he will carry MY GENES and because Kari is not married, he will also have MY SURNAME.

Kari is returning HUMBLED AND CONTRITE. She was such a sweet baby, but she began to rebel before she was baptized. I will see to it she never forgets the FOLLY of going out on her own and leaving the gospel and the guidance it provides. She says the father's name is Delmar "something" and he left as soon as he found out Kari was *pregnant. If he ever shows up to make any trouble, Kari can just deny he is the father. It would be hard for him to prove anything, what with the free "love" they practice in those hippie groups.*

"Grandpa says Kari was a sweet child, but then he repeats that she started to rebel around the time of her baptism. It seems something must have happened around that time," Robyn commented.

"Like I said, I wasn't born then. I can't remember anyone saying something happened then. All I remember about Kari was that she was angry at the world as long as I knew her. She was constantly doing things to aggravate both Mom and Dad, but especially Dad. I remember that one time she told him that she was going to have an affair with a black man and bring home a black grandchild—only she used the 'n' word. Grandpa was very patient with her; he let her get away with a lot of things that he wouldn't let anybody else do. She always used what Dad called, uppity language, just to aggravate him … especially when she would misuse some of the words. When they got into their frequent arguments, she would end them by shouting, 'end of discussion' and walking out. Dad would be furious, but there was nothing he could do about it. It was very difficult for my parents to get her to do anything that they wanted her to do. But I don't think that she would've run away on her own. Dar ran away first, and Kari found out that Dar was in San Francisco. That's when she decided to follow."

"Grandpa seems to be really fixated on having male children."

"He mentions it in the journal, but I don't recall him ever talking about it. I don't think he is that fixated; it's just the way he writes."

"In the journal, Grandpa said he was going to adopt Kari's baby, but I never heard anything about him doing it?"

"There was a lot of tension about that issue. Kari threatened to go back to California if my dad forced the issue. Dianne was on her side, and finally he had to give in. They stayed in the area for a couple of years, and my father took care of Kari and her baby, Frank. He really came to love Frank and was a real father to him. Then Kari heard from Frank's father, so she went back to California, and she and Delmar got married."

Robyn began searching the entries leading up to the divorce to see if she could find any information about the affair.

Jan 29, 1980; Tuesday: *Today I was going through some genealogical family group sheets at the stake genealogy library. I want to get a genealogy file together because the Church is beginning to put more emphasis on that principle of the gospel. DIANNE'S SHEETS SHOW HER GREAT GRANDFATHER ON HER MOTHER'S SIDE WAS A FULL-BLOODED MEXICAN! I CANNOT BELIEVE SHE KEPT THAT SECRET FROM ME ALL THESE YEARS!*

Feb 2, 1980; *I approached Dianne about her genealogy. SHE SAID IT SHOULDN'T BE AN ISSUE. NOT AN ISSUE? THAT MAKES MY CHILDREN ONE SIXTEENTH MEXICAN!! I CANNOT FIGURE, FOR THE LIFE OF ME, HOW SHE COULD THINK I WOULD NOT MIND THAT ALL MY CHILDREN ARE PART MEXICAN!! SHE KNOWS WHAT A LAZY GOOD FOR NOTHING RACE THEY ARE. THIS MAY EXPLAIN SOME OF THE PROBLEMS WE HAVE HAD WITH THE CHILDREN.*

"Mom, did you know Dianne was part Mexican?"

"Yes. I found it in her genealogy. I think it was a grandfather or great-grandfather, but it's not something we ever talked about."

"I just read in Grandpa's journal where he found out about it. It's pretty clear he was extremely upset."

"Let me see that." Jo read the entry. She seemed visibly moved. "Everybody knows that he was somewhat prejudiced ... a product of being raised in Texas. All his family and friends were that way to some degree. He has changed and mellowed over the years. Those old feelings don't make him a child molester."

"Well, I was raised partly in Texas."

"Yes, you were, but times change. The civil rights laws of the Kennedys and Johnson were all passed before you were born. You have basically grown up with integration. When Grandpa was growing up, they still had segregation. He has told me that he can still remember when the restrooms and even the drinking fountains were marked for white and colored. You had to obey the signs; they were legal then. The change in attitudes since civil rights laws were passed makes a big difference in the way people look at things."

"This entry is just before the divorce."

"Yes, but it doesn't mean anything ... he never treated us differently."

"But you all carry his genes ... you are biologically a part of him ... Dianne is only related to him by marriage ... and I guess that was fixed by the divorce."

"If you're trying to imply that's the reason for the divorce, you're in left field. Dianne was having an affair, and she refused to break it off."

"I wonder what Grandpa wrote when the Church gave the priesthood to the blacks. I bet he was shocked."

"I'm not sure what he thought, but you can be sure that he accepted whatever the prophet said. He never questions the authority of the Church leadership on any matter."

Robyn looked to find an entry for that event, but Jo didn't think it was important and Robyn couldn't remember the date the proclamation was made.

There were a lot of entries in the journals that were self-righteous and overbearing in Robyn's mind. She realized everything Grandpa put in his journal was there to create an image of himself for his posterity. There was a lot about that image Robyn didn't like, but it seemed impossible he would ever molest a child. Robyn was almost convinced he had not done anything to Debbie, but she still had that nagging little doubt in her mind. She still had her own personal questions about the temple. She was still determined to meet the other members of her family— now even more so than before. The references in the journal only increased her curiosity about them and what had happened. She still had a few days before her scheduled trip to California. She decided to talk to Grandpa before she left. She told her mother to make the arrangements for the meeting and asked her to be there.

CHAPTER 8

1950s – The Letters; Janice

Miss Trudy Kilgore   Oct 19, 1984

    I am so sorry to have to inform you that your friend Janice Guest passed away three days ago. She died of complications from AIDS. She wanted to write to you. She knew her time was short and writing the letter was physically difficult because of her condition. She asked me to mail the enclosed letter to you if she was not able to finish it. Before she started on this letter, she wanted to do everything she could to locate and warn everyone she had had intercourse with over the last five years. This was a big job for her—I do not judge the people I care for in this unit. I think there is way too much judging going on against victims of AIDS—this is especially cruel for someone who is facing an unpleasant death. Jan wrote her brother, Joshua Godwin, a letter informing him of her condition. She completed and mailed that letter on her own. Joshua recently moved to San Antonio, but he never made an effort to answer her letter or comfort her in any way while she was alive. I met him when he took control of her funeral. After meeting him, I was tempted to read the parts of Jan's letter that she had completed before I started helping her. The part I typed for her gave me some clues that something they did was relevant to the problems in her life. I remain in the dark, but I didn't like Joshua—not just for my suspicions, but for the uncaring, overbearing way he handled Jan's funeral.

    Jan insisted that she write the enclosed letter without any help because she wanted to keep the contents confidential. She worked several days on this letter using a portable typewriter from her bed. She typed it one letter at a time and used a blackout pen to color out mistakes. She worked at it for ten to fifteen minutes and then rested an hour or so before taking it up again. When a page was completed, she put it in an envelope. Near the end she couldn't type anymore, so she let me type that part for her as she dictated it. For several days she was alert, but she tired quickly, so the work went at the rate of a sentence or two per day. Near the end, it got so she couldn't carry a thought. I felt there was a lot she wanted to say to you, but for the final two days she was not able to continue. Sorry that it ended in mid-thought. After her death, I put the last page in and sealed the envelope without ever looking at the part she wrote. I am mailing it with this letter. Jan told me to be sure to tell that you she does not intend for you to do anything with Joshua about the letter. She was happy with her life and accepted how it was ending.

Some would say (by the lists she made) that she was a very promiscuous person. That's not for them to judge. I knew her at her most vulnerable time, and I will say she is the most moral person I have met. She dedicated the last, most difficult days of her life, to warning others—and who knows which of them infected her?

Sincerely,
Nurse P. Tanner

* * *

Dear Trudy,
I was so happy to hear of your success in South Africa since I returned. The news on my home front is ▮▮▮▮▮ not so good. I have a lot of things I want todo adn not much time. I discovered I have AIDS and along with it a massive dose of tuberculosis and hepatitis C. Mail being what it is, I probably won't be around tto get a response from you. Don't be sad Trudy, I have been able to prepare myself; pretty much. I am writing this letter to tell you some important things.

The doctors are pretty sure I got the AIDS while I was down there. Its important to notify all the guys Iw as with whenever I was down there. There was Jerry, Tom, Reginald, Richard, Larry, and Carson. You know all them. Have them get checked. Daniel Kaufman, Steven Brooks, Lynn Foster, and Robert Elwood are some others you didn't know. Maybe you can find them if they are still around. I also used to hang out at Red's Bar, Durban Lounge, and the Umtata Bar. I had a lot of one night stands. I don't kknow haw many or how to contact them—maybe post my picture with a warning about AIDS. Whenever I look back of that part of my life, I'm a bit imbarrased, but I have to fess up to it and do all I can to warn others. There is smoething else that no one else knows. It has been my private secret ~~for~~.

This goes back to the 1950s. At that tiem I was in grade school and Josh was a teenager. It all started whenever Ruth got married and moved out. You remember Ruth; she was Josh's big sister. My dad and ~~my~~ Josh's mother (my mother also) both worked and so Ruth was responsible to tak care of me. Josh was the next ~~nex~~ oldest and so he was in charge of me whenever Ruth left to get married.

Right away—the first thing on the first day he wanted to ██████ give me bath. Well, at first he just wanted me to leave the door unlocked so he could get in iif there was an emergency. But right away, he came in while I was still in the tub. He said that was not a problem because he couldn't actually see anything, but then right away he started to escalate his activities, but he said it wasn't a bad thing because I was still a little girl and that since he was a man and I was little girl everything was ok and that we were not actually playing nasty. Playing nasty was a term my mother used whnever she told me that boys and girls shouldn't play with each other's private parts, so what Josh was saying made some kind of sense because Mom never said anything about men and girls notplaying that way—at least that's what Josh said and I bought unto it because he was my big brother, after al.

After that he always wanted do what I will call inappropriate touching whenever I took a bath—him touching me and me touching him. He said he was doing me a favor because he was teaching me what to do whenever I got married, and I didn't know how that would make being married better, and so he explained intercourse and how thats hwo babies are made, and then after that he wanted to try to have intercourse with me.

Right away we started doing IT, and this was to further help me be ready for being married, and he said I was lucky to have a brother to help me, beause it would be playing nasty id some boy who was not related to me did it. he taught me secrets of how to make my future husband feel good. But what I didn't get was mostly i was jus making him feel good.

    Josh had a polaroid camera and right away he started to take pictures of me. I was afirad someone else would see them,b ut he said he had real good hiding place for them. It wasn't too many pictures because film was expensive. Then he had me take some pictures of him. Then he set the mirror up so he take pictures of us together in the reflection of the mirror. It was fun and scary. I worried a lot about what if we were caught.

    Sometimes I would complain that we should stop it and tell our parents we made a mistake. Josh said he would get all the balme and be in a lot of trouble if I said anything, so I kept my mouth shut. All mu life till now I have carried guilt about all that. I wonder often if that is the reason I've haven"t ever been able to have of good relationshop with a man. My divorces have been a real problem for me, but then,if I was married now, I guess I wouldn't be able to live my life as free as I do.

    Whenever I began to show signs of maturing physically, he told me we would have to stop doing what we were because I could end up pregnant. I was relieved and also sad. Some of it I missed. And he started to show attention ot neighbor girl younger that I, but I don't know if they did anything – maybe I shouldn't of wrot about it. Oh well.

    Shortly after, Josh found out he was going on a mission for the Church for two years. I was starting to have nightmares about that someone would find the picturs whenever he was gone and I was pretty sure he couldn't take those pictures on his mission. One day I told him i was so worried about those pictures I thought we should tell our parents and the Bishop so we could repent and have it all cleared up, before he left. He was dead set against that, so he came up with th idea that we should burn them then there wouldn't be a risk.

    So the firday before he was going to leave the next day we took them to a park and burned them all. He got all excited looking at them but we couldn't do intercourse because I had started to get my period. So he just kissed me and I kissed him and did oral sex, and that was the last time.

    After josh bot married, I became more aware of the worldly things. I began to wonder if he was a pedophile, or if what happened vetween us was just childish experimentation. Wehenever his daughter Kari was boorn, that;s when I really began to worry about

Josh. Sometime after Kari got in grade school i started to make oportnities to talk to her privately. That's when I let her know that she could tell me if ayone every wanted to play nasty with her and I would step in to help. Well nothing ever happened and I was relieved tjat it didn't, because I knw I would have really turned the family on its head if Josh turned out to be a pedophile and tried anything with my any of my nieces.

Though Josh isn't a pedophile, what he did helped cause my first divorce. All that stuff aobut making it so I would be ready for sex when I got married completely backfired. On our wedding night with Daryl ███████████████████████████████████████ ███████████████████████████████████████ ████████████████ well lets just say I wanted to show Darryl how good I was. Big Mistake!! He was a virgin, and he expected his wife to be one too. So when it didn't hurt me and I didn't bleed, he was angry. He planned to be gentle to help me get through it, and he was expecting me to bleed and he for sure didn't want me to know how to make him feel good, and so he was mad as hell whenever I started to show him what I knew. He wanted to know who popped my cherry and how I knew so much about men and there was no way I could tell him that Josh and I had ███████████████████ done IT for years, so I told him it was a guy in nineth grade and he wanted to know who. I told him just a guy and that he moved back east right after. I never herd from him again. I don't' know if that marrage would have lasted if things was more normal on the first night, but ███████████████████ it it went downhill from the first night.

Beginning with this page, I, Nurse Peggy Tanner, typed for Jan. I haven't looked at any of the other pages in the envelope per Jan's request.

The other two marriages, well it seemed the problems were different in their different ways, but there were always issues about sex. I wrote that letter to Josh about it because I just think he should know and I want to talk to him about it before I go. I haven't heard back, yet. It was kind of hard because I had to take my time and do a perfect job with the typing and all. Josh is a bit of a headache when it comes to writing, grammar, spelling and all like that. I didn't want my last letter to him to leave him with a bad reputation of my writing. It was easier to write then—I could never have done it now.

I know there were times whenever you and I had our problems and you didn't understand why I did some of the stupid things I always seemed to do—I hope this letter gives you a better feel for where I was coming from.

There have been some times when I have been really in the dumps about not having a good marriage and children but other than that my life has been great. Now as I think about this damn AIDS, I am deeply grateful that I didn't have my dream of having children. I don't think I could bear dying and leaving them behind. But, then maybe if I had a stable marriage and children, I would never have been in the position – just forget it.

I think my life was the best it could be and I am so glad you are my friend. I guess my main regret now is that since Geraldine Ferraro is nominated I would like to see if she will be the first woman US VP. I don't think I'll be around that long. Looks like a shoo-in for Reagan anyway.

Josh and I shouldn't have done what we did, but I didn't suffer too much by it and Josh has gone on with his life in a normal way. That's a good thing. My letter to him will

That time at the dance. I didn't mean much. Not what you thought.

It was mean for Josh to start making me stay away from his kids. I was a bad reputation, but he taught me everything. I wasn't going to infect his kids with what he taught me. I did miss them and then there was the divorce and

Junior was my friend. He tried to understand – please tell him

The thing with Fred. I need to explain that. He was the one who

Dear Trudy,

    Jan made a few fits and starts on other subjects, but I couldn't figure anything from what she babbled. I don't know if the bits and pieces I did include will mean anything to you; I put them just in case. She became very lucid just before she passed. She seemed to be speaking to herself. She said, "Joshua was wrong. He took advantage." I know she was very disappointed that he didn't come to visit her. There was something important she wanted to hear from him. I hope her letter to you is helpful. We on the ward all miss her.

Nurse P. Tanner

* * *

Robyn – July 20, 2012

Robyn was nervous about seeing her grandfather. This would be the first time she had been with him since that awful night. She knew this meeting was necessary, but she didn't have an idea what she was going to say.

    Grandpa had a rambling, single-story house on the outskirts of San Antonio with almost an acre of wooded land giving the feeling of seclusion. Robyn had visited the house often when she was growing up. Many fun times had been spent playing hide and seek and other games with her cousins in the woods. It was strange to think she had other cousins she had never met, and they probably had similar fun times in California, perhaps at Dianne's house.

    Jo answered the door when Robyn rang. She had never just walked into Grandpa's house as she did with her mother's house. There was a formal entry inside the door. Jo led her into the living room where Grandpa was seated in the large leather recliner. Except for the recliner, the room was done in Queen Anne, very similar to Jo's house—pretty but uncomfortable. Grandpa got up to greet her, but Robyn did not approach him for the accustomed hug. She sat quietly on the Queen Anne couch, content to let someone else start the conversation.

Grandpa started. "Your mother has told me about what you think you saw at your house. I'm a little surprised you would think I could do such a thing to a baby. That's the sickest thing I could imagine. Anyone who would do such a thing should be put out in the desert with no clothes and no food or water. He should be tied to a stake and allowed to die slowly and be eaten alive by ants. I really mean that too. I'm sure you've read what Jesus says about anyone who offends just one child. It would be better for him to never have been born."

There was no doubt in Grandpa's voice. He was convincing. "I've had some problems in my personal life since Mary died and left me. This has been an extremely hard time for me. I've been left alone, and I haven't dealt with the loneliness very well. But I have never had impure thoughts or actions. I have strived to live a life as perfect as possible for a human being in this imperfect world. I've always corrected my mistakes, and I have my temple recommend proving it." His fingers shook as he pulled out the piece of paper with the signatures of the bishop and stake president declaring the holder righteous in the sight of the local church authorities. "I've suffered a great deal over this accusation. Worst of all, I've had to have that detective at the police force prying in the very private and personal parts of my life. I'm sick of this now. I've never done anything to harm a child!" His voice had built to a crescendo, but then he followed in a quiet but firm tone. "You need to tell that prying policeman you're not going to press charges and to close the books on this case. And that's another thing, thanks to you I now have a record in the police files. I don't blame you. It was just an unfortunate thing you walked in at the wrong time. But what you saw was not what you want to make of it. You didn't see me doing anything wrong. It was just an illusion and nothing more. I'm not going to say any more about this because it's just too embarrassing for me, and I hope you will just drop the whole thing now too."

Grandpa was angry, no doubt about it. He was also convincing. "I have been thinking I would drop it. It seemed so real to me at the time, but I didn't actually see anything going on. I'm really sorry for all the trouble this has caused you. I just didn't know what to do."

"Well, it's a shame after knowing me all these years, and after all I've done to help you and your mother, that you would doubt me this way. I guess it's just the way this imperfect world is. I only hope you have learned to put more faith in me in the future. I forgive you.

"Your mother tells me you have been planning to go to California to meet Dianne and those other girls. I hope this conversation has convinced you that is not necessary."

"I'm not going to see them because of what I thought happened to Debbie, and I don't plan to discuss this private business with strangers. I just feel there is something incomplete in my life until I at least meet them. I just want to know a little about them and who they are. I have a whole bunch of cousins out there who are my generation who I don't know. Maybe I might …"

"Whom," Grandpa interrupted.

"What?" Robyn asked.

"It should be; cousins *whom* I don't know. If you're going to use the language, at least do it correctly."

It seemed nothing ever got in Grandpa's way when it came to correcting poor English. "I have a lot of cousins out there *whom* I don't know. It would be great if I could bring one or more of them back to the Church. It would be great to see some of them come back to the family. They had nothing to do with things that happened before they were born."

Grandpa got out of his chair and walked to the fireplace. His back was to Robyn so she couldn't see his face, but the tension of controlled anger was evident in his voice. "Those women attacked me … a priesthood leader in the Church, and in so doing they attacked the Church and Jesus Christ! They did it just to force me to sell the house so Dianne could get her 'thirty pieces of silver.' Well it worked. I did have to sell the house and leave Utah. God will make them pay for that. They are in the power of the devil, and it would be folly on your part to have anything to do with them. My advice is for you not to see them ... ever. If there is anything you want to know about them, you can ask me or just read about them in my journal. There's no need to tempt God by exposing yourself to the enticements of the devil."

Jo added, "They're very convincing, especially Dianne. They appear to be your friend, but slowly and insidiously they plant their lies and false doctrine. Dianne is a believer in reincarnation and other devil-inspired doctrines. She almost had me entrapped in her little coven. It's very dangerous to tempt the devil by putting yourself in the power of his servants. I'm telling you, don't do it."

"I'm not worried anyone can take me away from the Church just by meeting them. I just want to meet them. I especially want to meet my other cousins. I'm determined to do this." The past years had been hard for Robyn because she had gone against her mother's and grandfather's will on several important issues, especially the temple. Each time she did it, she felt stronger—more in her own power.

Her grandfather turned from the fireplace and faced her. The muscles under his eyes were twitching, and it was obvious he was fighting back tears as he spoke with an unsteady voice. "I've seen too many people entrapped by the wiles of the devil. It says in the scriptures that in the last days even the most elite of God's children will be ensnared by the lies of the devil. I beg you not to tempt the Lord by purposely putting yourself in danger."

"I'm not going to put myself in any danger. I'm just going to meet some of my relatives. Masla, Mike, Joshua the Third, Jill, Janice, Ralph, and John ... all the cousins I know, have all lived around them all their lives. I don't see them going to the devil. I need to do this for myself. I can't be kept in a bubble all my life. I am the only one left out."

Grandpa was beginning to sweat, and he began to twitch more as his emotions began to swell. Jo got up and stood beside him. "For God's sake," Joshua said, obviously fortified with Jo beside him, "do not tell them anything about what has happened recently. It's none of their business, and they will just use it to make my life more miserable. You can't imagine what happens to a man who is falsely accused of incest. There's no defense. For this crime, a man is presumed guilty by society until he proves himself innocent. How can a man even begin to prove himself innocent of such an accusation? They just wanted to force me out of the house so Dianne could get some money. I don't think they even cared that it would ruin my life in Utah. They couldn't prove a case in court, because there was no case, so they just attacked me publicly. I couldn't prove myself innocent, so I carried the taint of this false accusation for as long as I was in Utah.

"No one else in the family needs to know anything about this recent misunderstanding. Nothing happened, and it's none of their business."

Jo added, "When Marli moved to California she was active in the Church and had a temple recommend. I am certain that if she would have stayed away from Dianne's influence, she would still be active in the Church and have a temple recommend today."

"Maybe so ... there's no telling ... it's all speculation. I understand Marli's son, Michael, is planning to go on a mission. I would like to spend some time with him too. I'm going, but I will be careful, and I'll take whatever they say about religion with a grain of salt ... if it even comes up."

After the conversation was over, Robyn consented to have a prayer with her mother and grandfather before she left. Her grandfather said the prayer, and in it he blessed her with the power to discern the truth through the Gift of the Holy Ghost. When she left, she felt good about what had happened and the way the conversation had gone. Nearly all doubts about her grandfather were gone.

CHAPTER 9

2012 – The Three Sisters; Robyn

Marli

The day of Robyn's trip had finally come. There had been more admonitions from her mother and especially from her grandfather, but she would not be dissuaded. Mike, Marli's son, picked up Robyn at the Burbank Airport. He was a year younger than Robyn. Sometimes he seemed to take life easy, but generally speaking, he was very responsible for his age. He knew the freeway systems around L.A. like Robyn knew the local streets of her neighborhood in San Antonio. He was taking classes at California State University Los Angeles, working toward a BS degree in Criminal Justice.

He had a high forehead with bushy dark eyebrows. He combed, or rather brushed his hair straight back, but it had a mind of its own and would immediately fall from the top to the sides, some going to the right and some to the left, but there was no distinct part to provide organization. His hair was dark brown from the roots to the tips. He had Grandpa's cheeks. His nose was just short of being bulbous. He had a large mouth with full lips; sometimes the left upper lip would pull up into a faint sneer, as if he tried, unsuccessfully, to imitate Elvis Presley.

His favorite sport was golf. He said he took it up because he heard it would be a good way to meet the right people. He came to the airport dressed in a white golf shirt with a ribbed polo collar. On the left of the chest was a back-swinging Mickey Mouse whose club was bigger than Mickey.

Robyn was happy to see him, and he seemed excited to see her, but he gave most of his attention to Debbie. It was the first time he had seen her, and he was completely taken by her.

Masla, Mike's older sister, was married and lived in San Diego. It was a family tradition that all the family (except the alienated members) would get together for a big family reunion on the July 24th at Grandpa's house. For the few days they were in town, Aunt Marli and her family would stay with Robyn and Jo. Masla was five years older than Robyn, so they didn't have much in common, but she was like a big sister to her while her family was there. Junior also brought his two daughters, Janice, four years older than Robyn, and Jill, two years older. Though Grandpa had room at his house, Uncle Junior and his family stayed in a motel near Jo's house. The parents always took the four girls on a special girls' only outing sightseeing or shopping. As the cousins got older, they had more in common. When Masla moved out to live on her own she stopped coming to the reunions. Masla was married now and had two daughters of her own. One was five and the other was three. It was also a family tradition that Grandpa would pay for a new baby and the mother to fly to see him in San Antonio as soon as the baby was old enough to travel. Masla had also begged off on that trip each time, so Robyn hadn't seen Masla for many years. She had never seen either of her daughters except in pictures.

Robyn would have liked to see Masla and her girls, but there was no time, even though Mike was willing to take her to San Diego for a day visit.

They arrived at Aunt Marli's house in Glendale at about three. Aunt Marli was out shopping. The house was a one-story, rambling four-bedroom, three-bath home with a den and a family room. It was built in the early sixties when shake roofs were legal and popular in Southern California. The outside had a mauve stucco finish. It was a pretty house, one Robyn always loved.

The front yard was large. There was a meandering sidewalk from the street to the front door with snapdragons on both sides. There were two Mexican fan palms on the parkway. Up near the house were several large green plants with big leaves. Robyn didn't know what they were called, but they really set the house off in an attractive way.

The backyard had a large patio with a built-in barbeque. The natural ground sloped up from the house so when they leveled it for the patio, they built a small eighteen-inch high retaining wall. On the slope behind the retaining wall there was a lush groundcover with an orange tree and an avocado tree. There was no grass in the backyard. There was a small vegetable garden on one side of the house and the other side was a concrete parking space for their twenty-four-foot fifth wheel. Robyn had watched the trees grow and the landscaping age over the years as she came to visit on various occasions.

Robyn and Mike spent the time discussing the differences between California and Texas, all to no conclusion. They both felt they came from the best place. Robyn agreed California was a fun place to visit.

Aunt Marli got home around 4:30 p.m. Like the other Godwin girls, Aunt Marli had a very thin upper lip that almost disappeared when she smiled. Her eyes were large, dark, and spread wide apart. She wore her hair full and permed so it covered her ears. She liked pearls and usually wore a faux pearl necklace with long matching earrings. Today she was wearing a full, flowing dress with a V- neck and, of course, the pearls. She had white teeth that went well with her pearls. She was just slightly overweight and attractive. Robyn hoped she would look as good when she got to be that age.

Aunt Marli had not seen Debbie before, and she went crazy over her. "It's kind of too bad the family quit having the annual family reunions at Grandpa's house. It's so hard to keep up with everyone anymore," Aunt Marli said.

Uncle Jack barbecued chicken for dinner; it was his specialty, and he was proud of his work. He was a big man; about six foot three and around 240 pounds. He was getting a bit soft around the middle, but in general, he was in good shape. They had a nice visit at dinner, talking mostly about the earthquakes and fires of Southern California.

After dinner, Uncle Jack and Mike went to play tennis and then go out for ice cream. They volunteered to stay and visit with Robyn and maybe watch a video, but Robyn assured them she would be just fine with Aunt Marli. After the dinner dishes were cleaned up and Debbie was down for bed, Robyn had an opportunity to talk to Aunt Marli about some of the questions bothering her. Robyn began her inquiries in the living room. She was seated on a very comfortable chair, and Aunt Marli was lounging on the couch. Marli's house was comfortably decorated. There was a fireplace, and although there was no fire in it tonight, she could see by the smoke stains on the brick that it was used during the cool months of the year.

Robyn began, "I'm very interested in finding out about the history of my mother's family. I know I have been left out of knowing some of your sisters and your mother. They are my aunts and my grandmother, and it's time for me to know more about them. Do you mind talking to me about them and some of the things that have happened in the family?"

Aunt Marli seemed a little surprised. "Does your mother know you planned to get involved asking these questions?"

"She and Grandpa both know. They aren't too pleased about it either, but I want to get a broader perspective than they have been willing to give me. I'm an adult now, and I feel I have a right to know about my family."

"Well, it doesn't surprise me they are not encouraging you. This is all serious stuff, and I don't want to get sideways with your mother on it. What have they told you about the rest of the family?"

Robyn explained how they described them as being in the power of the devil and how they were concerned they would unduly influence her.

Marli asked, "In what way did they think they might influence you?"

"They think Dianne and the others will try to talk me into leaving the Church or influence me not go to the temple to be married. Mom and Grandpa think they are all servants of the devil."

"I know what you're talking about. I was married to my first husband in the temple, but as you know, that didn't work out. Your Uncle Jack and I are not very active, and we don't hold any positions or pay the required offerings. Jo and Grandpa think it's because we stay in contact with my mother. The truth is, Mom couldn't care less whether we go to church or not."

"I plan to visit Dianne, Aunt Kari, and Aunt Dar. Do you think they would talk to me?"

"I'm sure they would be delighted to. Your mother would have a fit though."

"She already had it, and so has Grandpa. I'm not a baby anymore. I have been a bit confused about a number of things in my life, and I feel part of the confusion has to do with the stories I have been told about the family. Everything I hear is one-sided. Would I be prying too much if I asked you about some of those things?"

"Well, if you do start to pry into things I don't want to talk about, I'll tell you."

"It seems so strange that two daughters would run away from home. Did you ever think about running away?"

"I suppose the thought came up, but never seriously. I knew Karianne was unhappy. In fact, I was surprised Darlene was the first to run away.

"Things in our house were about the same as with any good Mormon family but a bit stricter." As an example, Marli explained it was a strict rule in her family that the girls could not go on date until they were sixteen and they could not date any nonmember boys. On her first date, she was excited and thought everything would be okay because the boy was a Mormon boy from their ward. When he showed up, her father interviewed him and decided he wasn't faithful enough, so he sent him home.

"I couldn't believe he would do that to me. Mom always seemed to back Dad. She said I should be thankful I had a father who took such interest in my wellbeing.

"Everybody in school heard about it, so it was almost a year before I got another date. So, yeah, I felt like my life was too controlled, and I sometimes thought about running away."

"But you didn't actually do it."

"No, I got through it and came to realize that was Dad's way of showing his love."

"But now he doesn't want to have anything to do with two of his daughters, and he doesn't want me to either."

"Well, do you know what they accused him of?"

"That he molested them is all I know."

"He feels they conspired by creating a detailed story and supporting each other in it. Mom believed it hook, line, and sinker. So, it was a major battle."

"And you don't believe he molested them?"

"Their story comes from what's called repressed memory. Most of those memories are stimulated through hypnosis, and the person doing the hypnosis actually leads them into a false memory and reinforces it."

"You think this is a false memory, but Grandpa and my mom both believe it was an intentional lie."

"Well, like I say, it's a subject that's forbidden territory in this family."

"It must be pretty hard for you to be in the middle of all this."

"I've seen a lot of trouble that could've been avoided, and it's really a shame. For instance, when your mother and Gail got married, it was a complete fiasco that could've been avoided."

"What happened at my mother's wedding?"

Marli explained that it was all planned to exclude Dianne. Dianne was living in California, and Joshua and the family lived in San

Antonio. The wedding was arranged to be in the Salt Lake Temple in Salt Lake City. Marli's family lived in Salt Lake so Joshua stayed at her house. Dianne wasn't supposed to know about the wedding. Marli supposed that Junior must have informed her, because she came uninvited and stayed at Junior's house.

"Well, Mom showed up at the temple when Jo and your father to be came out after the ceremony," Marli explained. "They posed for pictures outside the temple, and Mom took pictures and visited with some of the people she knew before the divorce. But the thing that really pissed Dad off was that Mom visited with Mary and even gave her a hug."

"It doesn't seem Dianne tries to crash parties anymore," Robyn said.

Marli explained Dianne decided the upset was not worth it just to make a show of interest. When Mike was baptized, she stayed away from the main event Joshua attended. She sponsored a smaller family party and celebration about a week later.

"Dad always forced choices to exclude Mom and our sisters from those kinds of events, but he could not force Lori, Junior, and me to break our relationship with them. It wasn't a secret that we stayed in touch. Finally, it just became a general consensus we wouldn't talk to Dad, or Jo, or you about the part of the family Dad banned."

"Do you mind talking about the divorce?"

"There were a lot of accusations and counter accusations, so it was impossible to know exactly what happened."

Marli told Robyn approximately the same story about the affair and the divorce that Jo had told her.

"What is your relationship with your mom now?" Robyn asked.

"I have a strong relation with my mother. I love both of my parents, but each of them meets different needs. I feel sorry Jo has not been able to have the same kinds of experiences I have."

Robyn's feelings about her grandpa were similar to the things Marli said about him. He was definitely a man above the common. But he was human and had his imperfections.

* * *

The next day, Robyn spent the morning with Mike. They played tennis and had brunch. At brunch Robyn asked Mike, "Why haven't you or Masla ever said anything to me about Dianne?"

"That's forbidden territory. I don't know all the particulars. I know Grams has followed your life very closely over the years. It was she who made us promise not to say anything about her until your mother said it was okay. Once you found out about them, Aunt Jo still didn't want any of us to discuss her. Grams just told us to abide by what Aunt Jo said until she got over whatever was making her so mad."

Robyn realized Mike was not going to be much help.

* * *

Robyn was lucky. Mike had some things planned with his friends, and Uncle Jack had to work overtime. Robyn would have Aunt Marli to herself most of the evening. They got together in the kitchen where Aunt Marli was fixing a stew. Robyn began by asking, "Do you know why my mother is so adamant about me not talking to Dianne?"

"I can't say what goes on in her mind. Haven't you asked her?"

"I have, but she doesn't want to talk about it. She said Dianne abandoned her."

Marli thought a few moments and then explained that in her opinion, Dianne hadn't really abandoned anyone. The breakup was a surprise to Marli, and she thought everyone else was also surprised. There was no lead up or sign of tension before it all broke. Once it started, Joshua had plenty to say, but Dianne was close-lipped about it. Marli felt the two little girls, Jo and Lori, were very susceptible to Joshua's stories.

"My mother said Dianne told Grandpa she didn't want to be her mother … that Dianne didn't have time for her," Robyn said.

"That's the problem when you only have one story. Dad may have said he thought she was too busy, but I'm quite certain Mom never said that. I think the whole thing may just be poor communication or a misunderstanding."

"What about when Dianne blamed my mother for being almost raped?"

Marli stopped chopping potatoes and put her knife down. "I never heard anything like that."

"Some high school boy tried to rape my mom in his house. Dianne said she deserved it, and it was her fault because she was such a flirt."

"This is the first I ever heard of anyone trying to rape Jo. This is one thing I'm absolutely sure of; my mother would *never* have said anything like that about any girl under *any* circumstance, let alone one of her daughters. I would be willing to bet Mom never knew. She would have tried to get the guy arrested. She has a real thing about stuff like that."

Robyn didn't know where to go with that answer. It was as if no one in the family ever spoke about anything—everything was a secret. "My mother says Dianne was the one who came up with the story about Grandpa molesting the girls. She says Dianne did it to force Grandpa to sell his house so she could get some money."

Marli put her hands up with the palms out and waved them back and forth. She said she stayed out of that. She was sure Dianne didn't come up with the story. As far as Marli was concerned, Darlene and Karianne were messed up by some kind of hypnotism. "Unfortunately, you can't shake the doubt it implants. For instance, even though I don't believe Dad ever molested a child ... well, you know there's that tiny doubt that nags. We lived in Southern California, but when we were around Dad, we made sure we could watch Masla. When Masla got older and had other activities, we never made her go to those family reunions either. I know that was unfair to Dad, but it was something we couldn't help. And though we never talked about it, I think Junior was careful in the same way.

"I don't blame Mom for believing Karianne and Darlene." Aunt Marli picked up the knife and went back to fixing the stew. "I would probably support Masla if she had a story like that. I supported exercising caution around Dad and trying to help the girls deal with their false memories. However, their attempt to ruin Dad's reputation in the Church and with the police was overstepping the situation … it's just too far to go when there's no real proof."

"Well, I really do appreciate you talking to me about it," Robyn said. "You have helped me to understand more about my heritage and my family. Do you know how Dianne feels about my mother? Is she mad or something like that? My mom says she never tries to communicate with her."

"I'm sure Mom still loves her. She asks about her regularly. It's a real sad thing you never got to know her. But it's a two-sided coin. Dad has never got to see some of his grandchildren. I just don't understand how this can be. It's so not like the family I thought I grew up in. It's been a shock to see how things really are in our family."

"How much does Dianne know about me?"

Marli laughed. She put the potatoes in the pot and started chopping some carrots she had peeled. "She knows almost everything about you. She knows where you went to school. She knows you play the piano; she knows you were on the tennis team, that you got married before you graduated, and she knows about Debbie. She even knows when you're in town."

"How?"

"Robyn, she always knows when you're in town. How else do you think she avoids coming over when you're here?"

"So, she intentionally avoids seeing me?"

"If you had been allowed to meet her, your mother promised she would never let you to come to California again. Mom has honored your mother's wishes regarding you. I don't think it has been easy for her though."

"Well, I'm over eighteen now, and I can see whomever I want to."

"That's right, but Dianne is in Europe now."

"She is? For how long?"

"She and her husband, Kent, go to Paris for a couple of months every year."

"She's married?"

"She married a man named Kent Mansell back in ninety-eight. He made a fortune in some computer business he started back in the eighties. They live in Westwood in the foothills above UCLA. Kent has a painter friend named Randal Anderson, and they take their wives to Paris every year to mess around and study art. Mom and Randal's wife take side trips around Europe while they are there. They'll be back in late August or early September."

"Of all the people in the family, I most wanted to talk to Dianne."

"I can see your disappointment, but she takes her laptop with her, and we Skype a lot. It's almost like being there."

"No. I think I would much prefer to wait. I need to talk to her face to face. I would still like to meet Aunt Kari and Aunt Dar. Would that be all right with them, do you think?"

"I know they would be thrilled to meet you. Mike has arranged his time to do whatever you want. And now that he has a car, he enjoys shuttling people around to the sights of Southern California. I'll be happy to set it up. Oh, and they don't like their nicknames. They are Karianne and Darlene."

"Thanks, I'll remember that."

<u>Karianne</u>

Robyn hardly slept. At breakfast, she was so on edge and she didn't want to eat, though she did manage to get through the bacon, eggs, and toast Aunt Marli prepared for her. She had thought about this meeting a great deal; she was not sure what she expected to get from it. Aunt Marli had offered to take care of Debbie, and since Debbie got along very well with her, Robyn agreed to leave her.

Mike drove Robyn to Karianne's house in Irvine. The trip required Mike to drive about fifty-five miles south on Interstate 5. Though Robyn had never been to Disneyland, she recognized and the Matterhorn after they had been on the freeway for over an hour. It was a Friday morning and traffic was bad, but the worst of it was the first five miles or so until they passed downtown Los Angeles. They exited the freeway about five minutes after passing Disneyland. Another ten minutes put them in front of a beautiful Mediterranean-style, two-story house in an expensive neighborhood.

As they got out of the car, an overweight woman came from the house. She was wearing black Capri pants with a loose hanging, maroon V-neck tee shirt. Her dark brown hair was streaked with gray and was pulled back into a wavy ponytail that hung just below her shoulder line. She wore no makeup. She had the Godwin thin upper lip with beautiful dark brown eyes.

"This is a day I wondered if I would ever see," she said to Robyn as she got out of the car.

"Aunt Karianne?"

"Robyn, you are prettier than any of your pictures depict. Would it be acceptable if I gave you a hug?"

Robyn stepped forward with her arms open. "Sure," she said as she hugged her newfound aunt.

Karianne took her by her upper arms, stepped back, and looked at her up and down. "If I remember your mother, you resemble her a lot."

"Aunt Karianne, I've got a friend over in Huntington Beach that I'm going to hang with. Is that okay with you girls?" Mike asked.

"That'll be perfect. Why don't you return around five, and we'll all get something to eat."

"Great, see you then." Mike got in the car and drove away.

"How are you doing?" Karianne asked, as she led Robyn to the house.

"Well, to tell the truth, it's kind of weird to be walking up the walk with an aunt I didn't even know existed until I was twelve. I've looked forward to this for many years."

"I sort of know what you're talking about. Here I am in a situation whereby I only know you by means of stories and photos. But we'll make a good start at repairing that, what do you think?"

"That's what I'm hoping for."

Karianne took Robyn on a tour of her house. As they walked, she talked about her family, describing her children, Frank and Frances. Frank worked in management at Disneyland and lived in the city of Orange. Frances was a nurse in Loma Linda. Her husband, Del, was in upper management of the Stater Brothers supermarket chain in San Bernardino. Karianne was a little disappointed that Robyn had not brought Debbie, but it was agreed she would get a chance to meet her before Robyn left. It was an interesting tour, not just to see the house, but many of the pictures and decorations led to interesting family stories.

"Well, from what Marli told me, I guess you came here to acquire information," Karianne said when the tour was over. It had taken almost two hours, but the time had flown as Robyn tried to absorb as much as possible about Aunt Karianne and her life.

"My mother's family has been a mystery to me," Robyn began. "I found out about the lost members when I was twelve, and I have been in a quandary since. Mom and Grandpa have refused to give me any information, except they claim you, Darlene, and Dianne all lied about Grandpa to get money. I'm a grown woman, and I have a daughter of my own. It's time for me to break down the walls I did not create."

"How can I accommodate you in your endeavor?"

"I want to know about the things that broke this family apart."

"This is not a story you will like. I would hate to have it unfold in a way whereby it puts a wall between us after just meeting you."

"I have an inkling of what it's about. I know you accused Grandpa of molesting children. I'm not here to judge anyone. Whatever you say will not create bad feelings from me."

"Why do you want to hear this?"

"Because I'm tired of being in the dark, and for personal reasons I'm not free to divulge at this time."

"I will share this narrative with you, and then I'll ask you again to tell me why you want to hear it. Maybe you will answer me, maybe you won't. You will have to decide.

"I will tell you that Joshua is a child molester." Robyn held back a gasp. The accusation was so blunt and forceful it shocked her. "That's my functional description of him. I live a happy, productive life, but it is not the life I would have lived absent his abuse. It's the little things that occasionally pop up that demonstrate the existence of his influence on my inner soul. For instance, I really like musicals. Last week the movie *Gigi* was on TV, and since I had never seen it, I arranged to watch it. Well, the plot was initiated with a song by Maurice Chevalier titled 'Thank Heaven for Little Girls.' Before the song concluded, I became nauseated and couldn't proceed with the movie.

"I acknowledge I was a rebellious child." Aunt Karianne stood and walked to the sliding glass window and looked out. Robyn stared at her back as she walked. It's not that she didn't expect there would be accusations; it was that she hadn't thought about how they would feel. Her blood was thumping through her ears and her head seemed to be spinning. "I didn't want to conform with anything that my parents wanted me to do. Joshua and I had a particularly stunted relationship, which rendered most of our encounters distastefully offensive. It was never about *what* he wanted me to do; rather it was just that if *he* wanted one thing, *I* universally wanted something different. My life, from the last years of elementary school until I left home after high school, was an arrangement whereby I wanted him to know that he couldn't control me." She turned and faced Robyn. "As regards my mother, I didn't focus on her. She pretty much was just there to render support to Joshua. I had a false impression of her from an experience whereby I went to her for help, and I thought she betrayed me. Only after I had grown up and was a mother myself did I learn it was a miscommunication.

"I was the oldest in the family, and my parents attempted to instill in my mind a desire to set a good example for my younger brother and sisters. For all their attempts, the only responsibility that I wanted to put forward to my siblings was one of rebellion. Yes … I wanted them to rebel. I did not feel like either of my parents were worthy of respect. I freely admit that."

Aunt Karianne walked to Robyn's chair. It seemed to Robyn she was proud of her rebellion. "I've been told you eventually ran away," Robyn said.

Aunt Karianne sat on the couch across from the chair where Robyn was sitting. She told how she had run away to follow Darlene to San Francisco. Karianne described Darlene's lifestyle. That was unacceptable to her, so she moved in with the man she was dating, Delmar. She talked about having a baby with him. After some troubles, she and Delmar were married.

Darlene also had a son out of wedlock, but she stayed in California. She had returned to Salt Lake when she was pregnant with her second son. Her third child was a daughter, Cindy.

"Cindy was killed in a car accident. Because of Cindy's death, Darlene went to therapy wherein she discovered the extent of the behaviors that Joshua subjected her to when she was a child. The story she told rendered my cozy life unbearable. Because, and I've never revealed this to anyone in these terms ... I mean, I've told the wretched story to Mother, Darlene, a bishop, and even a police detective in Salt Lake. I hinted to the bishop, but I never elaborated to anyone the universal guilt I had about what happened to Darlene. I guess I haven't been ready to talk about that before."

"You feel guilty about what happened to Darlene ... how come?" Robyn could see Karianne's eyes were brimming with tears.

"Joshua's deviant behavior always unfolded on Thursday nights because on that night Mom was always at a church meeting. When he couldn't use me anymore, Joshua bluntly suggested to me that I should remove myself from the house on Thursday nights. I cherished those nights away from home and him. This created a circumstance whereby Joshua could substitute Darlene for me. This was something that never darkened even the deepest corners of my mind ... that he would transfer the trauma I experienced to my little sister. If I had only remained home during those nights ... well, it's a universal mystery to me what would have happened."

Robyn had not expected the stories of the molestation would be this nuanced. "You think at that age you could have stopped him?"

"Coupling what I knew then with what I found out later, it's obvious to me now that I possessed a great deal of power over him. Back then, I had a sense of it, but I didn't understand the source or its full reach. I pushed the limits throughout my teen years."

"What power did you have?"

"I told my mom exactly what was happening when he was molesting me from my point of view, but she didn't get it. My vocabulary, at that age, was not advanced enough to convey clearly what was happening. Layered on that was the fact that my mother grew up in the 1950s ... a time when parents were not forthright in explaining the birds-and-bees to their children, and even the news media was self-censoring in putting forth any news about what was happening in that particular brand of abuse. It's not like today, where pretty much everyone knows what child molestation is and that it's not uncommon. Back then, the very idea of such a thing was unheard of in some circles. Right after I revealed the details of my Thursdays with Joshua to Mom, there was a ... well, let's call it a final act that conveyed a quantum escalation in the severity of the abuse. Then Joshua tossed me aside. I soon discovered I could challenge him like none of the other children in the family. Maybe he experienced some guilt about what he did to me, but most probably, he was concerned about what would transpire if I got upset enough to reveal his repulsive secret to the Church or the police. If I had been home on Thursdays, I suppose he would have found ways around me, but I think Darlene would have experienced much less trauma if my presence in the house would have prevailed upon him to create arrangements that were difficult.

"Once the truth that he had carried his perversion forward with Darlene was revealed to me, I realized my mistake ... lamentably, too late. I realized that Joshua was a chronic pervert, and so I contacted his bishop and told him the entire, revolting story of my childhood relationship with Joshua. I was supposed to trust the bishop and the

Church to handle Joshua, but I think Joshua had concocted a story whereby Darlene and I were adversely impacted by a hypnotist to create our stories. I guess the bishop must have accepted that line, because I'm not aware of the Church doing anything about Joshua. I felt it was necessary that I inform everybody of the danger Joshua could perpetrate on a child and I did ... familywise. Mom and I contacted the police, but we had no case. The detective did agree to interview Joshua. I hoped that would create enough fear to deter him to some extent. I don't know if it did or not."

"Where did the hypnotism thing come in?"

According to Karianne, the proposition that repressed memories came from hypnotic suggestion was a "cockamamie" story that probably popped up when repressed memories started to rub the noses of molesters in the consequences of their psychoses. She explained that her earliest memories were repressed. Some of those come up occasionally to join "the flotsam" of her life when they are triggered. However, the Thursday memories had always been with her and were never repressed.

Aunt Karianne revealed some of the details of sex games that came from Walt Disney characters. Robyn felt like she was sitting in an alternate universe. She couldn't match those memories to her grandfather, but Aunt Karianne was very convincing.

"When I was immature, I was into Walt Disney. Mostly short cartoons of Mickey Mouse, Donald Duck, Pluto, all those. The games Joshua played with me stemmed from the Disney animated feature movies like Snow White, Cinderella, etcetera. My friends were consumed with those ... the princess characters. Not me. I couldn't tolerate them. I maintained a big poster of my version of Walt Disney in my room. I think it was kind of like something pure and innocent ... a dream world I could mentally escape to."

Robyn expected it would be obvious the stories were either lies or shadowy false memories, but instead, they sounded detailed, true, and real. Rather than clarity, she was sinking into an impenetrable fog of endless mystery. "Have you ever tried to recover the repressed memories?"

"My young mind compartmentalized them because they involve experiences that it could not support. From my later memories, I know what transpired ... all I need to know. I have dealt with my experiences enough to make a good life. Darlene occasionally suggests I will be better off if I pull them all out. She thinks they hold a key to my weight problem. I have had a weight problem most of my life. I eat too much. I am not convinced seeing more of the ugliness of that trauma would improve my circumstances. I think the only thing I could achieve would be more pain."

"Do you know what happened to cause the divorce?"

Karianne had the same problem as Marli—lots of information from Grandpa and almost nothing from Dianne.

Aunt Karianne refused to believe there was an affair. From her personal knowledge of Dianne since they had been in California, she knew Dianne was not a party girl and had little time for relationships with men. At the time, Dianne was working on an MBA and developing a career. A few years after getting her MBA she was recruited by a headhunter to manage an expanding computer tech company with a six-figure salary.

The owner of the company, Kent Mansell, was great at the technical aspects of the company, but he had always depended on the business manager to keep the company going. In the beginning it was Randal Anderson, but he moved back to Salt Lake City and started his own company. Years later, when Dianne took over management of the company, it grew like gangbusters. She managed the company through the time of the Silicon Valley tech bubble. Because of her management skills, the company flourished even when the bubble burst.

Kent's wife died in 1994. In 1998, Dianne and Kent were married. They bought a mansion in Westwood overlooking the UCLA campus. After they retired and sold the company, they spent much of their time working in philanthropic pursuits all over the country, mostly in the areas of education and abused children.

"So, I have rendered my story. At this point, do you feel safe enough to elaborate on the reasons for your interest?"

"I'm sorry, but not at this time ... I have some other things I need to resolve first."

"Okay. I understand you can experience reservations, especially with someone you don't know. I hope a door has been opened whereby at some time circumstances will unfold to alleviate the aforementioned reservations."

"I certainly hope that we can get to know each other better now that we have met."

Aunt Karianne gave Robyn a hug. "I'm sure we will. Mike will be here soon. What kind of food do you like?"

Darlene

Robyn couldn't sleep again. Her mother's warnings about listening to these women pirouetted through her mind with the same warnings from Grandpa. The feelings she got from the stories Aunt Karianne revealed were evil—almost menacing. She couldn't tell if that came from the fact that they were lies or from the dark reality of what it meant if they were true. She was certain about one thing; she was more confused than ever. She was in over her head, and this search was hurting rather than helping.

Debbie stirred in the bed beside Robyn. Robyn pulled her next to her. Soon Robyn drifted off to sleep.

The next day, Mike took Robyn to Darlene's house in Sherman Oaks. Marli had a previous commitment, so Robyn took Debbie with her. Robyn decided to give up trying to seek any more information about Grandpa. She could see there was no way to find the truth. She would meet Darlene just to get to know her, and then go home or take Mike up on his offer to drive her to Masla's home in San

Diego. She was not ready to delve any deeper into things for which she could never get a definitive truth.

Mike was excited about the preparations for his mission, and he talked about it most of the way. Darlene's house was built into the side of a hill above the street. A short driveway led to a three-car garage. The left part of the house was on top of the garage, and the right side was on a flat space cut out of the side of the hill with the floor at the same level as the top of the garage. The garage served as a partial basement on that side of the house. Concrete stairs circled up from the front of the garage to the front door. Mike parked on the street. "What a beautiful house," Robyn exclaimed. "Is Aunt Darlene's husband really rich or something?"

"She's never been married."

"She and her boys live here by themselves?"

"The boys were grown and moved out before she ever bought this house. She lives here with a woman she has been friends with for years … since she was at the University."

University? That didn't sound like the Darlene she had heard about from her mother and Grandpa. She got Debbie out of the car seat and followed Mike up the stairs as he carried Debbie up to the front door. As they reached the door, a woman opened it and stepped back startled. "Mike!"

"Hello," Mike said.

"This must be Robyn and her daughter," she said. She looked about fifty-years-old with brown hair. Her dark brown eyes sparkled as her full lips pulled into a smile, revealing teeth that had been whitened. She did not look like a Godwin girl. "Do come in. I was just going up the street to have breakfast with a friend."

The lady stepped back so they could go in. She walked past them and out the door, shouting behind her as she left, "Darlene, your long-lost niece is here with Mike. I've gotta run. See you this evening."

"That was Claudia, Aunt Darlene's friend," Mike said. "She's sort of a weird bird, but she can be really funny." He handed Debbie to Robyn.

"Robyn, is that you?" They were in a large living room with French windows and French doors looking out over a patio and swimming pool in the backyard. To the right of the door was a large brick fireplace that took up half the distance between the front door and the windows at the back. The fireplace had an open walkway on both sides, leading to another large space behind it. On the left, in the area that would be over the garage, was a wall of bookcases that went floor to ceiling and a door leading to a long hall. The woman who spoke was walking from a space behind the fireplace. She was wearing denim Bermuda shorts rolled up to just above the knees and a coral, sleeveless work shirt tucked in the front.

"Aunt Darlene?" Robyn answered.

The woman's face lit up. She was definitely a Godwin girl. She looked a great deal like Aunt Marli. She was about Robyn's size and shape. As she came over, Robyn set Debbie down and they hugged.

"This is Debbie?"

"Yes."

"What a cutie. Is she okay with strangers …? I mean do you think she would let me pick her up?"

"She's usually pretty good."

Darlene squatted in front of Debbie. "Hi Debbie. I'm Aunt Darlene." She held her arms out. Debbie hesitated and then cautiously stepped into them.

Behind the fireplace were the kitchen and game room. Mike left and Robyn followed Aunt Darlene and Debbie into the kitchen. "Have you had breakfast?" she asked.

"Yes, we had Aunt Marli's eggs and toast before we came."

Aunt Darlene turned on the TV in the game room to a children's show. "Wow, this is really a nice house," Robyn commented.

"My friend Claudia and I are buying it. I have the west half of the house. It has the bedroom that opens onto the patio and swimming pool. I like to get up early and swim a few laps every day, and Claudia couldn't care less about the pool. My bedroom would be like the maid's quarters. It has a full bath, but it is not as big as the master bedroom where Claudia sleeps. We've been friends since 1986, and we've lived together and shared expenses since 1994. In fact, even though we aren't gay, we have officially entered into a domestic partnership."

"Really? I don't think I've heard of anything like that before."

"We've both had really terrible experiences with men. As for me, I've had … or I should say, have been had … by enough men to last me three lifetimes. So, I hear you are trying to make up for lost time."

"Mostly, I'm really interested to get to know the family I haven't met."

"Well, that is a very wide territory."

"Aunt Karianne gave me the lowdown about your early years and the breakup of the family. What was your life like when you came to California with your mother?"

"Before that happened, my younger years were a mess, and things were only getting worse until my daughter, Cindy, was born. It was through her that I got into serious therapy. I was still on shaky ground until I came to California with Karianne and Mom."

Darlene explained that when they first got to California, she and her sons lived with Dianne. It was crowded, and Darlene was anxious to be on her own. She got a job working as a maid in a motel while she was working on a GED. When she completed the GED, all the family in Southern California got together at Karianne's house for a big celebration and Junior came down from Salt Lake. They made a bigger deal out of it than most people do for high school graduation. That really inspired Darlene and gave her the motivation to go on with an education and career. She started with some remedial courses so she could get into college.

She moved up to a job as a waitress and learned how to treat people in ways that made a good impression and resulted in good tips. After the remedial courses, she was accepted at Cal State Irvin. She started with General Ed courses as she tried to decide what she wanted to be. One day she was talking with her mother about her job and how she really enjoyed working with people. Her mother suggested she look at careers that involved people.

Darlene admired the therapist who helped her through the emotional upset after the death of her daughter, so she majored in psychology and got a Masters. She got a PhD while working part time in the mental health field. Her mother helped with finances until she got her Masters, but Darlene was proud she was able to get her PhD solely on the money she made and student loans. Even though by that time her mother was making good money and could easily help her, Darlene refused her help. "I wanted to do it on my own, and I was really proud when I succeeded. Imagine. Of all the people in the family, I was the only one to get a PhD. If you could see me in 1983, before Cindy, you would say 'no way,' and you'd be right. I owe everything first to Cindy for triggering my memories to begin to surface, my therapist for helping me find and confront my past, to Karianne for morally supporting me and providing a way to get out of Salt Lake, to Mom for insisting I start taking responsibility for myself and getting an education, and finally to me for completing it."

"It seems you really did make some major changes in your life."

"I did have a lot of help … not just in finances, but in moral support and advice."

Darlene explained she worked in research for a couple of years after graduation, and then in 2000, Dianne and her husband, Kent, encouraged her to open her own private practice. They loaned her the startup money, and her mother helped her learn how to run the business.

The practice was so successful Darlene was able to pay the money back in just four years. The real estate bubble burst in 2008. By 2009 the stress on people caused by the downturn created a lot of new business for Darlene. With a nice savings account and stellar credit rating, she was able to take advantage of the slump to get a piece of prime property and build a beautiful office building. She took the space she needed for her business and leased out the rest. As her business expanded, she came to a point where she occupied about two-thirds of the building. The lease payments from the rest of the space paid the mortgage.

"It seems life has really gone well for you."

"Beyond my wildest dreams ... that's for sure. It allowed me to do something really satisfying for me."

"What?"

Darlene told Robyn the story of her friend Judy. "I made a promise to myself the day I discovered she had died that I would get revenge on that preacher. At that time, I was thinking about finding him and killing him. It was many years later before I was ready to act on my promise. I had changed by then and killing was out of the question ... actually, it was always out of the question, I just couldn't think of anything else. It wasn't revenge I wanted anymore, but justice. When I had the money, I hired an attorney and a private detective to follow up on the preacher. The woman detective they sent was an expert. She soon found two girls having the typical problems victims experience. She got the parents to cooperate with a therapist, and her suspicions were shown to be accurate. With just a little work, she and the attorney were able to build a case against the pervert. Before the case went to trial, he committed suicide. Though, for him, justice was served, I did feel bad for his family, but that bastard was still molesting girls when he was caught. So, though it was bad for his family, it wasn't soon enough for the world to be rid of him. No telling how many girls he molested or how many more he would have."

Robyn wondered if Darlene felt that way about Grandpa, but she didn't want to bring the subject up. That preacher had left a trail of destruction that covered decades. Robyn couldn't picture Grandpa being that evil. He was so spiritual and active in the Church, and that freak was—. Robyn felt sick.

"Marli and Karianne called after you talked to them, so I understand you wanted to meet with Mom."

Robyn was glad Darlene had changed the subject. "That was one of the things I most wanted to do, but I guess that'll have to wait."

"Well, we called Mom on a conference call after you talked to Karianne, and Mom has invited you to meet her in Paris for a couple of days."

"That's a real nice offer, but I can't go. It was a real strain on our finances to come here. There's no way we can afford a trip to Europe."

"This is an all-expenses-paid trip."

"I'm sorry, but I don't even know Dianne. I can't accept a trip from her just out of the blue."

"Mom knew that."

"She did?"

"So, you can pay her back."

"No, I don't know when I could ever pay it back and besides, I can't commit George to that kind of debt."

"You could pay it back today with your own money."

"That's funny. I'm just sure I could pay that back with the seventy-five dollars I have in my purse."

"I want you to take a short drive with me right now. We'll have lunch when we get there."

"Where?"

"Mom lives in Westwood, about twenty minutes from here. The staff is there, and they're expecting us."

"But Dianne isn't there. What's the point?"

"She has some things there she wants me to show you. She thinks they will help you understand some things about the family you probably don't know."

"You sure it's all right with her?"

"She set it up."

"Staff?"

"You'll see."

Robyn was reluctant to go to Dianne's house with Dianne out of town, and she was more than a little reluctant to get any more involved in the family controversy, but she was caught up in Darlene's enthusiasm and curious about where the mysterious Dianne lived.

* * *

Thirty minutes later, Darlene pulled into a driveway with a huge iron gate. They had come by what Darlene called the "scenic route" along Mulholland Drive and North Beverly Glen Boulevard. After a couple of seconds, the gate opened, and Darlene drove through to a circular driveway and parked in front of a large mansion. "Holy cow!" Robyn exclaimed. "My grandmother lives here?"

"Not too shabby." Darlene turned off the engine.

A middle-aged man in a maroon blazer opened Robyn's door. "Mrs. Briggs, I presume."

Darlene called across the seat, "Yes, Fred."

Fred opened the door for Robyn and helped get Debbie out of the car seat Darlene had stored in her garage; Darlene was on her own to get out on her side of the car. "The keys are in the car, but you could probably just leave it here. We'll only be a couple of hours," Darlene said to Fred.

"As you say, Miss Godwin."

"I've never been greeted like this before," Robyn said as they followed Fred to the front door.

Fred opened the front door for them. "Oh my God, this is just beautiful!" They were standing in an entryway that was bigger than any room in Robyn's house. The ceiling was a full two stories high.

They walked from the entry into a large living room with a granite floor of warm brown tones. Large floor to ceiling windows looked out the back of the house to a covered patio with an outside barbeque that included a bar and a refrigerator. It was like an outdoor kitchen. To the left, a wide staircase led up to an indoor bridge that stretched in front of the windows across the room. There was a balcony on the left that had three doors. On the right was a large open space, but from Robyn's angle she couldn't see what kind of room it was. It was similar to Aunt Darlene's house, but on a grander scale.

As they stood there, a middle-aged woman in a knee-length dress came through an archway to the right. The color of her dress matched Fred's blazer. Darlene introduced Robyn to Dianne's personal assistant, Jenny. Jenny took Robyn's hand. "It's really a pleasure to meet Mrs. Mansell's granddaughter. She is so pleased you have come."

"Did you find what Mom wanted us to see?" Darlene asked.

"Oh yes. I put everything on the table in the downstairs library."

"Jenny will fix us lunch. She does excellent sandwiches: roast beef, ham and cheese, tuna, BLT, whatever you want."

"Ham and cheese sound good, and Debbie likes tuna fish," Robyn said.

"I'll have the roast beef," Darlene said.

"I'll have them in a few minutes," Jenny answered.

"Follow me," Darlene said.

"To the downstairs library?"

"Right this way." Darlene led Robyn through a double door at the foot of the stairs. The library was about fourteen by sixteen feet. The wall to her right as she stepped into the room was all windows with a French door looking out on the backyard. Outside the window Robyn could see part of a tennis court. The ceiling was nine feet high. The wall with the door through which they had entered and the wall to her right were filled floor to ceiling with bookshelves. The bookshelves were about one-third full of books, and the rest of the space was filled with small statues, figurines, silk flowers, and family pictures in expensive-looking frames. The wall directly in front of her had another door, a wet bar, some filing cabinets, and a round table with two chairs in the corner by the windows. Over the wet bar was a large painting of a southern plantation home with magnolia trees on each side of a dirt roadway that led to the front veranda. In the center of the room was a large library table with eight wooden chairs. Three decorative file boxes were on one end of the table.

"Wow!" Robyn exclaimed. "This is really impressive." Debbie began to squirm in Robyn's arms. Robyn put her down and she ran to the widows.

"Go outside?" Debbie asked.

"Not now," Robyn answered. "Where does that door lead?" Robyn asked, pointing to the door across the room from them.

"That goes to Mom's office. Besides the office there's a bathroom … it actually serves as a dressing room when she wants to play tennis or take a swim in their pool."

"She still plays tennis; I mean she's got to be pretty old?"

"She turned seventy-one this year. She only plays two or three times a week. She's still pretty good, but her knees and elbows get inflamed if she plays too much."

"And this is the downstairs library?"

Darlene described the rest of the house. It had three floors including a basement entertainment area with a game room and a home theater. The upstairs had a large formal library and the master bedroom. An elevator serviced the three floors in addition to the stairways.

"Wow! I never thought I would ever know anyone who could own a house like this," Robyn said.

When they were seated, Darlene said, "As you can see, Mom and Kent did exceptionally well in their business. They both started with nothing. By the time Mom met Kent, he was already a very rich man. However, working together they amassed a fortune. Kent has only one child, his daughter Susan. Mom has six. They don't plan to leave their fortune to their kids. They think people should learn to take care of themselves and make their own way in life."

"I was just making conversation," Robyn interrupted. "I'm not in any way looking to get any of this."

"I didn't think you were, but what I'm saying is important because it pertains to those boxes. Mom and Kent have put their possessions and fortune in trusts. This house and practically everything in it go to the Wounded Warriors Foundation. Their other money and investments will go mostly to foundations to help abused children, battered women, and support education. Though they do not plan on leaving their fortune to their posterity, they are very generous. Christmas and birthday gifts are substantial. They help in other ways. For instance, they loaned me the money to start my business, but not only that, Mom and her financial manager helped me lay the foundation of a good business plan, get all the paperwork, set up the accounting, and meet all the legal requirements. They were almost indispensable, but I had to make it work. And I worked hard to get it going ... seventy to eighty-hour weeks in the beginning. But every time I had a business question or needed some advice, they were right there."

Jenny came in with a tray. "Thank you," Darlene said as Jenny put the tray on the table.

"If you like, I can take Debbie out to the picnic area," Jenny suggested.

"Mom has a children's play yard out back with a playhouse, swings, teeter totter, etc. What do you think?" Darlene asked.

"Debbie is very good with strangers. Do you want to go outside with Jenny?"

"Yes, yes," Debbie responded.

"Okay, you can eat your lunch out there. You be a good girl and do what Jenny says."

"Let's get a bite to eat before we tackle the boxes," Darlene said as Debbie ran out the door with Jenny right behind her.

"Okay, but I'm not sure how I'm going to contain my curiosity." Robyn noted the boxes were labeled: Joanne, Robyn, Mrs. & Mr. Briggs.

The food was delicious. Aunt Darlene was curious about Robyn's life. Robyn talked about George and Debbie as Aunt Darlene questioned her and encouraged her to talk. Robyn noticed some pictures on one of the shelves. She got up to go look at them. "Oh my God! This is me at a tennis tournament."

"That's right. Mom is quite the photographer."

"She was at that tournament?"

"She went to a lot of your school activities. She was very good at disguises. I guess you could say you had a stalker."

"This blows me away." Robyn reached up to a framed picture on the shelf above the one she was looking at. "This is Dianne, isn't it?"

"Yes."

"Something about her looks very familiar."

"If you look at pictures of your mother compared to pictures of my mom at the same ages, it's hard to tell them apart. They were very close before the breakup. They not only look alike, but they talk a lot like each other. This picture is like a picture of your mom in the future."

Robyn walked back to the table to finish eating. When they finished, Darlene led Robyn back to the table with the boxes. "These boxes contain Christmas and birthday cards to you and your mother. They were returned unopened, and so Mom put them away, waiting for the time when the barriers would finally be broken down."

"What are you saying?"

"Mom never forgot your or Jo's birthday or Christmas. These cards … the ones to Jo go back to before you were born. The ones for you start from your birth, up to this year. In the Mr. and Mrs. Briggs box there are ones to Debbie, your wedding card, and anniversary cards."

"I've never seen anything from Dianne."

"She has always respected Jo as your mother. So, she sent everything intended for you to her, even after you were married and living on your own. She has this thing that she would not bypass your mother, but since you are now seeking her out as an adult … that's different, and she has told me to give these to you."

"But Mom always told me Dianne never tried to make contact with her."

Darlene opened the box with Jo's name on it and handed a handful of envelopes to Robyn. She looked at them. The postal cancelations were in the 1980s and "Return to Sender" was written in bold black letters across the front. Robyn recognized her mother's handwriting.

"All of these cards? They're all the same … return to sender?" Tears of pain and disappointment welled in Robyn's eyes.

"I don't know what to say," Darlene responded.

"My mother flat out lied to me about this. I just don't get it."

"I wouldn't hold that against her too much. She's so committed to Joshua, she's incapable of discerning truth. As a professional, I will tell you one potential reaction to molestation is to become inordinately attached to the molester. It seems totally counterintuitive, but it's called traumatic bonding, which describes a strong emotional bonding from victims to the person who threatens, intimidates, or abuses them. Stockholm syndrome is a version of this, where hostages form a bond to the person holding them. This also develops in some cases of spousal abuse."

"She wasn't molested. I'm sorry, but she lied to me. I don't know how to excuse that."

"Suppose she was."

"Saying she was molested is a stretch, and I don't see how that leads to protecting him."

"Let me explain the basics. For traumatic bonding to occur there has to be an imbalance of power that involves sporadic abuse with intermittent reinforcement characterized by highly intensive positives."

"Sorry, you're talking above my head." Robyn did not want to be trapped into a conversation involving accusations against her grandfather.

"Let's look at a father-daughter relationship. The father shows intense kindness and affection. These are the kinds of positive reinforcements you typically see between a father and his daughter, and they are exactly what a girl in our culture expects from her father. There is a marked imbalance of power in the relationship favoring the father. But now let's suppose the father sporadically sexually molests his daughter. This creates traumatic abuse that is so horrible, humiliating, and so far removed from the daughter's normal expectations of life that she needs some tool to cope with the contradicting behaviors of her father. Most of the time he is intensely loving, but there are those recurring episodes that cannot be explained in a sane manner. One way to resolve the issue is to psychologically disassociate from the abuse. This is a form of cognitive dissonance where the girl fulfills her need to justify her position in the relationship by completely distorting and overriding the truth. However, the most radical solution is to wipe the abuse from her memory."

"So, then you're saying Grandpa molested my mom?" Robyn's curiosity overcame her resolve. The dynamics Darlene was explaining interested her despite hearing them in the context of accusations against her grandfather.

"I don't know that. I do know Joshua molested me and Karianne. I also know that child molesters are chronic repeaters. If Joshua molested your mother, it would explain her claim that the cards were not a real attempt by Mom to contact her."

"So, then you're saying she has to lie about everything?"

"What I'm saying is that in cognitive dissonance the victim automatically distorts everything that threatens her made-up ideal of the relationship with the abuser. Jo can see the cards coming on birthdays and Christmas, but in her mind, they are disingenuous acts intended to mislead others into believing her mother cares. She doesn't see them as sincere attempts to contact her. So, when she says her mother never tried to get in touch with her, she would believe this is a true statement."

"That's crazy." Robyn wanted to end this discussion.

"It's not a real sane act, but it is a common coping mechanism for people in those kinds of situations."

"So then, perhaps *you* have cognitive dissonance, and you can't recognize the truth."

"Maybe. There are a lot of ways to deal with trauma. I was promiscuous and involved with drugs, and now I can't envision having an intimate relationship with a man. Karianne externalized her pain and was rebellious about everything. My friend who was molested by her minister internalized her pain ... thinking she was fat. Some women have panic attacks and problems with trust. Some have difficulty saying no to unwanted sexual advances. Some have problems making up their minds about life decisions. There is a cornucopia of responses, some more serious than others. There are plenty of problems to look at, but I was just offering a possible reason why your mother told you something that was patently untrue. I could be totally in left field. Maybe it was just to protect you from the weirdoes in California. I don't claim to know the answer."

"But do you think my mother was molested?"

"I suspect it, but I'm not in a position to make a judgment."

"Why do you suspect it?"

"I know from personal experience and other evidence that Joshua is a child molester. Jo's ability to disassociate from any evidence that Joshua molested children is astounding and unexplainable in the realm of normal behavior. Finally, she appears to lack any interest in forming an intimate relationship with a man, which could mean a lot of things. It's just a piece of a puzzle."

"My existence proves that last statement to be untrue."

"When she married, she chose a truck driver who was practically never home. After his death, she has not pursued another relationship."

"That's because she loved him so much no one can replace him."

"A valid answer, Robyn. I put the idea out there, not as standalone proof, but only as a bit of evidence that when all collected together suggests something to examine more deeply. It doesn't prove anything. I'm just telling you what I think and why, but I have been wrong enough in my life to allow that I may be totally off base here."

This search to find if Grandpa had attempted to molest Debbie was turning far afield. Anger boiled, and she desperately needed to change the subject. "Does Dianne want me to read these, or what?" Robyn held up the cards in her hands.

"The ones addressed to you and Debbie are yours to take with you. The ones addressed to Jo are to remain here, unopened. However, there is another point to these cards."

"What's that?"

"You will find a check in each card. According to Mom, in the early cards, the checks are for amounts of less than a hundred dollars. As her personal wealth increased, the checks increase to amounts in the thousands. Of course, all those checks have had a stop payment put on at the bank. However, each time Mom issued a stop payment, she deposited the amount of the check in an account she set aside for you ... the same thing with your mother. In addition to the money Mom put in, the account has been earning interest, so your account, as of today," Darlene picked up a paper that was in the top of the box, "is $53,234.89." Robyn swallowed. This was impossible. "Mom has authorized her financial manager to transfer the name on the account to Robyn Briggs. Here is the paperwork. All you have to do is provide the required information and identification to the bank and sign the signature card, and the money will be available for you to use to pay for all the travel expenses from here to Paris and back to San Antonio and anything else you wish to use it for. Tickets and arrangements have been made for you and Debbie to leave tomorrow from Burbank Airport. You will fly from there to San Francisco and from there non-stop to Heathrow. From Heathrow you fly to Charles de Gaulle Airport, and then a thirty-mile train ride gets you to Paris. Mom will meet you at the airport."

Robyn took a deep breath. "I can't accept that amount of money."

"Mom doesn't want you to feel pressured. All the arrangements have been made to expedite the trip. Everything can be cancelled at your say-so. I know it seems like a lot of money, but it's money that was given to you over your entire life. You haven't been treated any differently than all of Mom's other grandkids, and truth be told, you have missed out a lot."

"How so?"

"Because she has been involved with them. She has sent them on trips and many other things, such as family days at Disneyland. You might be surprised that she has committed some money each month to help Mike on his mission. I would have to say you have been shortchanged."

"I'll have to talk to George about this."

"Yes, of course you should, and he's expecting your call."

"What?"

"Marli already called George yesterday. She briefly told him about the possible trip and that it would cost nothing. She asked about passports and he informed her that you got passports for a trip to Cancun last year, and he agreed to get them together. She asked George to hold off calling you until you call him so I would have time to explain all this to you. Mom had a man from their satellite office in San Antonio pick up your passports and make arrangements to have them delivered to my house by nine tomorrow morning. Naturally the trip is not a go until you and George decide. You can call him now."

"I don't know what to say. I set my flight back for Thursday, and it's already Saturday."

"Obviously, George knows about the trip now. He is waiting to hear from you. If you decide to go, you must be at L.A. International Airport by 11:30 tomorrow morning. You can spend the night at my place, and I can take you to the airport. We can do some travel shopping this afternoon. With layovers and travel time, you'll be in Paris by Monday in the afternoon, and you will fly to San Antonio with an arrival at 9:45 on Friday morning ... severely jet lagged. Mom will meet you at Charles de Gaulle airport and take you back there for the flight home."

"What about my ticket from here back to San Antonio?"

"Don't sweat it."

"Dianne works fast."

"She has people," Darlene laughed.

CHAPTER 10

July/August 2012 – The Trip to Paris; Robyn

Monday: July 30

As the plane began its decent into Charles de Gaulle Airport, Robyn looked out the window hoping to see the Eiffel Tower or Notre Dame and thinking about the past couple of days. George was excited about Robyn's trip to Paris, once he understood it was to be paid for out of gifts Dianne had sent to her over the years. Robyn didn't even hint at the total amount of the gifts. It would be much better to tell him in person. Aunt Darlene had taken her on a shopping extravaganza that she would long remember though she only filled a carry-on suitcase. She signed the paper taking ownership of the account Dianne had created for her. The flight from San Francisco to Heathrow took nine hours. She slept part of the way but was too excited to sleep enough. Debbie slept most of the way. After a three-hour layover in Heathrow, they had a short flight to Paris.

Robyn waited until nearly everyone was off the plane before she pulled her bag from the overhead compartment. It was kind of a hassle to get the carry-on and Debbie off the plane. She managed to get them both to some seats near the security gate where she sat down with Debbie on her lap. Shortly after sitting down, she saw a woman she recognized as Dianne from the pictures she'd seen at her house. She was pushing a baby carriage toward her. How strange it was to know her grandmother only from pictures she had seen just a couple of days before. Dianne recognized Robyn. She hugged Robyn as if it were a regular occurrence. "I'm so glad you could come on such short notice," Dianne said. "And is this my little great-granddaughter?" She kneeled in front of Debbie. Dianne was prettier than her pictures. Though she was seventy-one years old, she looked like she was in her mid-fifties. Robyn became aware of a warm feeling. She had wondered what this meeting would be like. It somehow seemed natural.

"I don't even know how to thank you for making this trip possible and for all the other money you gave me over the years," Robyn said.

"It was just money. I wish we could have been close during all those years, but perhaps we can make up for lost time. Hi Debbie. I'm your great-grandmother." Debbie gave her a weak smile.

Dianne picked up Debbie and stood. "This has probably been a rough trip on her. We only have a couple of days. Is there anything in particular you want to see while you're here?"

"Of course, the Eiffel Tower, Notre Dame, and maybe eat at a café somewhere along the Seine."

"We definitely have time for all that. I could have had my driver bring me to pick you up, but I think you'll get a better feel for the city by using public transit. We'll take a train into the city and have my driver pick us up at the station there. I rented this stroller … it will make things easier for you and Debbie. Dianne gently put Debbie in the stroller. "This is called a voiture d'enfant. Do you want to ride in it?"

"Yes," Debbie answered hesitantly.

"It's kind of like your stroller at home. It will be fun," Robyn said. "I'll push you."

"Do you know much about Paris?" Dianne asked.

"Just the Eiffel Tower, Notre Dame, and the Seine."

"Well then, we're going to have a wonderful time. Do you need to pick up your baggage?"

"Since it's just for two days, I only brought a carry-on."

"That?" Dianne pointed to the medium-size suitcase beside Robyn.

"Yes, the handle extends, and it has wheels."

"Good, because the Gare ... the train station, is about a quarter-mile away. Highly inconvenient, but at least the walk is all indoors." Dianne took the handle of the carry-on and led the way with Robyn pushing Debbie at brisk walk.

Dianne purchased the tickets. As they were maneuvering onto the train, a man rushed out, knocking the stroller backward. Robyn just managed to keep it upright. Dianne shouted at the man in French. The man turned around, and Dianne flashed a look at him that caused him to apologize and offer to help get the stroller on the train. Robyn could see Dianne's eyes as she shouted. The look was not just anger; it was directed and controlled. Robyn had only seen a look like that one other time in her life. Suddenly, she realized she had seen Dianne before.

As the train started off toward Paris, Robyn asked Dianne, "You know they still don't have any female players in the NFL?"

Dianne returned a puzzled look, and then her eyes opened wide. "Are you remembering something about a boy bullying you and your friend?"

"Yes, and a green dress with a wide hat ... both worn by someone I thought of as sort of a guardian angel. But mostly I remember what you said about women not being held back by outdated barriers. Though, I have chosen a traditional role of being a mother, the relationship George and I have is anything but traditional."

"The whole point I was making was not whether to choose a tradition role or something else; the point is that *you* should choose ... never let other's ideas about who you should be put you where you don't want to be."

"How did you happen to be there that day?"

Dianne explained she went to great lengths to keep track of Robyn. She had made friends with Mary, and Mary was willing to keep her informed about Robyn's progress in school and her activities and interests. She and Kent opened a satellite office for their company in San Antonio that Dianne visited regularly, allowing her to attend many of Robyn's activities in person. That morning long ago she was in San Antonio on business. On a whim, she dropped by Robyn's house just in time to see her leaving for the school grounds with her friend. "When the boy pushed your friend down, I decided I needed to intervene."

"Did you really know Kung Fu?"

"Not a bit, but I know men like him."

"When I was in the library at your house with Darlene, I saw some pictures of my high school tennis tournament," Robyn said.

"Mary informed me that your tennis team was playing in a championship tournament, so I flew there in one of my great disguises and managed to snap a few pictures of you. I was only about four seats away from Joshua and Mary. She knew I was there, but he didn't have a clue.

"I was at Mary's funeral, also in a great, professional disguise. She and I were not friends, but she did me a lot of good turns for which I was not able to repay her during her life. She thought family was most important. She never believed that Joshua was a child molester, but she disagreed with him about shunning members of the family. She thought that everything possible should be done to bring the family together."

Robyn looked at Dianne a little differently. "I never recognized that in Mary, but I know she always tried to see things from the other person's point of view. You couldn't pay her back during her life. Does that mean you paid her back after?"

"She helped me with my daughter and grandchild, so after she died, I looked after her child."

"Ronald?"

"Yes."

"But he's in a care facility."

"Yes. I know. As long as Mary was well enough, she took care of Ronald at home, giving him special personal care. As soon as her health began to fail, Joshua had him institutionalized."

"Yes, but he goes to see him every week."

"Do you go with him?"

"Sometimes, but it's pretty difficult because Ronald doesn't seem to remember us."

"There's a log of visitors at the facility. Sometimes I check to see how many outside visitors see him. The log may give you a clue as to why he doesn't act like he knows Joshua."

"What are you getting at?"

"When Kent and I retired and sold the business, I was looking for some philanthropic investment to provide the excuse to visit San Antonio regularly. When Ronald was institutionalized, I became one of the institution's biggest donor. I also got involved in much of what it was doing. I became a silent member of the board.

"I got to know Ronald and gave him the personal attention that I knew Mary would want for him. At first, I did it to repay, in part, the debt I owed Mary, but over the years, Ronald and I have developed a relationship. He is such a special boy ... well, young man ... he'll be thirty in October. He has come a long way. When I visit him, he takes me to lunch. I drive, but he tells me where to go, orders the food, pays the bill, and leaves the tip. Sometimes he takes me to Brackenridge Park and guides me on a tour of the zoo, which he never gets tired of. He has a lot of friends and a part time job with a landscaping firm that pays part of his keep and provides spending money. But he doesn't have many visitors from the family."

"What about Grandpa? Don't you run into him sometimes?"

"No. He's easy to avoid, he only comes a few times a year."

"That's hard to believe."

"It's easy to prove ... the logs are accurate, and they are maintained years for legal purposes."

Robyn was surprised and disappointed. If what Dianne said were true, that would mean Grandpa had lied about his relationship with

Ronald. Maybe Dianne was lying, but then why would she tell her how to prove it with the logs?

Robyn and Dianne talked about Mary and Ronald as they rode through the French countryside. Then Dianne pointed out the Montmartre hill on the horizon. "From the top of that hill you can see all of Paris," Dianne said. Robyn was surprised at how quickly the thirty miles to Paris passed. "We will disembark at the Gare du Nord station. My car should be waiting for us," Dianne said. The train went underground before they arrived. "It's only a short drive from there to hotel Timhotel on Montmartre where we're staying. I got a room for you and Debbie next to our room. The Timhotel is in the shadow of the Sacre-Coeur basilica. That's a famous landmark, because it's located at the top of the highest hill overlooking Paris. It can be seen from almost anywhere. The Place du Tertre is pretty much right between the hotel and the basilica."

"I don't think I've ever heard of that."

"It's quite famous in the world of art. Many of the early impressionist artists used to hang out there. It's also just a short walk from the hotel to the Moulin Rough."

"I've heard of that," Robyn said. "The movie *Moulin Rouge* with Nicole Kidman is one of my favorite movies … along with *Phantom of the Opera*, which also takes place in Paris."

"Well then, we'll have to make sure you see the Moulin Rouge and the Paris National Opera. Sometime when George is with you and you have more time, we can get tickets to the opera and see a show at the Moulin Rouge."

"That'd be great. I can't even imagine what that would be like."

"Kent and I usually go to the opera at least once on our annual trip. When we get to the hotel, our rooms are on the top floor. From up there you can see the Eiffel Tower and the panorama of Paris. We have a powerful telescope that will let you get a pretty good view of Notre Dame, the Louvre, the Pompidou Center, and of course, the Eiffel Tower."

"It sounds like you could have a whole vacation from right there."

"When we come to Paris, we always stay at the Timhotel. Kent's best friend, Randal, owns an apartment not far from the hotel. It's quite convenient for us to get together while we're here. Kent has some business in Boudreaux and Randal and his wife are in Berlin, so it's just us. I think it's a good thing that we can have a couple of days together to get to know each other. Kent is looking forward to meeting you and your family back in the U.S. and I hope we can arrange a trip to Paris with you and George sometime."

When they got to the station, a young man was waiting for them. "This is Armand. He will be our driver for the next couple of days. Armand, this is Robyn and my great-granddaughter, Debbie." Robyn carried Debbie. Armand put the suitcase in the stroller as they walked to the car.

The ride to the hotel was short, and before she knew it, Robyn was looking out the window at the Eiffel Tower in the distance. It was dark but the tower had lights all over it. It looked very small from her window. Dianne helped Robyn locate Notre Dame in the telescope. She also helped her locate the Pompidou national art and culture center. It was hard to make them out among all the lights. Robin was eager to see them in the light of day.

"I imagine you and Debbie are pretty tired," Dianne said.

"Debbie slept a lot of the way, but she's acting tired, and I'm kind wiped out myself. I guess it's stress of all the traveling … along with the jet lag."

"Do you want me to order up something from room service before you turn in?"

"No, thank you. Debbie and I had a pretty good dinner at Heathrow during our layover there."

"Okay. You rest. I have arranged to have a professional nanny go with us tomorrow to help with Debbie. She speaks English and is very good with small children."

Tuesday: July 31

It was light when Dianne tapped on Robyn's door. Robyn got up gingerly, so as not to wake Debbie, and let Dianne in. Dianne was dressed, and there was a young woman with her. "Are you ready for a day of sightseeing?" Dianne asked.

"As soon as I get dressed. Did you have anything in mind?" Robyn asked.

"We can get around to the things you want to see quite quickly on the Metro, but it's underground, so it involves a lot of stairs or hot elevator rides and you don't get to see anything along the way. I've arranged for Armand to drive us around. This is Véronique. She is a professional nanny, and she will help take care of Debbie."

"It's a pleasure to meet you," Robyn said as she held her hand out.

Véronique took Robyn's hand. "I am also happy to meet you." She had only a slight French accent. "I am trained in the care of small children," she said to Dianne. "I can take care of Debbie very well."

Debbie cried out from the bed, "Mommy."

"Good morning," Robyn said as she picked her up from the bed. "Do you want to see the pretty city?"

"I'm hungry," Debbie answered.

Véronique sat on the edge of the bed. "Hi Debbie. My name is Verny. What do you like for breakfast?"

"Cakes," Debbie answered.

"She likes pancakes," Robyn clarified.

"I'll order breakfast while you dress," Dianne said. "They have a nice breakfast room, but it'll be faster if I have it sent to my room. What do you want?" she asked Robyn.

"Scrambled eggs with hash browns and toast. I like orange juice and Debbie likes milk, if that's possible."

Véronique said, "I have already eaten breakfast." Then to Robyn, "Would it be all right if I help get Debbie ready so we can know each other?"

While Robyn dressed in the bathroom, Véronique made a game of dressing Debbie. By the time Robyn was ready, Véronique and Debbie were laughing and playing.

Breakfast was quick, and they were soon in the car driving down the streets of Paris. "We're going to start with the Eiffel Tower," Dianne said.

When they crossed the Seine, Dianne informed Robyn they were going from what was called the Right Bank to the Left Bank. They drove along the river and then crossed back to the Right Bank as they got near the Eiffel Tower. Armand let them out at a place Dianne called Tocadero Square. From there they had a beautiful view of the Eiffel Tower on the other side of the Seine. Véronique took several pictures of Dianne, Robyn, and Debbie with Dianne's camera. Then they walked down to the Seine River to the sounds of a street musician playing some French music on an accordion. Robyn dropped two euros into his hat from money Dianne had given her before they left. They crossed the Seine on the Pont d'Iena Bridge. From the middle, Dianne pointed out the Sacre-Coeur basilica on the horizon.

There was a long line waiting to go up the tower. Adjacent to the tower was a large park with a pond. Véronique offered to take Debbie to play in the park. After waiting about fifteen minutes in the line, Debbie was more than happy to run off to the park to play. The elevator ride to the second level was quite interesting. For the trip to the first level, the elevator went up the slanted leg of the tower on an angle, though the inside of the elevator was perfectly vertical. At the first level, the angle of the slope changed to go to the second level, and they had to wait in the elevator until the elevator was adjusted to go up the new angle. Dianne pointed out many of the important sites in Paris. From level two, which was only about halfway to the top, they could see many of the famous sites of Paris.

Dianne had several other tourists use her camera to take pictures of them with the tower and Paris in the background as they strolled around the second level platform. She pointed out Notre Dame, but it was quite difficult to see and would be even harder to see in the photos. "I totally forgot about getting pictures' Robyn said. "I should buy a camera to get some pictures for George."

"You're on Facebook. I check in on your wall often. We should be friends, and then I can just post all my pictures to you on Facebook."

"That would be great," Robyn said. *What an amazing world*, Robyn thought.

As they walked, Robyn asked Dianne about the divorce. "I don't talk about that much. Let's just say that after so many years together we just found that we were not made for each other."

"Mom and Grandpa say it was because you were having an affair."

"That was an accusation that Joshua made to cover other problems that we had. It showed a real lack of sensitivity on his part to defame a completely innocent man. He backed down very quickly when he was faced with his bishop and stake president."

"What problems was he covering up?"

"Personal problems, my dear."

Her tone was bland, so Robyn did not think she was offended. She decided to probe. "I read Grandpa's journal just before the divorce happened. He was clearly angry because he had discovered you were part Mexican."

Dianne snapped her head around. "He actually wrote about that in his journal?"

"Yes, he did. And if I were a betting person, I'd bet what he wrote had a good deal to do with the divorce."

"He never said that it was a reason to me, but if I were a betting woman, I wouldn't bet against you." Dianne stopped and leaned against the rail. "Over there is the Arc de Triomphe. Napoleon ordered it to be built so his army would have the honor of marching through it into Paris after their victories. By the time it was complete Napoleon's army had been defeated and he was already dead." Dianne took a picture of Robyn with the arch behind her. "We can post these pictures to your Facebook and George can log on so he can sort of enjoy the trip with you instead of having to wait until you get back.

"Thanks. That's a great idea ... I'll just post them directly to his Facebook. Is there a reason why you didn't you tell anyone about Grandpa's feelings about Mexicans?" Robyn asked as they continued walking around the platform.

"It'd be pure speculation. That's reason number one, but not the most important reason."

"What was that?"

"I had three young daughters still at home. Can you imagine the kind of damage it would do to them to find out that their father was so upset by the fact that their mother was part Mexican that he divorced her? Think of what it would do to them; after all, they also had a Mexican heritage."

"So, you took the heat for the divorce to protect them?"

"Is that so strange?"

"But then why didn't you get custody?"

Dianne leaned against the railing looking out over Paris. "It would be difficult to win that battle without addressing the cause and making it pulic. I was naïve, and I thought that even if I fought for custody and won, I'd be in a very difficult way trying to support them. Joshua was the kind of man who could completely wash his hands of responsibility if he felt that he could get away with it. He and his attorney convinced me that things would go much smoother if I didn't get my own attorney ... more naiveté on my part." Dianne pointed out Sacre Coeur. "We should get a picture of you with Sacre Coeur in the background for George ... since it is so close to where we're staying.

Robyn leaned with one arm on the railing while Dianne took the picture. "Do you think he treated the kids any differently after he discovered the Mexican connection?"

Dianne put the camera in her purse. "The divorce naturally changed everything. It would be impossible to judge whether changes in his behavior toward them were influenced by their heritage or the divorce. Joshua had made up some formula in his mind that the Mexican genes in our children were sufficiently diluted. However, it's possible that he still had some issue about their bloodline." She looked out at Paris. "I know that he wanted boys. He thought it was my fault that we had so many girls. He was incredibly disappointed when I couldn't have any more children. Then he learned that I had Mexican blood. He was getting older. It would not be beyond my imagination that he wanted to get a new wife as quickly as possible to start having more children ... genetically pure sons. The Mexican connection may have been a way to excuse the divorce in his mind."

Dianne looked at her watch. "I have reservations for lunch, and there's a stop that I think you'll find interesting on the way there. The view at the top of the tower, while spectacular, doesn't show much that we can't see from here. I hope that you don't mind if we move on, because the wait for the top is going to be pretty long." It was clear to Robyn that Dianne didn't want to continue this conversation.

"Not at all," Robyn answered. "In fact, I was beginning to feel concerned about Debbie."

"Oh, you needn't worry; she's in very good hands."

"I know, but it's all very unfamiliar for her, and I don't want her to be without me for too long."

"A good point."

Before they started down, Dianne called Armand to pick them up at the foot of the tower on Quai Branly. He must have been waiting somewhere pretty close, because he pulled up as they reached the sidewalk.

Armand drove them back across the river to the Arc de Triomphe on the Right Bank. At the Arc, he took them around the circular intersection three times while Dianne took pictures for Robyn and then he exited on Champ-Elysées. At the Place de la Concorde, where much of the work of the Madam Guillotine had occurred during the French Revolution, Armand turned onto Rue Royale, then made a couple of turns to the Opéra Garnier. Armand let Dianne and Robyn out. Robyn recognized the exterior from the *Phantom of the Opera* movie starring Emmy Rossum. When Dianne explained they could see the grand staircase without waiting to go on a guided tour, Robyn couldn't resist.

"There's a lot more to see if we stay to take the tour, but there just isn't time on a two-day vacation," Dianne explained.

"If there's one thing I most wanted to see in the opera, it's the grand staircase. I am so glad you thought to stop here," Robyn explained as they hurried back to the street. They had only been there a few seconds when Armand drove around the corner with Véronique and Debbie. It was a short drive from there to the Les Bouquinistes restaurant next to the Seine. "You can't see the water from the restaurant because the river is below street level, but the view is nice. I have reservations in the Quai de Seine Room, which looks across the river to the island called the Île de la Citè. That's where Notre Dame is located. We are only about a fifteen-minute walk from Notre Dame. It will make a nice, after-lunch stroll."

The restaurant was elegant. Dianne warned that serving sizes were small, so they ordered an appetizer of white asparagus with marinated, smoked trout. Robyn ordered roasted salmon for the main course and chocolat parlin for dessert. The portions were small, but it was still more than she could eat. Dianne informed her that takeout containers were frowned upon in France, so they left the leftovers behind.

During lunch, Dianne talked about some interesting points of the history of Paris. After eating they crossed the Quia des Grands-Augustins bridge and walked down a ramp to a walkway along the Seine. After a short walk they went back up to street level and crossed the Pont au Double Bridge, which led to the courtyard in front of Notre Dame.

Inside the cathedral, the air was much cooler. Robyn was amazed at the size. It seemed the ceiling was high enough to put a skyscraper inside.

There were so many things Robyn wanted to talk about and so little time. While Véronique was pushing Debbie's stroller around, she started another conversation. "My mom thinks you abandoned her."

"At no time did I abandon any of the kids in my heart. I tried to be there for them, especially for the ones who were not out on their own. I was working and going to school, I was drastically short of money, and I had no transportation. But the main thing was that Joshua would not work with me in any way. Instead of making visitation easier, he seemed to glory in throwing up roadblocks."

"Did you know someone tried to rape my mom?"

"Not until a few days ago, when Karianne told me what you told her. At the time of the divorce, I had no idea of the kind of man Joshua really was. If fact, until I heard about this, I still had no idea how devious he is."

"What would you have done if you had known about the attempted rape?"

"I would have made sure that the law held the boy accountable. Not out of any feeling I had about punishing him, but so that it would be clear to Jo that he was the guilty party. She had no reason to ever feel bad about herself because of what the boy did."

They took their time, enjoying the coolness of the cathedral, and Dianne talked about what the family was like before the divorce, and how she managed to change her life and build a career after the divorce. Robyn mentioned that *The Hunchback of Notre Dame* was one of her favorite novels. "You know we are only about a half mile from where Victor Hugo lived," Dianne said. "Would you like to have Armand take us by?"

Robyn liked Hugo's works, especially *Les Misérables* and *The Hunchback of Notre Dame*. She was happy to get a chance to see where he lived.

When they were done with Notre Dame, they walked across the Pont d'Arcole to the Right Bank where Armand picked them up. He drove them a short distance and let them off at a small park. "This is Place de Vosges," Dianne explained. "It's the first open space that was created in ancient Paris."

Debbie had begun to get fidgety while they were in Notre Dame. "This would be a good place to let Debbie run free for a little if we have the time," Robyn suggested.

"We definitely do."

Robyn and Dianne sat on a bench and watched Véronique play in the grass with Debbie. They talked about Paris and other cities in Europe that Dianne had visited. Dianne again expressed the hope that Robyn and George would be able to visit those places with her and Kent in the years to come. It was almost too much to think about at this time, but Robyn really enjoyed the conversation. It was a needed break from the tensions of the past weeks since Grandpa's accident.

When Debbie was through playing, they went to see where Victor Hugo lived near the southeast corner of the park. After that Dianne led them on a short walk to the Place de la Bastille. "The Bastille was torn down, so there are only a monument and part of the foundation stones," Dianne explained. She called Armand and he picked them up there.

Robyn was surprised at how close Hugo lived to the Bastille and Notre Dame, both prominent locations in his novels.

It was getting late when Armand picked them up, but on the way home he drove them past the Moulin Rouge.

When they got back to Robyn's room, Véronique prepared a snack for Debbie. Debbie was exhausted and fell asleep soon after. Dianne suggested she and Robyn go to a small restaurant near the hotel for dinner.

After a short walk, they arrived at the Cafe Restaurant Buvetè located at one end of the Place du Tertre. Robyn was not very hungry, so she took a chance and ordered escargot. It turned out to be quite tasty, but it came with just six snails and practically nothing else. It was a good thing she wasn't hungry.

Robyn wanted to stay away from any more conversations about molestation, but she was interested about the entries in the diary. She asked Dianne about Grandpa's perception of the role of women in a marriage and if she had a problem with it.

"Was that a problem? He broke me from my dreams within the first months of our marriage. I was definitely overpowered, because he used the Mormon Church as his backup. I was thirteen when we met, and from that day forward he began to exert control. He was nineteen, and I was impressionable. Even when he was on his mission, he wrote me two times a week and expected me to answer.

"I was so ... when we met, I felt so important because this man ... for me he was a man, not a boy ... this man showed so much interest in me. When he got back from his mission, he was ready to get married, and he picked me. I wasn't in love, but on a level, I wanted to be, so I tried to be, and I think I was making serious inroads when we were married. The control issue was difficult for me, but he had me convinced that it was what God wanted ... that we each had a narrowly defined role to play. But my role was way narrower than his." Dianne winked. "It was a role where I had to sacrifice to fit in. At times, I think I probably really loved him, but there were the times when I chafed at my lot in life."

"It seems as though that part of your life was in total contradiction to your life today."

"I'm not changing the subject. We have seen all the things you thought you wanted to see. Tomorrow is already your last full day here. Is there anything else you really want to see?"

"I can't think of anything offhand. I have already seen much more than I planned."

"Well, you can't come all the way to France and not see the painting of Mona Lisa or the Venus de Milo statue. They're both in the Louvre. We'll go there tomorrow. The response to your last remark is there."

"I don't think I should leave Debbie for a long time. Do they let toddlers in?"

"Yes. In fact, if we take the stroller, we can bypass the normal wait at the ticket line."

At first, Robyn had a difficult time going to sleep. Clearly, Dianne's story about her relationship with Joshua and the kind of man he was differed drastically in several ways from the man she grew up with. How could she believe a woman whom she barely knew? But there was the journal and there would be the visitor log.

And on many levels, he was controlling. Maybe the truth would be found somewhere between the two extremes.

Wednesday: August 1

In comparison to yesterday, this morning had been laid back and relaxing. They had a leisurely breakfast in the Breakfast Room, which featured granite-topped tables that seated four. They sat in front of a window looking out on a cobblestone patio.

Once they got in the Louvre, Dianne led the party up the escalators from the Lower Ground Floor to the First Floor. They walked by an amazing amount of art on the way to the room with the statue of Venus de Milo. She was displayed in the center of a room with no other artwork. They walked all around her. Robyn was surprised at how close they could get.

"Most experts believe that she's a statue of the Greek goddess Aphrodite," Dianne said. "She is the goddess of love and beauty. They believed that Aphrodite was the personification of the regenerative powers of nature and the mother of all living things."

From there, Dianne led the group a short distance to the Grande Gallery. It seemed endless, but Dianne said it was just a small part of the museum. She led them to a side room called the Salle des États, the room where the Mona Lisa was. The portrait was high on a wall behind bulletproof glass. A curved wooden barrier kept the crowds back. After being allowed to get so close to Venus de Milo it was a little disappointing to be so far from Mona Lisa. Even so, it was exciting to see such an iconic work of art in person.

"The Mona Lisa is known for the mystery of who she is and her smile," Dianne said. "Up to that time, portraits rarely showed their subject smiling. The relaxed way she is holding her hands and the calmness of her face create a sense of serenity, but the background is anything but serene. Notice how the one side is like a wild alpine scene with rushing water and the other side is a sharply meandering path. It's not a scene of meadows and trees, but jagged rocks. The

Mona Lisa is the most famous painting by Leonardo da Vinci, but there is another very famous painting in the Louvre, also by da Vinci. It's called the Madonna of the Rocks. It's close by, so we'll see it next."

The painting was of two women and two infant boys in very rocky terrain. "The woman in the center is the Virgin Mary," Dianne said. "The child on her right is John the Baptist, the child on her left is Jesus, and the other woman is an angel."

"The boy on Mary's right is snuggled up to her, and she has her hand on his shoulder. The other boy is sitting away from her. Wouldn't you think the boy on the right was Jesus?" Robyn asked.

"The clue comes from the attitude of the two babies. John the Baptist's hands are together in prayer to Jesus, and Jesus has his hand up in the attitude of teaching or granting a wish. Also, Da Vinci made an almost identical copy of this painting, which is in London. He added some symbolism to that copy that explains this painting. In the copy, the child on Mary's right is holding a long cross, which is the symbol of John the Baptist. What is important about this painting to me … well, there are a couple of things. First, the scene is somewhat foreboding, like the background of the Mona Lisa. The second thing is that Mary has her arm around John the Baptist and Jesus is sitting away from her, but you can see that Mary has not forgotten about little Jesus. She has her hand stretched out over his head, ready to protect him. There is a similar painting done by Raphael, one of da Vinci's contemporaries. We'll look at it next."

Robyn followed Dianne to a painting of a woman and two male children. "This is La belle Jardinière. The woman is Mary, but this time the child to her right … the one she has her hand around is Jesus. The one sitting away is John the Baptist, and you can see that he is holding the symbol of the long cross. In this painting, Raphael paints a countryside that is a quiet farmland with trees and what appears to be a friendly village in the background. All is serene and happy here, with no threat on the horizon. Just one more thing I want to show you. We already passed it near the entrance to the Grande Gallery."

As they walked along, looking at exhibits along the way, Robyn noticed Debbie playing with Véronique. "Your nanny is really good with Debbie. A couple of weeks ago Grandpa was visiting at our house and he tripped and fell. He banged his head, which bled quite a lot. We had to have an ambulance come for him. It was only a concussion, and they released him from the hospital the next day, but Debbie hasn't been herself since. We've tried to talk to her about it, but as soon as we bring it up, she starts babbling about the blood. She can't seem to get beyond that."

"Has she seen Joshua since then?"

"Not exactly … we've been kind of busy, and then there was this trip." Robyn was still not ready to give the details of what she had suspected. She was already afraid Dianne knew she was interested in the molestation charges because Aunt Karianne was in regular communication with her. She wished she had not opened that subject on this trip.

"Maybe she's afraid that it was more serious."

"We've told her he's oaky."

"Well, she's a very small child. She probably just needs to see him to reassure her."

As they spoke, they arrived at a large staircase going down. On the landing partway down was a sculpture about nine or ten feet tall of a woman with wings, but the head and arms had been broken off. She was standing on what appeared to be the bow of a boat. There was a dynamic energy from the statue as it leaned forward. It captivated Robyn in a way that made her proud to be a woman.

"This is the Winged Victory of Samothrace. It's representative of a Greek goddess in celebration of a great victory at sea. You see how her body is thrusting forward, giving her a sense of action and triumph. Come sit with me on the stairs."

Dianne led the way, and Robyn sat beside her while Véronique took Debbie to the bottom of the stairs and pushed her around in the stroller. "The Louvre is so large you could spend the summer here and still not see it all. But we have seen what I wanted to show you. We still have some time, and there are some fantastic sculptures on the Lower Ground Floor that we should look at before we leave.

"Last night you wondered about how my life seems to have changed since the divorce. As a young girl I had a view of womanhood ... that I was to be the mother of my family, and that would be a calling worthy of great honor. I saw myself as I described Venus de Milo. I hoped to be the source of love and beauty in my home. I anticipated family life would be like what we saw in Raphael's La belle Jardinière. I'm not saying that I thought about these works of art, only that they typify what my thoughts were. I did have a notion of a particular role I would play in the family with my husband and my children. Taken alone, it was narrow. You could say the role Joshua had for me was not in complete conflict with what I was thinking. However, I also thought that in married life the wants, needs, and wishes of the wife would have some sway in how things happened. I thought the husband and wife would work as a team.

"That's where Joshua was in conflict with my hopes. He viewed me as an inept underling that required his constant oversight. He misused Mormon doctrine to subjugate me, and in my youth, I was not able to combat his logic. Deep inside, I had a sense that something was wrong.

"You could say that I quickly moved from the ideal of Venus de Milo to a Mona Lisa setting. On the surface was a quasi-smile, but in the background, there was an entirely different world. It was a world that I couldn't manage because I was trapped in the narrowness of my dreams and Joshua's false doctrine.

"It was only after I was living on my own that I could begin the process of recognizing those two issues and start to make new choices. I was removed from my children and had to content myself to try to keep my hand out to them ... hovering. This was as much because of my stupidity as it was Joshua's directed efforts to build a wedge. During those years, my world was surrounded by insecurity and foreboding.

"The road to Winged Victory was long and uphill. And now I have to say something to you. I say it in love, hoping it doesn't create a wedge … … Joshua is a child molester." Robyn stifled a gasp. It was a simple, unemotional statement of fact. "He has no compunction about exercising his perversion on children. It appears that he starts at a very young age. I am reluctant to say that I hope he doesn't recover full mobility and independence from his head injury, but I do hope that in his old age, sexual desires have left him. However, it would be unconscionable if something should happen to Debbie in the next few years because I was afraid to warn you."

This was it—the conversation Robyn did not want to have. She thought for several seconds, trying to decide what to say. Dianne waited in silence. Robyn had to say something. "My mom would be spitting mad if she heard you had said that. She says you encouraged Aunt Karianne and Aunt Darlene to make up lies about Grandpa molesting them so he would have to sell the house so you could get some money out of it. She says Grandpa had to sell the house and move from Salt Lake because of those stories."

"Do you believe that?"

"Mom says it's impossible that Grandpa could have done what they say. She says you needed the money … I guess there is no way to know for sure."

"I know … for certain … Joshua molested Karianne and Darlene."

"How can you know? Did you see him?" Anger was boiling below the surface. Robyn wanted an exit from this conversation.

"Karianne was a very sweet girl from her birth. She always wanted to please and was obedient to a fault. Darlene was always bubbly, excited about everything, and smart as a whip. She would laugh at anything even from before she could talk. Something happened to those girls … not at exactly the same time, but in grade school. I can remember the changes they went through, but thinking back, I'm not sure exactly how old they were when it started. They were very young, and the changes were not drastic. However, for Karianne there was a quantum change about the time she was baptized. It was like day and night. She just woke up one morning and, suddenly, she was independent ... argumentative. It was absolute rebellion from then all through her teen years. She gradually increased the intensity of the rebellion. It was a year or so after that time that she started to change the way she spoke. She changed her vocabulary, and then gradually she began to slightly misuse some of the new words. Joshua was a real stickler about grammar and English usage. Her language irritated him to the core. In high school she began to break off arguments with him using the statement, 'end of discussion' and stomping out of the room. Nothing irritated him more than that ... it was a challenge of the authoritarian way he ended disagreements with me by saying the same thing. Karianne was really good at tossing the phrase out just before Joshua did. I'll admit there was a part of me that wanted to laugh out loud when she did it."

"I'm sure all children change as they grow older," Robyn argued.

"You are right. Engaged parents notice and wonder about those changes. For instance, the scare Debbie experienced when Joshua hurt his head is something you noticed, and it concerns you. Of course, in this instance, you already know the cause, so you can move on."

It's not that simple, Robyn thought.

"Minor changes that you understand are one thing. Major, life-changing changes that you don't understand are different. For instance, I noticed the difference with Darlene at a younger age than Karianne. She became ... almost morose ... withdrawn.

"I was in a quandary about those changes. I suggested more than once that the girls, especially Karianne, see a counselor. Joshua wouldn't hear of it; he wouldn't even let them talk to the bishop at church. It was a family problem and, as the head of the house and spiritual leader of the family, he would handle it all."

Robyn wanted to say something—make an argument—defend Grandpa, but she was frozen. By evil? By the truth?

"In the summer of 1984 Darlene had some therapy, and she started to tell me exactly what Joshua did to her ... the details of the molestation. Without going into the details, I will say that he used children's stories to play out his perverted fantasies. As soon as Darlene started to relate the stories, a memory came to me. Joshua used to tell the children modified versions of children's stories. Sometimes he made them funny, sometimes scary … too scary for children. For example, he changed ending of Hansel and Gretel so that Gretel was baked by the witch and Hansel was lost in the forest trying to get away, or Little Red Riding Hood ended up being eaten by the wolf. I told him not to do that, but he thought it was funny to scare the kids, so he just kept on with it. He often used the stories from Walt Disney feature cartoons like Bambi or Pinocchio.

"One morning, and thinking back, this was about the time Karianne rebelled, she came to me complaining that Joshua was playing games about Snow White and Thumper. She didn't tell the details, but she said they were nasty games and they hurt Jesus. I confronted Joshua about it. He pooh-poohed my concern, but I told him that when it reached the point that Karianne was concerned that the stories were hurting Jesus, he had to stop it. He agreed at that point. I was thinking of nasty in terms of something unpleasant. In Joshua's family playing nasty implied sexual contact. That context never crossed my mind. Nothing in my background had prepared me to even consider something as vile and base as a father being sexually involved with his prepubescent daughters.

"As Darlene told the stories, she filled in the details in ways that I understood clearly. Then it dawned on me that those details were what Karianne was trying to explain to me way back when she was just a kid. I was sick with grief and regret. I had to call Karianne to verify what I then knew was true.

"When Karianne explained the details to me over the phone, she said that after she told me what was happening, Joshua abused her one more time … it was a violent rape. Karianne believed I approved of Joshua's behavior, because I didn't do anything about it after she told me. Joshua told her that I knew what he was doing, and I would not protect her. Karianne concluded that only she could protect herself. Joshua and I became her enemies."

Robyn thought of the warnings her mother and Grandpa had given her about Dianne. She wanted this conversation to stop, but she had an overpowering need to hear it all out. She sat quietly, drawing strength from staring at the Winged Victory. Dianne's voice droned on almost as a disembodied entity of truth or evil—Robyn couldn't decide which.

"As she told me this, I remembered a morning several days after I talked to Joshua about the games. When Karianne came to breakfast that morning, she looked terrible. Her eyes were puffy and red. Her nose was running. Her skin was pale. I didn't know what was wrong, but I wanted to take her to the doctor or at least keep her home from school. Joshua didn't want her going to a doctor. He became angry and adamant that she had to go to school and not see a doctor or even the school nurse. I do not for the life of me ... I can't imagine how I could have let her out of the house the way she looked. That must have been the morning after he raped her. Things were never the same between me and Karianne after that ... not until I found out the truth when she was an adult and fully able to take care of herself ... when it was too late. I was the mother. I should have done a better job."

It hit Robyn like a thunderclap. She was Debbie's mother. It didn't matter how improbable it was that Grandpa would do such a thing; she had a responsibility to protect her no matter whose feelings it might hurt. She had thought she would monitor Debbie and Grandpa. Now, for sure, no matter how Grandpa and her mother might complain, Debbie would absolutely never be left alone with Grandpa.

"If only I had spent more time with Karianne and her stories ... if I had just been more curious ... if only I had taken her to a doctor that morning ...well, I failed, and for a long time I blamed myself. Then, in a conversation with Karianne, she mentioned that she blamed herself for Darlene's experiences. It was then that I realized there is only one person to blame … not me … not Karianne. Karianne still grapples with blaming herself, though she is making progress.

"When I discovered the truth, I did all I could to warn others. I told all the kids and talked to a detective on the Salt Lake Police force. Karianne talked to Joshua's bishop and also to the detective. The detective said it was he-said-she-said and an old case, but he did interview Joshua. I worry a lot about the girls of every generation in this family. I know Junior, Marli, Jo, and Lori don't believe the story the girls told. But, at least Junior and Marli have taken precautions with their daughters out of an overabundance of caution. Lori doesn't have any daughters. Now a new generation is coming up. That's why I feel it's necessary to warn you to protect Debbie … even if only out of an overabundance of caution."

Sitting at the foot of the Winged Victory, Robyn felt she was sitting in a tub of defeat. The unbelievable story she had been listening to was so believable the way Dianne told it.

"Mom and Grandpa warned me you would be very convincing." Robyn was still not ready to divulge her concerns about Debbie. "While I am not ready to believe Grandpa is a child molester, I … … …" Robyn couldn't think of what to say.

"Well, I'm afraid I may have put you in overload," Dianne said.

"I don't know. Everything was all wrapped up in a package. Grandpa left Salt Lake because the accusations soured the bishop against him, and you got your needed money. I don't know what to believe … I mean, maybe he was a molester … or maybe he left because you involved the police." *He was so angry at me because I involved the police*, she thought.

"Joshua didn't leave because of the police or the bishop or anything to do with charges of molestation and his decision had nothing to do with the house in Kerns."

"Then why did he move?"

"The plan he always had was for us to move back to San Antonio, especially if his stepfather died before his mother."

"What do you mean?"

"From when we first got married, Joshua planned that one day he would own the mansion where his mother and Mitchel lived. He knew that Mitchel had two sons, and that he might want to leave the house to one of them. He was hoping that Mitchel would die first, and then we would move back to San Antonio to take care of his mother, hopefully living in the house with her while we did. That way, he could make sure that his mother left the house to him. When we bought the house in Kerns, he made it clear to me that it was temporary. He still planned to go back to get the house in San Antonio. Mitchel died several years before Joshua's mother. In late 1983, his mother was diagnosed with breast cancer. Her prognosis was not good."

"Are you implying Grandpa moved to get a house? He never got it."

"I know what his plans regarding the house were. I know he was preparing to move to Texas before the stories about the molestation came out. He left because of a house, but not the one in Kerns."

"How can you know that?"

"Darlene first realized in the spring of 1984 that Joshua had molested her. She didn't confront him until later in the spring or early summer. Joshua's attorney made a big mistake when he did the divorce. He didn't have the title of the house switched to Joshua. At the time of the divorce, I was probably just stupid enough to let them do that if they had insisted. In 1984, I was a joint owner, and he could not sell the house without my signature. He asked me to sign a release for him to sell the house. This was not long after he discovered his mother had cancer. I signed it in February of 1984 … several months before Darlene first confronted him about the molestation. The house was sold, and he had moved back to San Antonio less than a month after Darlene made the accusations. I suspect the house was already in escrow when Darlene spoke out. Mary told me that they were moving to San Antonio when I signed the release. I was thinking that with the money I would get from the house that I could also move back to San Antonio. That way I would be with the younger girls that were still with Joshua.

"Joshua and the family moved into the mansion, but as soon as Joshua spoke to his mother about leaving the house to him, he discovered that the house had already been left to Mitchel's youngest son, with the provision that Joshua's mother could live there until she died. As soon as Joshua found out about that, he moved to a rental house.

"When his mother died, Joshua got a very large inheritance from Mitchel's estate. He used the money to buy the property in San Antonio and build a custom house."

"How did you find out about those things?"

"For one thing, I signed the release, and I have a copy in my files at home. But mostly Mary and I kept in communication … about the kids. She felt bad about the rift in the family, and she hoped that someday things would be patched up. She was one of those who kept me informed about the things you were doing. She told me about what happened with Mitchel's house in San Antonio."

"I can't believe how much has been going on in this family … all around me, and I knew nothing. I keep getting more confused the harder I look, but I don't believe Grandpa would harm a child. That's not to say I'm foolish enough to ignore what other people believe." Bit by bit everything Robyn believed about her life and her family was crashing down. There would be records to back up what Dianne said about the house. Another lie from a man who she believed would never lie about anything.

"Why didn't you move to San Antonio?"

"The truth about Karianne and Darlene changed everything. My relations with Jo and Lori were so messed up I couldn't exert any influence on them. So, my options were to go to California with Karianne and Darlene, where I could be close to help them, especially Darlene, or go to San Antonio to try and help the younger girls, where Joshua would stand in the way of anything I would try. Neither of the younger girls trusted me. The only way I could leave them with Joshua was because Mary was so helpful in letting me know how things were going with them. Based upon what I knew about Karianne and Darlene, both of the younger girls had passed the age where Josh would have a sexual interest in them. Through Mary, I kept up with how they were doing in Texas while I was helping the others in California. The decision was ... one can't really put it in words. It's a decision I second guess all the time. I have a good relationship with all the children except Jo. I wonder if I had gone to San Antonio, would something have occurred that would have given me an opportunity to salvage that, but then what would have happened to the others, especially Darlene?"

Robyn was glad she only had one child as she looked at the pain in Dianne's eyes. She believed Grandpa had lied about Ronald, the divorce, and his reason for moving back to Texas. A little research would be enough to prove all of it. But the lies she could prove did not prove he had molested anyone. "I always thought being a parent would have its difficult days, but I never knew how difficult it could be, especially when the person you are married to becomes the problem. Thank you for your concern about Debbie. I'm not convinced Grandpa was ever a child molester. The stories on both sides are convincing, but unfortunately, I just don't see a possibility of proving anything one way or another. However, I will follow Marli and Junior's example. It will be more difficult because we are around Grandpa all the time, but I will see to it that Debbie is never alone with him." Robyn knew she had to do more. She would make sure Debbie knew what kinds of behavior were inappropriate and make sure she would feel safe to tell her if anyone ever attempted anything inappropriate with her.

"I'm glad for that. I have waited so long to begin a relationship with you. I was really frightened that this would spoil it."

"Actually, for the first time, I really feel like you are my grandma." Robyn leaned over and gave her grandmother a big hug. There were tears in both their eyes.

For another hour they walked around the Louvre. Robyn enjoyed the time with Dianne, but she was more confused than ever. Was she slipping into an incredibly prepared lie as Grandpa had predicted, or could he have really been the monster Dianne described? She really liked Dianne, and she loved Grandpa. How could she maintain a relationship with both of them? Marli did it by putting her head in the sand—by ignoring stories of molestation, pretending they didn't exist. Robyn didn't think she could close her mind to the possibility, and yet, that was the only option she could think of. In any case, she would have to confront the lies. She already knew her mother would find a way to twist out of it and excuse them.

Later, as they were working their way to the exit on the Lower Ground Level looking at French statues in the Cour Puget room, Debbie broke from Véronique and ran a short distance to a statue titled Aristaeus. It was a slightly larger than life statue of a man leaning against a tree stump with the skin of a sheep hanging from it. The statue was completely naked. Debbie pointed to his crotch and said, "Grampuh has that!"

"What?!" Robyn exclaimed, gasping in horror at the implications of those three words—three words that suddenly, irrevocably overturned a major paradigm of her life. As Debbie jumped back and looked at her with wide eyes, Robyn realized her own emotional state was flowing to Debbie. Her mind was choked, and she didn't know what to say.

Suddenly, her grandmother's hand was on her shoulder. "Take a deep breath. Let's not do anything to frighten Debbie or make this into a problem for her," she said in a quiet, soothing voice.

"But …" Robyn stammered, realizing her grandmother was right but realizing her emotions were out of control.

"Here, let me," Dianne said as she knelt down with Debbie. "Debbie, how do you know Grandpa has that?" she asked in a pleasant tone.

"Grampuh show me."

"When did he do that?"

"When he hurt his head."

"I'm glad he's better now. Do you want to look at some more of the rock people?" Dianne nodded to Véronique, who quickly stepped in and led Debbie to some more appropriately clothed statues. Robyn watched Debbie toddling away with Véronique holding her hand. Debbie was fine. Robyn was not.

"He was prepping her." Robyn was almost whispering, as though Debbie and Véronique were still there.

"I'm so sorry," Dianne said. "I think it would be best to consult an expert in these things to help deal with how to handle this with Debbie. In the meantime, is there anything I can do?"

"You know about Darlene's friend and the preacher?"

"Yes, I do."

"You know what I have to do, don't you?"

"Yes. I'll help all I can. You're not going to have a strong case."

"Doesn't matter, old as he is, he's still a threat. Win or lose, my mom will not have anything to do with me."

"Don't underestimate her." Dianne put her arm around Robyn, and they walked together to get Debbie and Véronique. The tour was over. The vacation was over. Her old life was over.

INTERLUDE

Joshua Godwin

Joshua Godwin opened the door to his office, walked in, and locked it. He walked to his desk but was too agitated to sit. Robyn and Dianne had just left. He began to pace in front of his desk. That Mexican whore had been in his house, and though she said almost nothing, he knew she was gloating as Robyn made her foul accusations.

That meddling little bitch! I warned her Dianne would trap her, but she just had to take that damn trip and put herself in Dianne's power. That slimy, twisted witch turned a silly thing a baby said about a statue into proof of a lifetime of ... Robyn just swallowed it. She believed Dianne's spin on an innocent comment from a baby rather than me. Thank God Jo isn't falling for that bunk.

Joshua walked to the French door and looked out over the patio into the dancing shadows of the afternoon sun playing in the forest.

Robyn is too stubborn. She and Dianne will never stop pressuring Jo. Dianne is the one who is pushing Robyn to press charges. She won't be happy until she destroys my life and turns everyone against me. Jo was strong today. She won't fall for that lame story from Debbie. But Robyn ... Robyn is a different thing altogether. She is the one who can file the charges, and she's in Dianne's power. Maybe Jo can make her pull back, but Dianne came all the way from Paris with Robyn. Dianne is not going to pull back. What if the police get a search warrant? That would be the death nail on everything.

Joshua unlocked his private closet, went in, climbed the ladder, and retrieved the box from its place on the top shelf. It was handmade of wood with metal reinforced joints. Brother Owen had made it for him to his specifications back when he lived in Salt Lake. It was fifteen inches long, twelve inches wide, and five inches deep. Though it was made before there was such a thing, it fit his secret laptop easily. It was bulky and heavy and though it had strong handles, it was becoming more difficult for him to put on the top shelf. It wouldn't fit in the fireplace, but the files and mementos could easily be burned in it individually. He carried the box to his desk and opened the combination lock. He opened the lid, took out the laptop, and pushed the plastic bag to the side. The file labeled DIVORCE was underneath the bag. He thought about the many times he had looked at the contents of the box over the years. He enjoyed the memories and the feelings they gave him. He leaned back and closed his eyes. He began to contemplate all the memories held in the box. He could feel the blood rush through his body and the excitement build just thinking about them.

Why should I have to destroy all this? Because of a damn Mexican woman? Well, she can't get in here to get anything. The police don't have enough information to get a search warrant. There has to be probable cause. ... But what if they find a judge who's easy to convince? Or ... when I was in the hospital ... what if I have to go again and stay a couple of days? What if someone finds it? What if Junior gets the box after I die and doesn't follow my instructions?

Joshua took the divorce file out and set it on the desk beside the box.

This file doesn't have any bearing on Robyn's charges. But ... it could be hard to explain to Jo if she found it. She was resolute today. I can depend on her, but she might find this hard to take.

He turned on the gas fireplace and pulled a chair in front of it. He put the divorce file on his lap and opened it. *One last time before I get rid of it all.* The letter from Sue Ann was on top. It should have been in his letters file—he must have rushed the last time he had the files out. He read the letter. Sue Ann was the only girl he had touched on his mission. It had been difficult to get separated from his missionary companion at the church picnic in order to be alone with Sue Ann. Once he accomplished that, the rest was easy. She had crushes on all the missionaries and fell for the line that he would go to college after his mission, and by the time he was through she would be old enough to get married and he would come back to get her. She followed his instruction not to write him until after he was released. Then she wrote him. It was just an innocent letter with no mention of the details. It was inspired by her infatuation. He wrote back, acting surprised she had written. He told her she was way too young to be thinking about dating and that he was getting married. Nothing in her letter admitted to anything, but Dianne might try to find Sue Ann, and the story she could tell would be hard to explain. Reluctantly, he threw the pages one by one into the fire and watched them burn.

The next thing in the divorce file was the first letter from Dianne. It was four pages handwritten. In it she pleaded with him to let her move back into the house. She talked about the accusations of the affair and the meeting he had had with the bishop and the stake president. She accused him of leaving her because she was a Mexican and that it was not her fault. She talked about getting therapy and meeting with church authorities. He imagined having her in his power again; groveling and pleading. He was the one in power and there was nothing she could do.

If Jo ever read the letter, she would ask some difficult questions. He threw those pages, one by one, into the fire. There was no relief in seeing them burn. Why should there be? This was not something he wanted to do. Robyn was lost. Jo was his only ally now. He had to get rid of anything that could cause her to doubt.

The idea of having to burn everything was giving him a headache. The air in front of the fireplace was getting warm, and the acrid smell of burning paper singed his nose. He thought about putting everything back in the box and hiding it someplace where the police would never look—maybe bury it in the backyard. His head hurt more. He realized trying to hide the box would be stupid; he had to clean up all of it—burn everything—it would be insane to keep evidence. He opened the file and picked out some more papers. They slipped from his fingers as the file slipped from his lap. He looked at them scattered on the floor. He felt powerless to pick them up.

CHAPTER 11

August 2012 – The Box

Opens door Leans into room
goodbye ... ... um
  Walks from door to bedside Speaking softly
I dont know what to call you anymore
  Turns toward window
I used to call you dad ... when Robyn was around I called you grandpa and it was Brother Godwin at church
  Turns back
you arent *any* of those ... all my life I have known you ... well I never ever really knew you ... you talked ... I listened ... I agreed and if ever I didn't you brought me sharply to your reality ... I didnt mind ... I hardly knew what I was doing ... now *Im* doing the talking
  Walks to window Looks out
from the third floor San Antonio looks calm ... peaceful
  Turns around Looks at bed
remember when you took me to the Alamo ... rules of reverence ... peaceful calm quiet ... not like the sixth of March eighteen thirty six with Santa Anna and all the chaos and death ... remember the Alamo ... a cry for revenge

Walks to bed
I saw those pictures that you took ... pictures that I dont remember I dont *want* to remember ... but maybe if I did remember ... maybe then this pain and chaos would leave me ... remember our trips to the River Walk ... the water on the top so peaceful but underneath prey and predators struggling unseen to survive ... ... an east facing window looking to a rising sun ... a new start ... for you its a sunset ... at least thats what the doctors are saying now ... ... brain dead ... the brain in your head cant run the organic machinery of your body they say that people in comas can hear whats being said ... I wonder if brain dead people can hear through their spirit ... I wonder if there even *is* a spirit ... can your spirit hear me ... ... can your spirit understand the depth of my pain
Blows nose
of the pain you caused ... you look so peaceful ... ... I guess I didnt mind accepting your reality and your spirituality ... which of course was all a lie ... now Im here with the truth and I dont know if you are hearing me ... you bastard
Walks to door Looks back
goodbye bastard
Pauses. Turns around Walks to bedside
is that a strong term ... is it too strong ... they say that there are two sides to every story ... I remember the story you told me about your terrible stepdad and Jace and how you had to dig him up when you were just a child yourself ... and yes that was *terrible* ... so what did you do ... did you try to ease *your* pain by inflicting pain on other innocents ... how did that work out ... did you have less pain because of it ... ... I think not ... you just made the pain grow and spread from generation to generation to generation ... you are such an asshole.
Walks to door Looks back
goodbye asshole
Looks at ceiling Walks back to bedside
you used me oh my *god* how you used me ... can you count the ways that you used me ... you used me to satisfy your disgusting perversion

then you compounded it ... you used me to cover it up ... god damn you ... you used me to isolate and punish your victims ... god damn you to hell god DAMN you to hell

Pounds her fists on her thighs
god damn you to hell ... FOREVER

Raises fists Backs up
you used me to cover your sins and while I was doing that you were using my daughter ... and then my granddaughter ... was that your plan ... oh JESUS GOD you used me to help you ... to be your accomplice with my daughter and my granddaughter

Quietly
children are so fragile ... did you know that ... in kindergarten the teacher had us sing a song ... where oh where has my little dog gone ... where oh where can he be ... with his ears cut short and his tail cut long ... the teacher asked the students to raise their hands if they knew what was wrong with the song ... I was the only one who didnt raise her hand ... I didnt see anything wrong ... the teacher made fun of me in front of the class saying Joanne is stupid she doesnt even know that you cant cut a tail long ... and the children laughed and I stood up for myself and I said that you can too cut a tail long ... boys cut their hair short but girls cut their hair long and the teacher made fun of *that* answer and for weeks ... the students made fun of me and I never volunteered an answer in school again ... that was so minor compared to what you did to your own daughters ... I wonder if it ever occurred to you how much damage you did to your little children ... and to all those others ... to hurt them like you did ... to deny it ... to just cover it up ... what an asshole you are ... you changed their lives for the worse and no one can know what their lives would have been without your evil ... how could I have been so *stupid* right up to the end ... when Mom and Robyn came back from France yesterday with what Debbie said and you convinced me that they purposely misconstrued what she said ... you stood there and allowed me to turn away from my mother my daughter and my

granddaughter ... what do I call you now ... shit face I think ... isnt that what you called him ... your stepfather

Walks to door Opens door

goodbye shit face

Pauses Closes door Walks to bedside

maybe you would be interested to find out how I found your secret trophy box ... maybe you already know ... you know ... the box with the big lock ... it must have been hidden somewhere in your office ... probably in the locked closet ... the box with the combination padlock and the letter taped to the top that instructed Junior to burn the box if he found it after you died ... because it had personal papers that were important to you but would cause unnecessary pain to members of the family ... unnecessary pain ... are you kidding WHAT A GOD DAMNED JOKE

Starts shaking Looks at him

you were trusting that he would fall for your guilt and follow your instructions as his eldest male heir ... yes that box ... Junior didnt find it ... *I did* ... oh yeah ... its going to come out now ... your whole god damned flood of perversion ... no ... I am not a snoop if thats what youre thinking ... if you can even think at all at this point

Sits on chair

what a frightful thing when Robyn and Mom came to confront you ... frightful for *you* ... you were so angry ... and then your tears ... phony tears ... and I dont even know what they were about ... probably faked up to manipulate me ... I was such an easy target for you ... they werent honest tears ... honest tears of regret would mean something ... you may have never been capable of *honestly* crying ... I sent Robyn and Mom away because I believed you instead of my own mother and daughter ... after they left you went to your office to work through your grief ... at least thats what I thought ... I heard the chair tip over and of course I couldnt get in to see what happened because you locked the god damn door and you didnt answer my calls or my knocking ... so I had to go outside to look through the window and see you sprawled on the floor with papers scattered around and the fireplace going full blast ... and I had to use a rock to break the window in the French door to unlock it so I could get in ... I didnt even notice the box on your desk until after the ambulance came to carry you away and I was getting ready to follow the ambulance and turning off the gas to the damn fireplace ... and I didnt notice ashes of the papers in the fire because I was focused on you ... I ignored everything else until I got back from the hospital and I went back to your office ... to see if there was something that I could do about the broken glass and there was the divorce file on the floor with its contents scattered next to the tipped over chair ... and I tipped up the chair and gathered the papers ... and I read them ... the ones that werent burned ... I know times change but only three hundred a month for a year in alimony ... are you kidding ... how was that enough for her to get an education and get on her feet ... you got everything in the house and both the cars ... I suppose that worked out real well since you never let her get a driver's license ... and she got three thousand dollars and a future interest in the house but only if you sold it ... what a rip off that divorce was ... the cars alone were worth more than you gave her ... and what about that pitiful letter from Mom after the divorce ... pleading for you to stop making it so hard for her to visit us ... the one with details of the rotten things you did to make it harder for her ... and the picture of Mom and me and you ... only the part with Mom was torn off ... I wondered where that picture had gone ... I cringe when I think of the things that you were telling me about her at the same time ... I was alone without Mom and you caused that ... you didnt think about *me* at all ... it was all about *you* ... all about making *you* look right and her wrong ... in a way it breaks my heart ... I just wonder what other enlightenment there would be in the pages you had already burned ... it didnt look like that much ... you must have just started

Gets up Starts pacing at foot of bed
the big combination padlock was lying open on the desk and the box lid was closed with the letter to Junior taped to the top and it said no one was to look in ... but I peeked ... no ... I went through everything.

Stops pacing
there was the plastic bag with your collection of little girls panties ... they were not new but they were clean and each one was marked with a letter of the alphabet just below the waistband on the front using some kind of black marking pen ... but what was really weird were the words written in the crotch ... prime ... choice ... select ... standard ... I think thats how beef is graded ... how sick *are* you ... I was thinking ... I dont remember *what* I was thinking ... for sure not what I discovered deeper in the box ... I put them on the big table in your office ... the panties ... and began to organize them ... trying to see if the letters put them in some recognizable order and as I was looking at them I noticed the panties with the letter F written on the front had the letter D stitched on the backside just below the waistband ... thats what Mom did to separate all our panties after the wash and that looked exactly like Moms D ... D was Darlene so I started looking for letters stitched on the back and sure enough I found a pair with a letter for each of the girls except Marlene. Karianne had an E written on the front and her K that was sewn on the back ... Darlene was F front and D back ... the panties with the letter I on the front had my J on the back ... you had *my* panties in your collection ... Lorianne had the letter L stitched on the back with a K written on the front ... Karianne and Lorianne were labeled prime in the crotch ... Darlene was only select and I was choice ... choice ... *Shit* ... the marks on the fronts started at letter A and went to W ... probably in chronological order
  Sits on chair
you had a fine old time of it collecting twenty three pairs of little girls panties ... four of them from your own daughters ... stupid silly me ... at first I was wondering how you got them ... thinking of maybe you stole them from clotheslines or something ... and what the hell were the sick words in the crotch for ... then it was obvious how you got them ... ... really sick ... when I was finished sorting them I went back to the box and there was a file folder labeled with the address of the house in Kerns ... and inside were the sales papers

with escrow and stuff along with a copy of the check that you sent to Mom for her payoff and then I saw the paper ... the release ...you know ... the paper Mom signed that allowed you to put the house on the market and she signed it the fourteenth of February nineteen eighty four ... you know what was weird about that ... of course you do ... that was months before Karianne and Darlene accused you of molesting them ... supposedly to force you to sell the house ... how was that supposed to be instigated by Mom to force you to sell a house that you had already started the paperwork to sell ... and there was no way she did not know it ... she signed the damn release you god damned slimy snail path ... everything about your relationship with Mom was a god damned lie ... everything from the divorce to the move back to Texas was a lie ... and Im glad you had to sell the house ... ... as Darlene would say ... you *fucker*

Walks to door Grabs doorknob Turns around
goodbye fucker
Lets go of door Walks to bed
Im not done yet you putrefied vulture bait ... the file underneath the house file was labeled letters and thats where I found the letter from Aunt Janice to her friend Trudy

Turns away
I would like to be a fly on the wall to see how you got that letter ... what was in Trudys mind to give it to you

Turns back Looks at ceiling
oh my god in heaven ... what you did to Aunt Janice ... you lousy stinking SON OF A BITCH ... what a heartless piece of steaming bat dung you are ... ... I cried as I read the letter that Darlene sent you when you banned her ... why did you keep those papers ... that doesnt make any sense to me at all ... is that how a pathetic dweeb bug gets his power trip ... by reliving and reveling in his abuse ... did you get your rocks off by reading your sisters description of how you statutorily raped her ... WHAT A GOD DAMNED SICKO PERVERT CREEP YOU ARE ... I cant stand to look at you another second.

Shakes head Walks to door
goodbye sicko pervert
　　Pauses Turns around
I nearly shit my pants ... or is that shat ... *mister* editor ... ... when I saw the letters I nearly shat my pants ... but that would come later
　　Walks to bedside
really ... your little sister ... what ... about seven or eight years younger than you ... just a little kid and you were teaching her to be a good wife ... to be a good sex partner for her future husband ... is that what you were doing ... no you sicko perverted piece of lice filled rat crap ... you were getting *your* rocks off ... and to think I didnt believe it when Karianne and Darlene said that you were playing perverted Walt Disney games with them
　　Turns away Walks to window
playing Peter Pan and Wen ... FUCKING SON OF A BITCH ... Darlene and Karianne didnt say a thing about Peter Pan and Wendy
　　Runs to bedside shouting in his face
THIS IS MY MEMORY ... it started to come back early this morning ... oh Jesus Christ on the cross you fucking bastard son of a bitch pervert
　　Slaps man on face Puts hands at side Steps back Clenches fists Door opens

"Hello, you must be Mrs. Charles. We're all so sorry about your father. I'm Nurse Thompson. Were you calling for a nurse?" Nurse Thompson walks into the room.

"Um ... no ... just thinking aloud is all." Jo is somewhat surprised at how relaxed and nonchalant her voice sounds.

"I just have to check a couple of things, and I'll be right out of your hair."

"No bother ... take your time." Jo walks behind the chair and stands with her hands on the chair back.

Nurse Thompson checks the instrument and writes in her chart. "I understand the rest of your family will be here tomorrow."

"Some will be here this evening, and the rest should be here tomorrow. Thank you."

"You're welcome. I really am sorry. And if you do need something, you can use the call button." Nurse Thompson leaves and closes the door.

Sits on chair

I wonder if I'm feeling sorry for myself too much. He's over there dead. Well, he deserves to be. He had all the chances in the world to come clean and try to make things right, but he just kept the lie up. He didn't care whom he hurt. He was planning to add Debbie's underwear to his perverted collection. Even up to the last day of his sick life he was putting his lies between me and my family. And he was burning his sick trophies just before he died? It's good he died. Otherwise we would never have known. I would never have known.

Walks to bed
you are one sorry asshole ... you know
Crying
all the time I wasted separating myself from Mom and Karianne and Darlene ... they dont like to be called by nicknames ... you always have nicknames for people ... is it because you want to put space between them and their real name ... the real person ... I can see why you would do that ... I have so many questions to ask you now that you are dead ... well as good as dead ... Im speaking to your spirit now ... did you EVER feel bad for what you did at ANY time ... I saw the laptop beside the box and turned it on and it was more than half charged ... I guess you looked at it often ... kept it charged ... there were several files of pictures ... mostly of the family and trips ... I lingered and cried over that trip to the world fair in San Antonia in sixty eight when I was just a baby ... I dont remember that trip ... I was too young ... do you remember the group picture with me in the stroller and Karianne standing a bit offish with that

look … you know the one … you called it the look of rebellion and Junior pretending to be the man of the family and Darlene … her slumped posture and sad looking eyes … only six years old and already burdened and Marlene leaning against Moms leg smiling and its all so revealing if you know what to look for … and thats my first trip to San Antonio … Im so innocent … so cute and my life is all ahead of me there … I tried to open the file labeled beauties but it was password protected … I noticed the string of letters numbers and characters wood-burned inside the lid of the box … for a smart man you are as stupid as the wood the box was made of … I put them in the computer and the file opened … … … what a … … a … Im speechless even now

Takes a deep breath

the first page was some scans of badly faded polaroid pictures … I couldnt recognize the girl … a little girl … naked and the header on the page was the letter A … dash … Jannie … dash … prime … Jannie was your nickname for Aunt Janice … I guess the letter A referred to the letter you put on the panties … the panties with the letter a on the front and prime written in the crotch … A … would that be the first girl you molested or just the first one whose panties you collected or whose picture you took … in the letter to Trudy aunt Janice wrote that you burned all her pictures … apparently you kept some you lying bastard … … I didn't want to see more … I couldnt help it … I clicked through the pages fast trying to focus on the faces … trying not to see more but unavoidably seeing too much in my peripheral vision.

… I noticed some things … the header pages were alphabetical and the first page for each girl was labeled the same way as Aunt Jannie … a letter followed by a name and a score … but the names looked like nicknames … there were a few other polaroids before the regular photos appeared and I guess that explains why you were so interested in photography at work … so you could take pictures and develop them at the newspaper dark room … what did you call them … quality photos of the family … quality photos … hell almighty ... quality photos ... you were so proud of your quality family photos ... well the beauties file certainly gave me a new perspective on quality photos ... I could tell when you finally got the tripod because thats when the pictures with you in them stopped being taken in a mirror ... from the panties on the table I expected Karianne's pictures to be labeled E ... the panties with the K sown on the back and the E written on the front ... I didnt want to see but I had to verify that my guess was right and on the screen in front of me was Karianne ... little Kari ... actually you labeled it peach fuzz ... her sad frightened face and her naked body ... I was frozen ... a petrified rock ... I expected it but it was a terrifying surprise to see her with that expression and know her perverted father had posed her and set her up and took the picture ... superficially knowing and actually being confronted with the irrevocable proof ... that was a chilling shock like being dropped on a block of ice and having it swallow you whole like water and you had eleven pages of her ... three to four pictures per page with subtitles ... I wanted to look away but I had to look ... I had to know ... subtitles of Snow White ... Pinocchio ... ... THUMPER ... you posed *that* picture

Sniffles

and ... ... good god I didnt even think that was physically possible with a girl so little ... oh ... you *are* going straight to hell ... I dont know how all the subtitles tie in but those pictures were soooo sick and Karianne looked so young so innocent and my eyes were burning ... and I could feel the tears on my cheeks and my nose was running ... like clear water ... I closed my eyes ... how could you demand that I shun her ... that I punish *her* ... how could I have let you ... thats the real question ... isnt it

Crying Gets napkin from beside table Blows nose

I didnt want to know this but I had to know it. Darlene was next ... F ... I gasped at how young she looked ... I started clicking through the pages as fast as the computer would go ... not wanting to see any of the pictures ... only the faces ... I stopped in the middle of the next group ... G ... I recognized Blossom ... Blossom ... I dont know if

that was her nickname or real name ... the little black girl from my school ... I clicked back to the front of the G pages ... G dash Blossom dash prime ... you perverted racist pig ... I started clicking to get to the letter I ... weird ... from the letters on the panties I knew I would be the I group ... and then there I was ... I swallowed bile as I looked through the pages ... Snow White ... Cinderella ... Peter Pan. ... that's when the fleecy memories began ... nothing I could get my mind around ... I could never imagine ... not in my wildest dreams could I have imagined that a grown man would do those things to a little girl ... then there I was ... doing Thumper ... my little face was pain ... I pulled open one of your drawers and vomited in it
   Speaking at almost a whisper
I went to the bathroom in the hall where my stuff is ... washed my mouth and brushed my teeth
   Speaking with normal voice
I walked to the fireplace to turn it on and I was going to burn your laptop but the light airy ashes showed that you had started to burn the evidence ... probably from the divorce file ... was it because you were afraid ... now that Debbie had busted you and Robyn believed her ... ... when I saw the quality photos of me I didnt suddenly get a clear memory of when you took the photos or even that they were ever taken ... only the glimpses ... the shadows of imperfect underdeveloped memories fluttered in my head and they are going to have to be recalled someday ... and it made me sick ... but it wasnt like the shock of seeing Karianne ... as I sat in front of the fireplace I was numb and I couldnt figure out why I was shaking so I left the fireplace ... I really didnt want to ... but I had to ... you know I had to find out ... no matter what ... I clicked forward and there was Lorianne and then Masla ... just a couple of nudes with Masla ... no games and no Josh ... she was saved ... sort of ... I pushed on and then there was Robyn.
   Collapses to floor by bedside Speaks into her hands
as Darlene would say FUCK YOU ALL THE WAY TO HELL YOU FUCKING MONSTER ... ... at that moment I totally

understood the language Darlene used … I made a sincere effort but I pissed my pants and shat on your floor … the whole mess running out of my underwear and down my legs as I ran for the bathroom and I sat on the hall floor outside your bathroom door in my mess and threw up again … in my lap this time and I was running from every orifice in my body except my ears

Cries on floor of hospital room … … Stands up

Somehow … I got into your bathroom … the one attached to your office and I tore the buttons from my blouse as I pulled it off and I dropped my skirt on the floor beside it and stepped into the shower … I filled my hands full of the body soap and began frantically scrubbing all over … then I stopped and stood under the warm water and felt the heavy blanket of years of self-imposed ignorance fall from my shoulders as I stood in my underwear in the light of the knowledge of the box … but it was more … it was a … a … knowingness of the depth of your evil and my part in it … and I pulled off my panties and dropped them in a corner of the shower and filled my hands with more soap … and I scrubbed my bottom with my hands as hard as I could and I filled my hands with more soap and scrubbed over and over until the soap was gone … and my bottom was sore … stinging … burning … like I had ruined it … like I hoped I would … … … … I stood crying in the falling water until the hot water turned warm and the black evilness of your house crept into me and I started to shake … I had to get out … I jumped out of the shower and wrapped a towel around me and grabbed my purse from the entry table and I fumbled for my keys … and somehow got in the car and I got it started and I drove home slumped in my seat … peering through the steering wheel … hiding in the shame of the coming of night as the sun started to set … I left my purse in the car and dropped the towel to the ground as soon as I got out of the car and ran to the door barefoot and I couldnt remember what happened to my shoes and socks … I fumbled with the keys again at the door and dropped them to the ground as soon as the door unlocked and I opened the door and took off my bra and flung it beside the walkway ... ... I went into my house with nothing that had been in your house ... nothing except me

Paces silently at foot of bed Walks to side of bed

my neck was tight from the shaking and the back of my scalp was pulled tight and aching ... I sat in my bath with the water as hot as I could stand and drained some when it started to cool and added more hot water ... I don't know how many times ... as I sat there a new knowingness came to me ... an epiphany of pain ... I had separated myself from my daughter and from my mother ... they didnt deserve it and I couldnt think of a way to make it up to Mom ... or to Robyn ... there was no way and I wanted to blame you but I knew that I played my part and I wanted so much to undo what I did and then it hit me ... my mother will welcome me ... she didnt put up the barrier ... I did ... I have to apologize to her and I know she will accept it ... but before I could do that I had to come here ... I had to say goodbye ... end it ... and I thought I would just stick my head in the door and say something like I know what you did and I hate you ... bye ... but now I find I have to purge what you did when you led me on that path away from her ... but at the same time I didnt want to have to see you at all but I knew I couldnt be whole without this goodbye ... but now it seems I have to do more to be whole ... I wish I knew that you could hear me ... you are like a mechanical man ... machines keep you alive ... empty ... heartless ... a cold empty robot ... ... remember when I used to watch Lost in Space reruns ... that robot would always shout ... danger Will Robinson danger ... remember ... it had more heart than you ... you should have shouted danger Will Robinson danger ... oh my god

Pulls hair

Im the one who should have shouted at the top of my lungs DANGER ROBYN DANGER ... Darlene woke from a memory repression and she warned everyone and even though Junior didnt believe her he kept his daughters from you ... Marlene didnt believe the stories but she moved away and tried to keep Masla safe ... not hard enough ...

Masla ended up in your porn box but only a couple of shots ... not like the others ... you are the essence of evil ... may you burn in hell

Walks to door Opens door

Goodbye

Steps through doorway Turns around Steps back in room Closes door

I guess Im still not done

Sits in chair Pauses

... ...when I got out of the bath it was very late ... past midnight so I dressed and drove to the shopping center down the street and threw your towel in the dumpster along with my bra and my purse and everything in it except my key and drivers license ... I had even cut up my credit cards and got rid of them ... I dont drink coffee but I needed something and I had seen that the Starbucks place at the Quarry was open till one am and I had some money in the car coin holder ... so I went there and they were just getting ready to close ... when I got home there was a message from junior on the line so I returned the call and he told me the hospital called him and said that they thought you might be brain dead ... the doctor confirmed that you *are* brain dead just before I came in here this morning ... I havent been back to your house but I suppose the battery is dead in the laptop and the water is still running in the shower ... with the mess I left by now the house must smell a fright but Im not going back in there again ... *ever* ... I will have Junior retrieve the box and laptop and make arrangements to get the house cleaned ... I wonder if we could get a permit from the fire department to burn the damn thing down

Walks to window Looks out

the world is a beautiful place ... you know ... maybe there is a god but why did he let you live ... shouldnt he have traded places between you and Jace ... what a better world that would have been

Slowly turns around

maybe its not right to blame you for everything. I sure had plenty of times ... plenty of chances to see the truth about you ... why was I so blind ... thats the unfathomable question as Karianne would say ...

but then maybe my incredible need to seek your approval at all costs was born in those Walt Disney perversions that hide somewhere in my mind ... for now ... but that still brings it back to you

Walking to bed

but it *isnt* all you. I *have to* bear some of the blame

At bedside

tomorrow they will all be here and I have to explain it all and I have to take my share of the blame ... but oh my god I *dont* know how I am going to do it ... not yet ... yes I have a lot of blame to bare for protecting you by refusing to face the truth even when my face was rubbed in it yesterday

Sits on chair

I have a fucked-up life ... you know ... I loved Gail and was anxious to get married ... but not putting a lot of thought or anticipation to the marriage bed because I just didnt have that kind of desire ... but I did like making out ... then the night and the marriage bed came and it was bad

Look at the monster laying there like nothing is happening. What did he ever care about his daughter's honeymoon? It's none of his damned business that my body didn't lubricate and that really made it hard and that there was no blood and I expected it ... and so did Gail. There was no blood when I was nearly raped and dad said that it was because the rapist didn't penetrate, but he didn't want me to see a doctor to verify it. So, on my wedding night I still thought that I was a virgin, and now I know that I wasn't, and he knew it too because he and Thumper took my virginity when I was just a kid. Gail had a problem because it seemed that I wasn't a virgin and the fact is, I wasn't a virgin for the same reason and by the same person as Aunt Janice wasn't, but I didn't know that, and my wedding night was spoiled by the same person who spoiled hers.

Sniffs

sex was always bad for me so it was good that Gail was away a lot of time traveling on his truck ... I grieved and it was real grief when he died ... but a part of me was relieved ... delivered in a way ... I let everyone believe that I would never marry again because of my feelings for Gail and I encouraged them to believe it ... the main thing was that I would rather live alone than participate in sex again and thats not normal

Turns from bed Throws up hands Lets them drop
well theres another lie on my part

Walks to window

I need to fess up to all my lies ... I see how you manipulated me to separate me from Mom but I also liked to have more power in the house which I had with her gone ... also I knew she would go after the guy who tried to rape me and I didnt want to participate in the legal mess and maybe even a trial that it would could cause ... not that I asked to be raped in any way but I did things that sort of set me up for it ... like I should not have gone to that guys house ... I knew he was not a good sort but I didnt think it would lead to anything more than making out ... but all you cared about was that I had tried to go out with a guy before I was sixteen so you were actually doing exactly what you said Mom would do ... blame me ... and thats not the only lie ... for sure I knew Mom wasnt having an affair and I didnt really buy into the partying crap that you put out either ... but I have kept those lies alive aaallll these years ... I got so tied up in the lies that I couldn't tell what was true so I let you manipulate me with your phony prayers ... I wasnt stupid either ... we all knew how you treated Mom ... no better than a slave you never gave her any respect nor did you allow her any serious part in family decisions and you said it was all per church doctrine ... you didnt think we knew about how husbands *should* treat their wives and that you were *completely* violating the doctrine ... youre the stupid one ... none of us girls would *ever* marry a man like you ... I told everyone that Mary was a great mother but I didnt really like her all that much and there were a lot of times I really wished I could talk to my real mom ... that was hard but it was mostly my fault

Walks to bedside
heres a truth for you ... I always suspected that you married Mary so you could have more children because Mom couldnt and we all knew too well that you wanted more boys ... well I guess Mary gave you quite a surprise with Ronald and I will tell you another thing ... you always made it look like you were making the sacrifices for Ronald ... refusing to have him committed while Mary was the one taking all the care of him while you went to work ... and when you got home at night you were always too tired to lend Mary a hand with Ronald ... yeah you were too tired but you never considered that Mary got tired working with him all day long and that she could use some help when you got home ... then you retired from work but Mary still did all the work for Ronald ... and dont think for a minute we didnt all recognize what was happening ... and you all the time insisting the family take care of him so he wouldnt be alone in an institution but as soon as Marys health began to fail ... it didnt take very long at all for you to have him committed ... I knew all that ... but I buried it ... ignored it ... made it go away ... why

Sits on chair

Sometimes I feel like I don't even know myself. I need some therapy. I need to take a long deep look at what really happened to me. There are so many questions coming up about myself that I simply cannot understand, and he isn't my whole problem.

well I want to blame you for everything
    Stands up Walks toward bed
I really think that you are the root of all my problems
    Stands by bed
but there is more to a plant than the roots.

He looks weak and pitiful laying all gray on the bed with tubes sticking out of his body. Tomorrow, we sign the papers to pull the plugs like a radio or a TV and the lights go out and the questions that I want answered go unanswered, but the most important questions are not about him. They are about me. My life must be my life not his, so now I have to figure out my own answers, answers about me, answers for me. I don't know how to do it. Maybe Darlene can help.

thanks to what you did ... and what I did ... I have a big bridge to cross to get back to Robyn ... in mythology the phoenix rises from its ashes to new life but sometimes it means regeneration and thats what I need ... all I need is a complete regeneration ... a way back to Robyn and Karianne and Darlene and Mom and I will do it too ... I look down the road years from now when no one thinks about you anymore or about the things that you did and life will be about other things ... I long for those days ... rules of reverence days ... there were so many good times with you but all of them together are not worth remembering the smallest of the bad so if I finally erase you from my mind it will be a good day ... a day without chaos and soul death ... a day when the cry for revenge has died ... all of my siblings will be here tomorrow when they turn off the switches and unplug you ... and just so you know ... Ive asked Mom to come ... not to watch you kick the final bucket but to talk with me and Im not coming back with the rest tomorrow because ... I have to start my new life and Im spending that time with Mom ... when they pull the plugs on you I will be with her ... starting to mend my bridges with her and as far as Im concerned you are on your own now ... but it would have been good if you could have confessed and asked for forgiveness from those that you hurt ... but its not like you didnt have all the opportunity ... you lived your life in the choking slime of your evil and now you slink out in the same slime having missed your opportunity to recover ... and no ... Im not sorry that I wont be here with the rest when they disconnect you ... disconnect you from life ... its a sad thing ... I guess

Walks to window Looks out

you know what I think ... I am going to leave San Antonio because there are too many reminders ... like the days we spent at

Brackenridge park bird watching ... picnicking on the grass around the pond ... the Alamo ... the zoo ... the Spurs games and I could go on and on but all together it doesnt add up to a hill of beans when those memories bring up the horrible truth of my whole life to date ... so I have to start a new life and create a new me ... a regenerated me ... someplace else

Walks to door Turns around

I wasted most of my life ... its time to build a new one ... does that mean I forgive you ... I cant do that ... you wasted your opportunity so you cant look for forgiveness from me to release you from the evil that you are

Puts both hands on sides of her forehead Presses fingers into scalp Pushes them over top to back of head Looks at him

Look at his face. Why is it so peaceful? He should be feeling my pain, all the pain that he caused me, all the pain that he caused everyone in his box. And it's not just the people in his box that he hurt, either.

Focuses on his face. Sighs
I will not forgive you and release you from your responsibility because you must work that out for yourself now... and god only knows how you will since you blew it in this life

Walks to window. Looks out. Walks back to door looking at him
when I think of the future ... a future where you are no longer in my mind ... I try to see it ... I want to see it ... why wont you let me see it

Throws head back Looks at ceiling

It's not him. I am holding the key. I can never find that future while I hold onto the things that he did.

Shakes head Swallows
I forgive you ... unconditionally

Wipes tears from her eyes with knuckles
its over ... ... good afternoon Mister Godwin ... bye

Opens door Walks out Closes door

* * *

Jo walked out of the hospital and sat in her car. She had said what she wanted to say and more. She had forgiven him, but somehow there was no release in any of that. The pain was still like a sharp knife cutting her heart on a muggy afternoon. Now what? She thought again about last night when she got back from dumping the towel and picking up some coffee. She had sipped the coffee on the way home. It tasted far worse than it smelled. She wasn't a coffee drinker, but she had heard it would perk her up and give her some energy. She was physically exhausted and mentally drained after her ordeal at Josh's house. It was past midnight when she listened to Junior's message on the phone and called him back. He told her the hospital called him because Junior was listed as Josh's Surrogate Decision-maker. The tests on Joshua did not show any brain activity. They were doing other tests to see if he was in irreversible coma and verify the proximate cause. Jo didn't understand what Junior was saying and neither did he. The best he could tell her was they were checking to see if he was suffering brain death. If they couldn't find any responses to the testing by morning, they would do something called an apnea test. If that was negative, they had a doctor at the hospital who was qualified to certify brain death. That would mean he was officially dead, and they would take him off life support.

Junior had agreed to call everyone in the family, but Jo wanted to be the one to call Robyn. She believed Dianne was spending a couple of days with Robyn before her flight back to Paris.

Junior had booked a flight that would arrive in San Antonio that afternoon around 5:30 p.m. Jo had agreed to pick him up. She told him she needed to talk to him in person when he arrived. Junior had to get some paperwork for the hospital at Joshua's house in case the outcome was negative and suggested they talk when they got there. Jo told him they could do their talking on the way there. She would drop him off, but she wouldn't go in with him. She suggested he drive the old Impala while he was in town. It was Joshua's pride and joy. He'd kept it in like new condition since he first married Dianne.

After Junior hung up, Jo had thought about Joshua and the paths his life had taken between the good and evil of his life. Surely there was some good. Once when they lived in Salt Lake, Josh had taken the whole family to dinner at the small café on Main Street where Joshua and Dianne had their first breakfast as man and wife. She tried to imagine their mutual joy and excitement as they began their life together when everything was new and love was ripe, before the strife and disappointments began to worm their way into the marriage. The old Impala had been new on that day. It was a family legend that the first song played on its radio after Joshua got the keys was the number one song that week. "At the Hop." The whole family had learned the lyrics and sang it in the Impala as they drove to the café to celebrate her parents' anniversary. Jo couldn't remember the name of the café—something with a K. A couple of years ago on vacation, she had gone back to see it, but it was gone like the life she thought she had lived was gone now.

Jo had sipped more of her coffee, trying to deal with the fact that her father may already be dead. There were so many things going through her mind, so many things she wanted him to explain. She had picked up the phone and dialed Robyn's number.

"Hello Mom, it's kind of late," Robyn had answered, following the caller ID.

"I know dear. Did I wake you up?"

"Not really. Grandma and I were just talking."

"You know we were concerned that Joshua would have another stroke that could be serious." Without thinking, Jo used Joshua's name instead of calling him Grandpa.

"Joshua?"

"I'll explain, but not tonight. He had another stroke, and he's in the hospital. They are testing him to see if he's brain dead, and so far the tests aren't going good for him. Could I talk to my mom?"

"Sure, just a minute." Jo could hear the surprise in Robyn's voice. "Hello?"

Jo easily recognized her voice. She had something planned to say, but her mind went blank. It took her a couple of seconds to gather herself. "Mom … I guess I don't know how to start, mostly we have to talk in person, but I just wanted to tell you how sorry I am for … for everything all these years. Joshua had a relapse … he might be dead, but they won't know until tomorrow. I found out some things today … I guess it was actually yesterday after you and Robyn left … I know I was wrong … I suppose I could blame Joshua, but in a way that wouldn't be fair because he's probably already dead, and I guess a lot of it's my own fault, and I'm just babbling away here because I don't know what to say. I really am a mess, and I just know that tomorrow is going to be worse, and I have some things that I just have to deal with. I have to clear things with Joshua, and I don't even know how, and I'm not trying to put you off, but I really want to talk with you once I find a way to deal with him and I pull myself together, so I was wondering if you are … can you stay around a few days or do you have to fly back to Paris?"

"Joanne, I'll be right here when you're ready. Don't worry about that. You just let me know, and I'll be there. Okay?"

"Thanks Mom, I'll get back to you. I have another call to make."

"Okay then, I'll let you go. I love you. Bye now."

Jo sat on the chair crying. Feelings she had buried for years began to surface.

* * *

When Jo had finally got to the hospital in the morning, the doctor informed her Joshua's tests were negative and he would be officially pronounced brain dead. Junior would meet with hospital personnel later in the evening to make the final arrangements. Jo asked the doctor if she could say goodbye to Joshua. He told her to take all the time she needed. She went to his room not knowing how to start or what to say—just "I know what you did, bye"? Knowing he was dead made it seem almost redundant, but she knew she had to say something if only to the air in the room where his body was still breathing.

Jo had been surprised at the emotions that poured out while she was with Joshua. She was lightheaded and the room seemed to be spinning as she stood looking at him from the door for the final time. As soon as she walked out the door, she felt some relief, but it was short-lived.

After sitting awhile in the parking lot at the hospital, Jo drove to the airport. She had called Darlene after talking to her mother. She told her she wanted to talk with her as soon as possible. Darlene was able to book a flight on the internet after Junior's call. They made arrangements for Robyn up to pick Darlene at the airport to talk and give her the results of this morning's tests. Jo arrived at the airport forty-five minutes early, which gave her some time to sip the second cup of coffee she had in her life and think about the events of last night and this morning.

* * *

Even after all the years, Jo recognized Darlene right away. The broad smile on Darlene's face told Jo that Darlene recognized her. They hugged and cried and laughed.

"You said there was something you wanted to talk about. Is now a good time?" Darlene asked.

"I've got something very important to talk to you about. We have about four hours before I have to pick up Junior. How about going downtown and walking on the River Walk?"

"Sounds great," Darlene said.

As they drove downtown, it seemed Darlene was pretty much up to date on Jo's life, so they talked about Darlene and her family. Jo discovered Colin was a dentist in Irvin, and Chas was a forest ranger in Washington State. They were both married, and Darlene had five grandchildren.

As they walked along the river, Jo told Darlene about Joshua's test results and what they meant.

"It's not much of a surprise now," Darlene said. "I'm sorry he died without ever making things right, but, for me, in a lot of ways, he has been dead a long time. I'm really sorry for you though."

"Don't be … not on account of the fact that he's dead. There is a lot more going on now, and I'm dealing with way more than his death. Here, let's sit down." Jo led Darlene to a park bench in a small space along the river. "I've been doing a lot of soul searching in the last few hours," Jo began. "Robyn is convinced that you honestly believe that Josh molested you. I'm so sorry that I have made things hard for you all these years. I don't know if you can ever forgive me, but I am sooo sorry."

"I forgave you long ago." Darlene turned on the bench and gave Jo a hug and kissed her on the cheek. "We have been a terribly dysfunctional family, Jo. It's not your fault. But I don't think it's too late to put all the pieces back together. We're not Humpty Dumpty."

"What do you think about Mom and Karianne? How can I make things up to them?"

"Of course, you know we have done practically nothing except talk about you ever since your call came. This is a very sad circumstance, but we're hoping this can help bring us together … that perhaps a door might open from this sadness."

"I talked to Mom for a few minutes last night, but I just didn't know what to say to her. I have been really unfair to her, and because of that she missed Robyn growing up. My stupidity robbed both Mom and Robyn of a relationship. Looking at everything from a new perspective, it was inexcusable. Junior, Marli, and Lori handled it so much better than I. I just can't believe how narrow-minded I was."

Darlene put her hand on Robyn's thigh. "I talked to Mom last night after your call. You didn't say much, but Mom is reading a lot into it. She is anxious to get with you and start a new relationship …

if you're willing. And don't worry a minute about Karianne. What is past is past with all of us. All we want is to start over."

"I have something else to discuss with you …something no one else knows. I need your professional assistance with it."

"What is that?" Darlene turned toward Jo and removed her hand.

Jo explained everything about the box and what was in it.

"I remember how hard it was for me when I discovered the truth," Darlene said, "but it was a process that went on several weeks with the help of an excellent therapist. I can't imagine what you are going through with this crap from Josh, along with the upset with Robyn and now Josh being brain dead. Let me strongly suggest you get some professional help."

"That's kind of why I wanted to talk to you. I was thinking you that could help me find a really good therapist. I mean, from the pictures, I know that something happened, but I don't remember them or when they were taken. I have had the beginning of something pretty awful with Peter Pan and Wendy. It's really scary, and I don't know how I'm going to face it, so I pushed really hard to force it back. But I know that I can't get through this by pushing it back, but at the same time, it's really hard to look at it."

"I know exactly what you're talking about from a professional standpoint and also from personal experience. I'll make a call today and get my people looking for the best therapist in San Antonio. By the way, Peter Pan and Wendy … that's a new one."

"I plan to leave San Antonio as soon as I get my personal situations in order. There's really no need for me to stay and a number of reasons to leave."

"How long do you think it will take you?"

"I'm going to sell my house, and I have some other connections that need to be worked out. I'm thinking about two or three months."

"Where are you planning to move?"

"That's one of the things I have to work out."

"Well, I usually don't much like to have a patient change therapist in mid-stream, but in this case, I suggest you start therapy as soon as it can be arranged. I'm guessing there will be some extremely stressful things happening in the next few days and weeks."

"Yeah, and this is sort of one of them. I understand that all of you have been keeping pretty good track of me, but I hardly know anything at all about you. I have some time before I need to pick up Junior. I would really like it if you would go to lunch with me so we can talk about what has been going on with all of you. I think it would be good for me to spend some time just talking about normal life. There are some really nice restaurants on the River Walk."

"I would really like that, Jo."

* * *

Junior stood up from his chair behind the table. "I'm happy to see all of you together. This is the first time we have all been together for many years. It's unfortunate that it took something like this to bring it about. Mom is also in town. She's with Robyn right now, which is another miracle of sorts. I'm sure you are all wondering why I chose to have the meeting in a hotel meeting room rather than at Dad's house. Jo requested we have it here, and I agree with her. I got all the necessary files and information here. There were some messes in Dad's house so it's being professionally cleaned. Jo has asked to speak to you." Junior sat down.

Jo stood in front of the table. "Thank you Junior. ... ... I'm sorry ... seeing you all here together ... well I just don't know how to start. Um ... okay ... I was at Joshua's house when he had the seizure. He was in his office going over some things. I didn't pay much attention to the stuff he was working on until I came back to the house after I left him at the hospital. There was a box on his desk ... this box." She pointed to the box on a table behind her. She picked up a paper on the table beside the box. "This letter was taped to the top. I'll read it."

Dear Joshua Jr.

    This box contains some private papers about my family, which are important to me but of no interest to anyone else. I do not give you the combination to the lock, because the information inside would cause unnecessary pain to some people without creating a compensatory good. My instructions to you are to put this box in the gas-fired fireplace in the backyard, put several logs on it, douse it with gasoline, ignite it, and turn the natural gas on. Allow it to burn until only ashes are left. I have given you instructions regarding my wishes in all that relates to the disposal and distribution of my property to my progeny, and you know where the will is. I trust you, as my eldest male heir, to comply in everything, especially this request.

"It is signed Joshua Godwin Senior. The combination lock was open on the desk beside the box. Perhaps I shouldn't have, but I looked in the box. It contains evidence that supports the stories that Karianne and Darlene told the family many years ago. I realize that I have been Joshua's staunchest defender against those stories. Rather than try to answer a bunch of random questions at this time, I will present what I learned and answer questions later. To start with, I am going to read a couple of letters. One from Aunt Janice's nurse and one from Aunt Janice. Both the letters were to Aunt Janice's friend, Trudy. Aunt Janice knew that she was dying when these letters were written."

When Jo finished reading, Lori broke in. "This is a very private letter. I don't see why you felt you needed to read it to us. Clearly it was about private things that happened between Dad and his sister, things that Aunt Janice already realized were just childhood experimentation. On top of that, she had checked with Kari to make sure Dad was not continuing his behavior as a grown man, which supports the claims he has made all along."

"If this letter were the only thing, I would never have brought it up. I remind you that I always supported Joshua … at a great sacrifice to my own daughter. This letter shows that Aunt Janice had doubts about Joshua and for good reason, based upon what he did with her. True, she didn't find any evidence that he repeated those actions with other little girls. Unfortunately, there is more. Darlene wrote her own letter to Joshua, which was in the box. Darlene has agreed to let me read it to you."

Joshua Godwin: July 20, 1984

Many years ago, a girl came to this earth. She was so beautiful and had so much promise. Her parents were proud of her and showed her off to anyone who would take the time to look at her. They both loved her and were willing to sacrifice their quiet, comfort, money, time, sleep, and anything else they had to make her happy and ensure she would have a useful, fulfilled, and successful life.

Very early in her life, something happened - something secret. Her father used her to meet a need of his own. She was young - it wouldn't hurt her - it would be done and forgotten. But then it was done again and again and again!

Something basic - something essential - something precious was broken at a very deep level. A shadow was thrown over the little girl. Still pretty - still intelligent - still precious, but now a seeded, subconscious, emotional crack was created. A power lost. A trust violated. A pattern of problems related to relationships, sexuality, and basic happiness was implanted. The potential for joy and satisfaction was reduced.

Had the father known the ramifications of his thoughtless acts; would he have done what he did? He sacrificed to give her a home, food, clothes, an education - all the things to contribute to a happy home and contented life. What do those things matter if, in the moments of his personal gratification he has pulled from her the emotional strengths most needed to form a core of happiness? What do those things matter if he has created deep, painful, festering, emotional wounds that deny her full happiness and produce instead failure where success should be?

Look now at the angry, rage-filled woman who finally denounces what you did. Do you see in her rage the glory of her spirit fighting for her happiness, for her sanity, for her wholeness, for her power? Will you now deny her those things just to protect your pride? Will you enlist others of her family to fight against her in order to keep your dark secret? If you do that - if you fail to stand by her now, knowing what you know, you are the most selfish of all men - no matter your other sacrifices.

Look again at this woman - see again the trusting beautiful baby girl that came to you totally innocent with such great promise so many years ago. Be a man - stand with her - give her back some of what you took. If you turn from her now, you invalidate everything else.

Darlene

"I took sides with Joshua to persecute this woman, and I am sooo sorry for that." Tears were streaming down Jo's face.

"So, are you saying you believe Dar and Kari now? The stories Dar wrote about are not new. How can you know this wasn't just a phony letter to make Dad look guilty?" Lori turned to Darlene. "Sorry Dar. I don't know what to think, but these questions have to be asked."

Darlene nodded.

"It's all right, Lori," Jo said, "in fact the day before yesterday I would have been the first to suggest that, even though it makes absolutely no sense at all."

"What do you mean?" Marli asked.

"If Darlene had made copies to pass around to everyone, or in some other way made this letter known to others ... okay. But this letter was a *private* letter to Joshua. You have never heard of this before, and no one else has. No, this letter was directed privately and directly to Joshua. She didn't go to this much trouble to try to convince Joshua that he did it. She made one last desperate attempt to find something in his conscience ... in his soul ... some self-redeeming spark of empathy. Sadly, it was not to be found.

"Darlene's letter is not all. This laptop was also in the box. It contains a file with scanned and digital photos that clearly show that the accusations Karianne and Darlene made against Joshua were true. The clear and detailed pictures showing the games that he played with each game labeled. There are pictures of me showing that I suffered the same games. Even now I don't remember them being taken or any of the things that happened in them, but some flashes of memory have begun to come up. Darlene is helping me find a therapist to get through it. The laptop was left on for nearly twenty-four hours, and the battery is discharged. I asked Junior to bring the laptop to me without charging it. No one has seen the photos except me. I don't think it would be appropriate for anyone to see the photos except the ones that they are in. There are no photos of Marli ... every other woman in this room is in the file."

"Wait a minute," Lori interjected, "you're saying there are explicit pictures of me?"

"I am so sorry Lori."

"What exactly do they show?"

"They are nude photos of you at a very young age. Several of them show you doing things with Joshua ... really depraved things."

"I don't believe it."

"If you want, I will plug the laptop in and let you see *your* photos when we are through here. I am really sorry to say that there are also photos of Robyn ... ... and." Jo started to cry. Junior stood beside Jo and put his arm around her. "And Masla."

"What!" Marli exclaimed. "He never was allowed to be near her alone."

"There are only a couple of nude pictures ... none of the real sick ones with Joshua in them. I think you were successful in preventing the real bad stuff. Now that the facts are out, you might want to ask her why she hasn't been to San Antonio in many years ... why she has *never* brought her daughters here."

"What kind of a messed up family is this!" Lori demanded more than asked.

"Joshua was the only really messed up one," Karianne said.

"There were a lot of other girls that he abused," Jo said, "but no other ones in the family ... except for Aunt Janice, of course. I don't recognize any of the other girls except a girl who was in my school. It appears he called them all by nicknames. All together there were twenty-three kids, all girls. As old and decrepit as he was, he was starting to prepare Debbie, Robyn's little girl, for when she got a little older. Against all the roadblocks I threw in her way, Robyn was able see him for what he was, but even then, I needed the photos to prove the truth to me. I am sorry, Marli ... sorry that I was protecting him at the time he was making his attempts on Masla.

"That's all I have to say for now. Junior has some information from the doctors." Jo stepped back and Junior came to the table.

"I'm as shocked as most of you," Junior said. "I just never would have thought this could be possible in my own family. I just ... I just want to go home now and forget all this crap ... but I can't.

"I've talked to the doctors, and Dad has been declared brain dead. He signed up to be an organ donor years ago. He told me not to mention it until after his death. In the case of an organ donor they have to leave him on life support until they can do an operation to remove them. That is scheduled for 3:00 p.m. today. Anyone in the family who wants to can be there when he goes to the operation room. Jo has chosen not to be there. I will be there, though I am going out of duty rather than anything else. If any of the rest of you choose not to be there, I will understand."

The meeting ended on a somber note.

* * *

Junior returned to his room at the motel after the meeting. Jo had prepared him somewhat for the information she planned to reveal, but he was taken aback by the breadth of Joshua's perversion. Junior was called Junior only within his family. He was called Joshua in all other areas of his life. Right now, he couldn't stand the sound of Joshua.

Joshua had purchased his burial plot and casket and paid for the funeral services several years ago. Junior had already called the cemetery and started the arrangements to have the body picked up and made preparations for the funeral and burial. He called his wife to let her know the things he had found out. It was difficult for him to finally admit that all the things of which his father had been accused were true. She had been supportive over the phone.

Junior walked into Joshua's room at St. Luke's at a quarter to three. The walls were painted a light teal. To his right there was a small bathroom near the door. Past the bathroom, the bed stuck out from the wall, also to his right. Joshua was connected to numerous tubes and wires coming from plugs in the wall behind the bed. There were two monitors on a table on the left side of the bed. Straight ahead was a window with a view a little north of straight east. It looked out over parking lots near the hospital, with trees lining the back. To his right was a hand-washing station with a medical waste receptacle on the side. When he had come in last night there was just one chair. Now there were two on the right side of the bed. Karianne and Darlene were sitting in them, facing each other.

"I didn't think anyone one would be here after the meeting this morning ... especially you two," Junior said.

Both of the women stood up. "Why would you be surprised to see us?" Darlene asked.

"Well, I guess it's because you have suffered the most and the longest from what he did."

"Maybe that's why we're here," Karianne said.

"I don't understand." They each gave Junior a hug.

Darlene said, "We've had a lot of time to process everything ... the good and the bad."

"The good? How is there any good in the fact that at least twenty-three little girls' lives were destroyed by a sick pervert?"

A nurse knocked on the door, opened it, and came in. "Oh, Mr. Godwin, I'm glad you're here. I just came to let you all know the final tests have been done, and they confirm the original diagnosis. The final preparations are being made to ... uh ... you know."

"Thank you," Junior answered.

Darlene moved her chair beside Karianne's and turned it so they both faced Junior. The two women sat down. "Should I bring in another chair?" the nurse asked.

"No. I really don't think I can sit right now," Junior said.

"Well, if you change your mind, the call button is connected." The nurse walked out, and the door closed behind her.

"Final tests?" Karianne said.

"Because he's an organ donor, they have to do several extra batteries of tests to make doubly sure he's dead before they remove the organs."

"That conveys a cold reality," Karianne said.

"So why are you two here, after all he did to you?"

"Well, we haven't seen him for … like about eighteen years," Karianne said.

"That," Junior pointed at the bed, "doesn't even look like him, which is appropriate given who and what he is. I find myself ashamed of carrying his name, and I only came because I might be needed to sign something or make some kind of decision. In fact, I think I'm a little old to be called Junior. From now on, I want to be known by my middle name, Jace."

"I get it," Darlene said. "Karianne and I found his nicknames for us offensive, so we don't use them. I kind of like Jace."

"Me too," Karianne said. "From now on, you're Jace."

"Thanks. It kind of seems weird to be called Jace, but I like it."

"Your reaction is perfectly normal," Darlene said. "Of course, you have had years to suspect something and come to terms with the suspicion, but now, to suddenly have the reality of it shoved upon you … yeah, that's a tough one. You, Marli, Jo, Lori, and many of the grandkids are getting a gut-shot right now. It will take time."

"Time to adjust to the fact that my father is an evil monster? Is there enough time for that?"

"You know what we have been doing here?" Darlene asked.

"No. I don't have a clue. I really don't even know what I'm doing in this room … not really."

"We have been discussing the good times we experienced with Dad when we were growing up," Karianne said.

"What possible good times could answer for the evil?"

"None," Darlene said. "But they were there all the same, and the picture is not complete without them."

"What good times? My mind is drawing a blank," Jace said.

Karianne stood up in front of him. "You remember how he always had summers laid out? It wasn't like an actual schedule, but every year he would make sure to take the family to Hogle Zoo and Lagoon."

Darlene stood beside Karianne. "And he took us to swim in Great Salt Lake … well, float. I guess it was too salty to swim."

"And what about the days at Liberty Park wherein we would experience a big picnic on the grassy area under the flagpole?" Karianne said.

"Yeah, and he would let us ride on the Ferris wheel or the merry-go-round and buy us soft ice cream cones at the concession stand," Darlene said.

"Oh! And you must remember he would always take us to see the Salt Lake Bees baseball team at Derks Field … until they moved away. And he always bought us messy hot dogs. Sunny days at the old ballpark," Karianne said.

"And the drive-in movies," Darlene added.

Jace walked to the window and looked out. "There are no more drive-ins. The Bees moved away when I was about five. My memories of them are pretty sketchy. Hogle Zoo has been completely rebuilt … I don't think there's a single display left from when we were kids. The only thing left of the old Lagoon is the rollercoaster. Everything else is new … they even got rid of the 'million-gallon' swimming pool. When we were kids, Sixth East ran through the middle of Liberty Park, now there's no sign the street ever existed. Even Derks Field was demolished, and Smith's Field was built to replace it. Nothing is like it was."

Karianne stood beside him and put her arm around his waist. "Nothing endures forever in the real world. But it's all here in my virtual world … in my mind."

Darlene stood on Jace's other side. Karianne continued. "My first memory of this life is the summer Dad took us to the Seattle

World's Fair. I was almost four and you were two. Darlene was three months, and she remained in Salt Lake with friends. The only thing I remember of that trip is eating in the restaurant at the top of the Space Needle. I experienced it as a slow merry-go-round in the sky. Every summer he took us on a major trip. We went to the '65 New York World's Fair. You must remember that one; you were five and Mom was pregnant with Marli."

"I do remember a long trip, and everyone making a big fuss about a tall building."

"What about the San Antonio HemisFair … you were eight or nine by then?"

"I remember that, and Bryce Canyon, and Yellowstone, and Disneyland, and yes there was always a vacation. But it's all spoiled when I think of the damage he did. He gave, but he took so much more than what he gave. He was an evil man … bottom line."

"He participated in evil," Karianne said. "He distributed it freely, I'll agree. But does that make him evil?"

"Evil is as evil does," Jace said.

"Yes," Darlene agreed. "In a real sense he was evil. In another sense he was good. In my life, the evil outweighed the good by a wide margin. I'm sure it's the same way with Karianne. We have worked years and years to overcome most of the effects of the evil … not everything. I suspect there will be residuals for the rest of our lives. But Dad is complicated. He is a troubled and wounded soul. He had this lifetime to work some of it out, but he wasted it … he sank deeper into a hole."

"Being the only son until I was fourteen, I have a lot of memories. It *was* special to share priesthood and scouting activities with him. When the accusations came out, I couldn't believe them, partly because of the special memories I had of him. I don't know why, but those memories were always a kind of lifeline for me. Now I just feel empty … they were lies."

"In my business, I have worked a lot with families like ours," Darlene said. "One thing I have discovered is that it's not just the children who are violated who suffer. It's common that some children are skipped because of their sex, or maybe there is just something going on in the perpetrator's life that causes him to skip some of the siblings. But those who are skipped, even when they don't actually know what's going on, end up with issues they have to deal with. I don't know what it is, but I'm guessing there is always a subliminal dynamic going on in an environment where sexual abuse is occurring, and that rubs off subconsciously on everyone."

"For many years, I lived in a way whereby I reacted in universal rebellion because of what he did," Karianne said. "But now I realize what he did cannot define me. I do not owe him devotion, nor do I owe him revulsion. I deal with the evil and celebrate the good. I make no conclusion as to whether Dad was good or evil. I look at him as a vehicle whereby I was able to come to knowledge about myself and use that to grow. I think for me, this trip has allowed me to look at and cherish the good for the first time in my life. I realized that just this afternoon talking with Darlene."

"Well, I guess I'm black and white on this. I don't see that the good means anything or that the bad serves any good purpose," Jace said.

The nurse and the doctor came in. "I'm sorry," the doctor said. "It's time."

"We're ready," Jace said.

The three siblings watched as Joshua's body was disconnected from the support systems and reconnected to similar portable systems. Tears flowed down Darlene and Karianne's faces.

"Oh my God," Darlene cried. "I never expected to feel this. If only he had somehow … you know … just made an effort."

"I know," Karianne said.

Jace stood between them and put his arms around them. They took one last look at Joshua, and then he was wheeled out.

"You can wait in the waiting room," the doctor said.

Karianne stepped back from Jace. "I think Darlene and I are done here but if you want, we'll wait with you until it's all over."

"No. You guys have given me some things to think about. I'm going to wait around until everything is done and all the i's are dotted. We'll get together later to figure out where to go from here."

"Take care, Jace." Karianne hugged him and kissed him on the lips.

"It'll take some time, but things will work out. You know I'm here for you." Darlene hugged him.

Well, buddy, you've got a lot to figure out, but you're not in this boat alone, Jace thought as he watched his sisters walk out the door.

* * *

Joshua was buried. The winter came and passed. Jo refused her share of the inheritance from Joshua's estate. All the other siblings joined her in that decision. They agreed to donate the whole amount to a charity for battered children in his name.

Jo also refused the money Dianne had accumulated for her. She explained to Robyn, "I want my mother back in my life more than anything in the world. The chasm I created is wide … wider than you can imagine. I know that Mom is fully open to me, but it will take me some time to flush the chaos of emotions I'm feeling, because I've created so many reasons to hate her and so many barriers. I know they are baseless, but I have to deal with them. I don't want anyone, especially me, to ever think that I am doing it because of the money."

Jo agreed to work with Junior to sell Joshua's house if she didn't have to go near the house itself. She also put her house on the market. Though she wasn't sure where she would go, she knew she could not live in San Antonio.

Robyn was also eager to leave San Antonio. She wanted to be closer to the family in California, especially Aunt Darlene and her grandmother. George began to actively seek employment in Southern California in March 2013. He found a job there in April with a start date the first week in July.

Shortly after the funeral, Robyn and Jo started meeting separately with Dr. Moffett, the therapist Aunt Darlene had recommended. Jo was making little progress when Darlene came for a visit. Jo talked to her in detail about her experience forgiving Joshua in the hospital. "It seems that should be enough. I am a survivor, but the pain won't leave."

Darlene explained many women in her circumstance proudly proclaim they are survivors. "But a survivor is a person who defines themselves as a victim … a survivor for sure, but the survival is based upon the victimization."

"I'm not sure what you mean," Jo said.

"You are an incest survivor. Some women are rape survivors, and so on. But in every case, the adjective they use to define themselves is incest or rape or whatever. And that works for some, but in my experience, the best and most stable recovery comes from letting it all go. When it ceases to define you in any aspect; that will be your major victory. Don't see yourself as an *incest* survivor. You are a competent woman; you have been a policewoman who saved a life; you raised a little girl to be a bright, intelligent, and powerful woman. That's how you're defined. And you will expand that definition. You let Joshua go. Now, you must let go of what he did."

As Jo began to focus on that aspect, her progress improved. She had been keeping Joshua's files as a reminder of the evil he had done. She made copies of the files that were on the laptop and papers in the box for those who wanted copies and then had the hard drive physically destroyed and burned all the papers.

Dianne and Kent arranged to have Ronald moved to California to live with them. They sent Derek Bateman, one their best facilitators, to make all the arrangements. Dianne had him stay on to help settle Joshua's affairs. Jo had started therapy and was making significant strides. As Jo and Derek worked on Joshua's estate, they began a personal relationship. A part of Jo that had been suppressed most of her life started to break free. She was lighthearted and happier than she ever remembered.

Robyn requested the files of her pictures with the private parts pixelated. Her face was sometimes sad and sometimes frightened. Joshua's face was exuberant. The pictures did not create any kind of flashbacks and since she felt her life was full and happy, she felt no need to recover the memories as part of her therapy. She also burned all her papers. She concluded her life was impacted in ways that were much different than her mother or her aunts.

* * *

One morning in early May, Robyn had a talk with George. "Are you feeling I'm pressuring you to leave San Antonio?" Robyn asked George.

"Actually, I'm kind of anxious to move on to a new life."

"Good, because all this mess in my family … well, I mean, I don't want to think this is causing you to have to move away from your family."

"You know the scriptures say a man should leave his father and mother to join with his wife and start his own family."

"Well, I kind of wanted to talk to you about scriptures and religion. I think, and I've talked about this to Dr. Moffett, and she kind of agrees … what I mean is, I think my doubts about the temple could have … probably came from an unconscious feeling of unworthiness that stems from my relationship with Joshua."

"Do you feel unworthy?"

"I think I did, but I never actually put my finger on it. I know I feel much better about myself now. I think I was lucky because I don't have nearly as many problems as the others had. My life has been impacted in a different way. I think there is a purpose for the trials we all face."

"Do you think you have overcome all you're supposed to?"

"You know what I think? I think I may have a kind of empathy for others. I think I want to do something with my life that will help other victims. Aunt Darlene is going to form a division in her company devoted to helping victims of child molestation. It will also look at prevention by working for prosecution and removal of molesters from society. They say child molesters can't be helped. Aunt Darlene is not so sure. She is also going to work with willing molesters to see if they can be rehabilitated. I have talked to Aunt Darlene about working in this division, and she thinks I could make a valuable contribution. She is going to help me expand my education in that area … perhaps even get a degree. In the meantime, she will mentor me and let me work with her in a sort of intern capacity."

"So, you're looking to be a career woman?"

Robyn laughed. "Well now, I don't know. Would you be threatened by having a career woman for a wife?"

"Only if you make more money than I do." George laughed.

"My main concern will be about Debbie." Robyn said. "All these changes could be difficult for her."

"Yes, there will be changes for her, but she will have us, and we can give her the attention she needs working as a team."

"Thanks, I was sure I could count on you, but it's great to hear you confirm it."

"And what about the temple? Do you think still you're unworthy?"

"Actually, my consideration now is whether the Church is worthy of me."

"What do you mean?"

"It has bothered me that … there are many instances where the Church seems to take the side of the perpetrator in these things. We should all act to protect the innocent, but the bigger question for me is to face the consequences of my experiences and grow from them. There is no question in my mind the Church is wrong for protecting the guilty. It does it based upon a conception that they can be cured. And maybe they can; that's what I'm interested it trying. I just don't think the solution has been found yet, and until it is found, every child molester needs to be in facilities that absolutely keep them away from children."

"So, are you saying you don't want to even belong to the Church?"

"The Mormon Church has a history of making radical changes. I guess you could say that started when it accepted polygamy back in Joseph Smith's time and then when it abandoned it in the 1890s. Until 1978, the Church denied the most important blessing, the temple itself, to blacks. These are examples of fundamental doctrinal changes. Balanced against the Church's attitude on molesters are all the other good things the Church does. I have a strong belief in God, and I want Debbie to be raised with a strong moral foundation. I think a church is an essential part of doing that. Given the churches that are available, my preference is the Mormon Church. So, I plan to maintain my membership and remain active.

"As far as the temple is concerned, if I have to bear testimony that I believe the Church is right in the way it has handled the issue of child abuse, I will have to forego the temple. I will discuss that with the bishop. I wouldn't be surprised to see the Church make a radical change on this issue."

"I'm sorry all this upset had to come," George said.

"A lot of things have happened since we had to miss *Chicago*. I guess when Joshua tripped in our front room ... well ... that's what started the series of events that exposed all the evil he did, and his fall, at a time he was preparing a child to be molested, is what eventually killed him; sort of a divine justice. But on the good side, the family is reunited, and we don't have to worry about Joshua hurting anyone else ... Debbie would have been his next victim."

"This is one time your persistence brought about a good result," George agreed.

"It's kind of ironic ... you realize all this was actually started because when you walked out of the door of our house that night, you forgot to pick up your wallet ... such a small oversight in the scheme of things."

* * *

The first week of June the escrows on the houses were closed, and all the impediments for Jo's move were overcome. By that time, she and Derek were dating, and Jo confided to Robyn that it was getting serious. Jo decided to move to Southern California where Derek and most of the family were. She looked forward to building new relationships with all the family there and spending more time with Derek. Robyn was happy she and her mother would be close to each other so they could build a new relationship.

Jo had no job and no place to live, so she put all her things in temporary storage, and agreed to live with her mother until she found a job. She recognized this would give her a chance to work on her relationship with her and spend time getting reacquainted with her half-brother, Ronald.

Jo and Derek flew out of San Antonio together bound for Burbank Airport on June 12, 2013.

* * *

Robyn's little family celebrated Father's Day with George's family. The following Monday morning they rented a U-Haul truck. They packed it and gassed the truck and the car. Before starting out the next morning, Robyn wanted to spend some time alone to say goodbye to her old life before starting anew. George and Debbie went to say the final goodbye to his family.

Robyn parked her car across the road from the house that used to belong to Joshua. A <u>SOLD</u> sign was stuck diagonally across the <u>FOR SALE</u> sign. The new family would be moving in next month. Robyn walked across the road. The doors were locked, and the secret key box had been removed from under the rock by the front porch. No matter, she wanted to forget the inside.

Robyn walked to the backyard and sat on the concrete bench across from the outdoor fireplace. It would be impossible to remember how many marshmallows and hot dogs she had roasted in that fire on sticks Joshua had prepared for her. Every year they had a big July 24 party at the house to celebrate the Mormon holiday commemorating the entrance of Brigham Young and the first group of pioneers into the Salt Lake Valley in 1848. Back in Utah, it was a recognized holiday with a big parade from Temple Square to Liberty Park, and a major firework show from the Liberty Park area. Joshua and

Mary always had games and treasure hunts planned for the children. Parties in this backyard were always filled with fun and laughter.

Robyn closed her eyes and tried to remember the good times—times when she thought Joshua was a powerfully spiritual man. She tried to recall the admiration she used to feel for him. That feeling—the mental picture of him formed, and then, like a cloud of smoke hit by a strong fan, it swirled into a hundred whirlpools dissipating into the air. She could not bring it back, and she felt she never would.

Robyn opened her eyes. Though she may find a way to forgive Joshua sometime, she knew the wonderful picture she had held of him and her pride in him was gone forever.

She heard a rapid, buzzy "tweah-tweah-twee-sy," the familiar call of the golden-cheeked warbler. It was a call Robyn had heard often when she was growing up, but the goldfinch of Texas, as Mary used to call it, had become rare. Much of its natural habitat had been destroyed by development.

Robyn looked into the woodlands behind Joshua's house. The call of the warbler began in April when the birds were nesting and then gradually dropped off, lasting into June. The birds would soon migrate into northern Mexico for the fall and winter months, and then return in the spring to breed again.

Robyn finally spotted the little bird perched on an oak branch. It was about five inches long, black with white wing bars, and a grey breast. It had yellow markings on its cheeks and its eyes, with a black eye-stripe from its black bill through each eye to its nape. It was proudly calling, "tweah-tweah-twee-sy, tweah-tweah-twee-sy, tweah-tweah-twee-sy." Then it suddenly flew off, flitting gracefully between the trees.

Robyn watched it flash through the shadows until it disappeared, and the forest was quiet. She knew it would be back next year, but she wouldn't.

EPILOG—JULY 27, 2015

"Hello?"
"Hi Robyn. Did you see the news today?
"No, grandma. What's happened?"
"The Arizona Cardinals just hired a woman named Jen Welter to be a coach on their team. That's the NFL, girl!"

Glen R Stott was born in Salt Lake City, Utah. He is a retired civil engineer who lives in Southern California with his wife. His interests include writing, including novels, short stories, poems, and more. He writes about things that he is deeply interested in. When writing novels, he chooses genres that best tell the story. In addition to the Neandertal series, he has written a psycho-thriller, "Dead Angels," a romance, "Timpanogos," and a general literature novel about a family trying to deal with a child molester, "Robyn."

www.ingramcontent.com/pod-product-compliance
Lightning Source LLC
LaVergne TN
LVHW091533060526
838200LV00036B/592